SWARM

JENNIFER D. LYLE

sourcebooks
fire

Published by Sourcebooks Fire, an imprint of Sourcebooks
P.O. Box 4410, Naperville, Illinois 60567-4410
(630) 961-3900
sourcebooks.com

Originally published as *Contribute* in 2017 in United States by
Jolly Fish Press, an imprint of North Star Editions, Inc.

Cataloging-in-Publication Data is on file with the Library of Congress.

Printed and bound in the United States of America.
LSC 10 9 8 7 6 5 4 3 2 1

For Denise, who has always been there for me.

1

I see the butterfly before the rest of my class. I see it because I am absolutely not paying attention to Mr. Shephard's droning lecture on some amendment or another. He teaches straight from the book, so there's no reason for me to pay attention. And that's dangerous for my anxiety, because my bladder is always like, "Bored? Maybe we have to pee!"

I'm staring out the window and jiggling my leg up and down. A group of kids are clumped together on the damp soccer field. They should be limbering up for gym class torture, but instead they are staring collectively at a point above the school. The gym teacher stares along with them, which is totally weird. I follow the general direction of their line of sight, tracing the route until I spot exactly what they're seeing on the roof of the north wing of the school.

It's a monstrously large butterfly. Butterflies are beautiful. Nature's masterpiece. There is nothing scary about a pair of colorful wings bobbling up and down on the faintest of breezes.

But, honestly, any insect is scary if you make it big enough. And this thing isn't big, but BIG, all caps, straight-out-of-a-dream type weird. And that has to be the explanation—I'm dreaming.

Except I can feel my twin brother Keene's big feet resting on either side of my chair and can smell my best friend Jenny's perfume, floral and light, drifting back from her desk in front of me. Those kinds of grounding details don't happen in my dreams. So I must be awake.

Crazy size aside, the butterfly seems normal. It has the coloring of a monarch: orange and black with speckles of white at the wing edges. It's perched on a chimney I know all too well from staring out the window all semester. The chimney is probably two feet tall. The thing is, with the butterfly's wings all spread out in the sun, I can barely see the chimney at all.

I kick Jenny's chair once, then twice, and she whips around, annoyed. "What?" she hisses.

I point. My whole arm vibrates, my hand shaking at the end of it. I didn't even realize I was freaked until I see myself quivering.

She gives me an odd look before turning and then visibly startles.

"Jesus!" Jenny cries, interrupting Mr. Shephard midramble.

Invoking Jesus is enough to get the entire class up and out of their seats. The kids on the far side of the room half stand, craning their necks, while those closer to us crowd over, probably expecting to see a fight on the soccer field. As gasps and shouts of surprise erupt, everyone in the classroom charges at the windows, trying to see what the fuss is about.

Kelly Teehan screams. Then she screams again. She claps a hand over her mouth, eyes wide with terror.

"Dude," Keene says.

"I don't like butterflies," she whispers from between her fingers. "They creep me out."

"People, please!" Mr. Shephard says. "Can we get back to the discussion?" He's not even curious about what we're all looking at.

"Mr. Shephard, you should probably see this," Jenny says. She gently takes Kelly by the shoulders and says, "Maybe you should go to the bathroom and splash some water on your face. It might be gone by the time you get back." Kelly gives the tiniest of nods. Her face has become a funny shade that kind of reminds me of Swiss cheese.

I wonder what color my face is right now. My heart is doing that thing it does when it's prepping for a full-on panic attack. Not quite racing yet but thinking about it. I'm not afraid of butterflies like Kelly. Nope. I'm afraid of things that break my sense of rhythm. I like my world orderly and neat, and this butterfly is...too big.

"It's only a butterfly," Keene says, putting his hands on my shoulders from behind and resting his chin on my head. He's very protective, especially when he senses I might be teetering on the edge of a freak out. I'm shaking. I put one hand over his. Our eyes are fixed on the thing out the window as we contemplate it together. "Just because we haven't ever seen anything like it before doesn't mean it's bad," he says to me. "Right, Shur?"

"Right," I agree, but it comes out in a whisper because my mouth has dried up.

Mr. Shephard comes to the window, and the annoyance painted all over his face dissolves into something more like disbelief, then morphs again into fear. This has a calming effect on me. If an adult is scared, then this is serious, and I am right to be paranoid.

Mr. Shephard navigates the desks and strides to the phone at the front of the class. Evidently, the gym teachers have decided not to take any chances with the oversized butterfly, because the class is being herded out of sight, back into the building.

Jenny pulls out her phone and begins to record the thing. It hasn't moved much, except to spread its wings even wider.

"I think it was just born," Jenny says.

"Why?" Keene asks.

"Have you ever seen a freshly hatched butterfly?" she asks. "Their wings are wet. They can't fly."

"Then how did it get up there?"

Jenny shrugs, unable to tear her eyes away. "They have strong legs. It probably climbed up there to get to a safe spot in the sun."

"Where did it come from, anyway?" someone asks.

"Is it alone?" someone else asks, and this sets my heart to jackhammering. What if it isn't alone? I can't even wrap my mind around one, let alone a whole swarm.

"The odds that there's only one in the entire world and we're the ones to witness it seem pretty low," Jenny says. "But unless you're a flower, you're probably in no immediate danger." She stares at me pointedly. "So there's no reason to freak."

"Everyone please return to your seats," Mr. Shephard shouts over the escalating noise.

We file back through the rows, resigned to more civics. A moment later, our cell phones begin to blat in unison, the sharp, honking sound of an emergency situation.

We've heard that nuclear noise a hundred times before, most often for an Amber Alert or, this summer, a tornado warning. Across our screens marches, "Take cover. This is not a drill. Danger risk is high. Do not venture outdoors. Seek the lowest, most secure point in your home. Stay away from windows."

And outside one unnaturally large butterfly suns itself.

"No reason to freak, huh?" I ask Jenny. A flood of adrenaline has chased away the thin calm that I'd felt a moment ago. Now I feel sick.

Before Jenny can answer, the loudspeaker shrieks with feedback.

"MAY I HAVE YOUR ATTENTION. This is not a drill. Line up with your classes following tornado shelter-in-place procedures. I repeat, this is not a drill. Everyone, proceed to the gym as quickly as possible. Do not return to your lockers; do not leave the building." The heavy clunk of the disconnecting intercom signifies the end of the order, and there's a moment when we all just look at each other, like one of us has an answer.

"This can't be a coincidence," someone says.

"I want to go home," I whisper to Keene. He tugs his cell phone loose with one hand. I turn in my seat, and we stare at the screen together. Around us, everyone is doing the same thing, trying to get an answer from the Internet. Jenny frowns at her own screen. Unable to resist, I risk another look at the window. The bug is still there, wings rippling slightly.

"Oh Jesus," Keene says.

The news says they're everywhere. We can only see the one, and it doesn't seem dangerous, but in the world outside our school, butterflies have erupted all over the place. "What does it say?" I ask. "Are they—"

"Everyone get in line at the door," Mr. Shephard shouts. Years of drills drop us into line almost instantly. We turn to the formation for comfort and protection. I feel a little better knowing we've practiced for this. Well, not *this*, exactly. But for danger. Right?

Because what I was asking Keene before we got interrupted was, "Are they dangerous?"

2

The class exits in a long, single-file line led by Mr. Shephard. Joining the tail of the stream in front of us, we march in an orderly fashion toward the stairwell.

The order lasts for about twelve seconds. It would have held if everyone were following the protocol we've practiced over and over since kindergarten, weather evac drills, active shooter, shelter-in-place and bomb evac, so that we'll automatically do the right thing when the time comes, kind of like muscle memory. Thing is, in a real crisis, you can never predict how people will react. I know that better than anyone.

At first, a few panicked stragglers pound down the hall, escaping into the back stairwell. Then, others start to step out of line, which starts a wave of chaos. It spreads down the hallway on a wind of whispers. *Should we go? Should we stay? What are those things out there?* The whispers rise to talking voices, the voices to shouts and screams. Still, the bulk of the line continues to worm its way to the stairwell down to the gym.

My throat is starting to constrict, turning my breathing into a high whistle. I tighten my grip on Keene's hand, and he looks down at me. "We're okay," he says. "We don't even know if there's a reason to panic yet. This could all be noise."

Always the reasonable one, while I am Miss Worst Case Scenario.

Nathan, my brother's best friend, emerges from the tide. His backpack is slung over one shoulder, and his face is grim with determination that turns to relief when he spots us.

"Dude, what are you doing? Let's go!" Nathan says, grabbing Keene's backpack and tugging him less than gently into the center of the corridor. I'm hauled along and grab Jenny's hand to bring her with us. I would never leave Jenny behind.

All around us, the line is falling apart, becoming a mob. Someone screams, "How are they supposed to protect us? Those are monsters, not a freaking tornado!"

We haven't practiced for this. Keene might be right—we might not even know if this is a thing to panic over, but the mob is barreling toward hysteria all the same.

A scuffle breaks out ahead of us. The fragile order shatters, and the mob stampedes up and down the hallway in both directions.

"I don't like this," I moan.

"We're out of here," Keene shouts, tugging me along in Nathan's wake. I can feel Jenny's hands weighing down my backpack as she holds on for dear life. The fire alarm goes off, and the emergency lights flash white-blue. I almost fall, tripping as we get through the door to the back stairwell. Jenny steadies me from behind.

Finally, we spill into the bright morning. There's a new housing development across the soccer field, a nest of interwoven neighborhoods. A group of kids, probably the ones who live over there, take off in that direction at a trot, bunched together. One girl puts her backpack over her head like a shield.

"Where are we going?" Nathan asks over his shoulder, barely slowing his pace.

"Our house," Keene says.

"No," I say. "We need to get Little." Our baby brother is at day care and he needs us. "We should get him so Mom doesn't have to stop on her way home."

Above us, more butterflies float up and down on a light breeze that rustles the early fall leaves. We turn away from the soccer field, following the sidewalk around the edge of the school to the parking lot, barely watching where we're going. Although they all share the same monarch butterfly coloring, they vary in size. Some are bigger than the first one I saw by the chimney and some are no larger than a squirrel.

"They're so...big." Jenny's eyes are wide, her voice awed.

"Yeah, I'd really like to not have one touch me," Keene says.

"Butterflies don't have mouths," Jenny says, snapping into lecture-mode. Facts ground her, and she's always ready with some trivia in any situation. "They have this, like, straw thing they put into plants, and it sort of sucks the juice out. They could not bite you if they tried."

"That doesn't make them any less scary as shit," says Keene.

"Mothra," Nathan adds. He's jumpy, twitchy, hands clapping together, off his thighs, on the straps of his backpack.

"Hey, maybe that's the emergency! Godzilla's on his way." I say. I try to sound jokey, like this is more fun than terrifying.

We round the corner to the parking lot, and Keene swears under his breath. Loads of people have ditched and are streaming to their cars. Almost as many cars are headed inbound, parents picking up their kids, spouses come for teachers.

Keene's beater is parked close. We hurry to it. Jenny and I slide into the backseat, Nathan and Keene climb into the front.

"Do you not believe in trash bags?" Jenny asks, slapping an empty Gatorade bottle into the debris field on the floor.

"Do you want to walk?" Keene counters, but his heart isn't really in it. This is their usual banter, triggered by reflex. He's eyeing the parking lot, the other drivers, the sky.

I tug my phone free from my back pocket. "No message from Mom yet. Should I call her?"

"Yeah. Tell her we'll meet her at home with Little," Keene says.

The phone rings and rings and rings. I hang up and try again. Nothing. No answer, no reassuring voice of my mother. This time, voicemail picks up.

"Mom," I say. "We're worried. The school was going into lockdown, so me and Keene left. We're going to get Little, and we'll meet you at home. Can you call me back? Love you."

I hang up.

"I can't get through," Nathan says, twisting to see around his seat back. "Just *Network Busy*, over and over."

Jenny frowns at her screen. "Me too. Keep trying. Everyone is calling at once."

Ahead of us, the line of cars inches forward as the light changes. I close my eyes and send up a prayer to the traffic gods that no one panics and pulls out into another car, causing a jam at the entrance. As we make the turn onto the main road, we pass a long line of cars waiting to get into the lot.

I try texting. *Left a voicemail - call or text, service sucks. Love you.*

As if to make my point, the text hangs for a long moment, then fails.

Jenny pats my knee.

I ask. "Should we have stayed?"

Keene grunts. "The last place I want to be during an emergency is trapped in a gym with 1,200 people I can't stand."

3

n and out, okay?" Keene says, as he steers the car into the neighborhood where Little's day care is.

"Yeah, yeah, no chatty-chatty. We don't have his car seat," I say. "He's going to freak." Little does not like rule breaking, and *always in your car seat* is a Big Rule.

"I'll tell him the cops said it was okay," Nathan offers. "He'll believe me."

Three cars linger at the curb outside of Ms. Caroline's house, a McMansion on a cul-de-sac. At the circle's center sits a huge island garden with a little bench, slate paths, and a sea of bright late-summer flowers. Above the garden, a pair of butterflies are doing butterfly things, one normal size and the other one of the monstrosities. So big, floating, and peaceful. The sun is warm, probably feels good on its wings.

I climb out onto the soft green grass of Ms. Caroline's manicured lawn, still damp with morning dew. A woman in a smart business suit and heels hustles her daughter toward one of the waiting cars, passing me without so much as a glance in my direction.

The day care has its own entrance down the driveway, into the finished basement. I slide my shoes off and gather Little's things from his cubby: Billy Bear, his backpack, his bright blue sneakers with Cookie Monster smiling up from the sides.

"Oh! Thank goodness," Ms. Caroline says as I come down the stairs. "I haven't been able to get ahold of your mother. We're trying to close early what with this...whatever is happening. Shawn?"

No one in the family ever calls Little by his real name, but he only wants to be Shawn at day care because "Little is a baby name." He emerges from the inner room, sees me, and shouts, "Shur! How come you're here? Where's Mommy?"

"Mommy's at work," I say. "We're going to take a ride with Keene and Nathan and Jenny back to our house."

"Nathan!" He claps his hands and darts for the stairs. "I need my shoes!"

I smile at Ms. Caroline. "Hopefully we'll see you tomorrow."

"Well, stay safe and stay inside," she says. "The news isn't saying much, but I don't like the looks of those things. They're too big and too...sudden."

Outside, the butterfly garden has more visitors, large and small. Little points at a butterfly the size of a chihuahua. "That's a big bug."

"You like butterflies."

"I don't like those ones. They're too big."

Jenny waits by the car door. "Hey kiddo, you get to ride with us."

Little frowns into the back suspiciously. "Where's my seat?"

"In Mommy's car."

"I can't drive without my seat. It's against the law."

"Well," Nathan says, leaning out of the car window, "we have a secret to tell you, but only if you super promise to keep it quiet. No one can know."

"What?" Little asks.

"Promise not to tell?"

"Promise!" Little says. "But what?"

"The police called us and said to pick you up and bring you home safe," Nathan says. "And when we told them you had no car seat, they said it was *so* important that they would give us permission this one time to *not* use a car seat. But they made us swear you would use a seat belt, and you would never, ever tell anyone that they changed the rules especially for you."

"For real?" Little asks, looking to me for confirmation.

I nod. "Yeah. And Keene will drive super-duper safe."

"Can we get ice cream?"

"We can eat some ice cream at home later, buddy. We need to get back to see if Mommy is there yet."

"Mommy is coming home early?"

"Yep."

With Little firmly settled between us, I reach over with the middle belt, cross it over his lap, and hand it to Jenny to click home. He bounces his legs. "This feels weird. I can see right up to the windshield!"

Keene glances in his side mirror and pulls out into the street. He maneuvers around the garden island, crawling along. The butterflies are harder to ignore. At least one floats over almost every lawn, most high up, but some lower to the ground and closer to the street.

We leave the neighborhood and pick up speed back on the main road. Keene says, "I think I'm going to take the back—"

A butterfly slams into the windshield, solid as a bird, and everyone screams. Little keeps screaming, his mouth open as wide as it can be, eyes popping.

The butterfly, easily two feet from wingtip to wingtip, clings to the windshield wiper, belly flat against dirty glass. On any butterfly, on any moth, there's a head, a thorax, and an abdomen covered in fuzz like fur, sometimes black, sometimes mimicking the coloration of the rest of the bug, but on this butterfly...

On this butterfly...

And the legs. Usually it'd be stick legs, delicate, ticklish on human skin, an innate sense of fragility, like the wrong move could snap one. But these. These are thick, bony, exoskeletal. The legs of a crab, but ebony, each ending in a claw that grips the rubber part of the wiper and cuts it away.

But the legs aren't why Little is screaming, screaming still.

The segments of the thorax split vertically and spread, revealing a mouth filled with jagged, pointed teeth. A line of saliva sticks, spanning the gash, and it snaps at the windshield uselessly, opening and closing. A black wriggle inside might be a tongue.

"Get it off, man!" Nathan shouts and lunges for the windshield wiper control, even as Keene stares straight ahead, hands locked at 10 and 2, completely frozen. The wipers begin to move, and the skeletal legs scratch along the glass, leaving a mark. The butterfly-crab does not let go, and Nathan hits the control again, setting it to high speed with a whack of his palm. On the return trip, the butterfly hangs on, but the next flip sends it sailing into the slipstream of a passing car. It tumbles away on the wind before righting itself. I turn in my seat to follow it. The maw has disappeared; the legs are tucked. It's just an abnormally large, but otherwise unremarkable, monarch butterfly once again.

And Little screams like he might never stop.

4

As we drive, the only sounds are road noises, wind whistling by, and Little's occasional snuffle. We are stunned into silence. Little is too shaken to truly cry, but anything could set him off. He presses his face to my side, not wanting to see any other butterflies. It seems wrong to call them butterflies, but I don't have a better word besides "monster," and I'm not sure I want to go there yet. I keep one arm around him, hugging as best I can with the seat belts between us.

The way home takes us through downtown. I expect a ghost town, for people to have figured out that these are not passive nectar-sippers but rather full-fledged prey beasts with dragon teeth. We roll to a stop at a light behind two other cars. Some of the stores are closed, like the noodle shop, which would ordinarily be prepping for the lunch rush. The consignment shop next store usually has a few things out on the sidewalk, an antique bicycle or refinished end table to lure pedestrians, door propped open in an invitation, but not today. The front window is dark.

But other places are still open, and a handful of pedestrians are on the sidewalks. Some are nervous, glancing at the sky, but many seem oblivious. Maybe we are making incorrect assumptions about the danger level. Maybe they know something we don't. But I don't think so. Nothing with that many teeth can be benign. My anxiety clicks up another notch watching them amble about their business like it's any Friday in early fall.

Jenny cracks her window, letting a slim breeze float in.

Nathan snaps, "Close that! You're going to get us killed!"

"Chill," she says. "It's open a millimeter."

"Close it!" he yells, metallic hysteria crowding his voice.

Jenny closes the window and says dryly, "Maybe close the air vents too. Don't want them coming in that way."

She's not serious, but Nathan doesn't catch the sarcasm and slams his vent closed. Keene whacks him and says, "Dude. She was joking. Nothing is getting in through the vents."

"How can you be sure?"

"That would be like a bird coming through a screen," Keene says, eyes rolling. "I know you're scared, but pull it together."

"No birds," Jenny announces.

"What?" I ask.

"There are no birds. No squirrels either. When was the last time you were downtown and didn't see a crap ton of both?"

Jenny is right: The downtown pigeons are borderline aggressive, especially outside the bakery, and the squirrels are bold almost to the point of tameness. But there are no squirrels or birds to be seen.

"They're smarter than we are. Look at these people, just walking along," Jenny says.

"Maybe they don't know yet," Keene says.

"We should yell at them to get in their cars," I say.

"We're not opening the windows." Nathan shakes his head, almost a spasm more than a deliberate motion.

"These people... It's like with a tornado warning," Keene says. "You know, there's always that one guy mowing his lawn because he doesn't believe it's going to happen."

"Bill," Jenny and I say in unison.

Bill Hockstetter is our across the street neighbor and a bit of a character. He does not believe in tornado warnings, climate change, or the need for taxes. He also has a very large gun collection, assembles his own bullets, and makes the best cheeseburger chowder in the state (a champion four years running).

"He's probably stringing up a crossbow," Jenny says, and Little brings his red face out from my side.

"Really?"

"Yeah, man," she says. "You kill monsters with a crossbow." And there it is. Someone has used the "m" word, and there's no taking it back.

"You kill them with a stake," Keene says.

"That's vampires."

"Werewolves are killed by silver bullets. Not crossbows."

"A silver crossbow bolt would work on either of those," Jenny says, warming to the topic.

"You may have a point," he says. "A bolt is pretty stake-like, and I guess silver on the pointy part is more or less the same as a silver bullet. But still, I mean, a crossbow for these? Wouldn't a shotgun make more sense?"

It's nice to have something like a normal flow of conversation in the car, to distract both ourselves and Little, even if the topic is Effective Monster Slaying.

The light turns. We're waiting for the front car to roll when a scream tears through the air.

In front of the bakery, a woman stumbles across the sidewalk. She swats at herself with one hand, trying to get something off of the sleeve of her red shirt. I recognize her. She owns the place and must have been in the process of closing up like the other downtown businesses. I can't come up with her name. That's what my brain chooses to focus on. *Sandra? Sarah?*

The woman streaks toward the front car at the light. *Her shirt isn't red*, my busy, busy brain realizes. It's the same shirt she always wears at work, the pink and brown one that matches the sign in the window. But it's drenched red with her blood.

"Holy shit, go around," Nathan whispers.

"What's happening?" Little asks, the pitch going up on the *ing* as it dawns on him that it must be bad. He cannot have seen, but I cover his eyes anyway.

"Keene!" Jenny says. "Go!"

Keene throws a wild glance over his right shoulder and pulls around, narrowly missing a parked car. The man in the front car is getting out to help. A large orange and black mass squirms on her arm, and I think of that maw full of needle-sharp teeth. Sandra-or-Sarah whipsaws her arm and a splatter-fall hits Keene's window, a red drizzle. It glistens like rubies in the morning sun, and I can't tear my eyes away. The droplets are speckled black like flawed jewels.

Then we're past and moving too fast, shooting through town.

"I need to get home," Nathan says.

Keene squares his jaw, teeth clenched. "We're not stopping."

"My parents!" Nathan shouts, turning on Keene.

"Jesus, Nathan. You just saw someone getting eaten," Keene snaps. "Do you really think I'm stopping?"

"But—"

"Nathan," Jenny says and drops a hand on his shoulder. "Think. They aren't home. They're at work. We're better off staying together for now. We can call them once we get to the Riordan's to let them know you're okay. They can pick you up the second the shelter-in-place order lifts. But Keene is right: We can't stop. We need to be somewhere safe."

His mouth moves, and I think he's going to argue more, but he slumps, deflated, and nods.

Jenny pulls her hand back and looks at me, eyes wide. I don't know for sure, and it might just be my paranoia piping up, but I don't think Nathan's parents are going to be picking him up any time soon. These things are hunters—and there are more of them with every passing hour. How long until they're everywhere?

5

On the way home, we witness two more attacks, but mercifully neither are gory: On the street outside the library, a boy on his bicycle narrowly avoids being grabbed by snapping claws when he swerves around a parked car at the last second. Then closer to our house, we see the UPS guy manage to slam the door of his truck in the face of another coming straight at him with outstretched crab legs. If there was any question before about what the butterflies are doing here, it's gone. These things want us.

Keene pulls in under the carport beside the house, bringing the car as close as he can to the kitchen door. It's a relief when the sky overhead is hidden from view. There are so many of them now, I want to cry then curl into a ball under the covers in my bed, in that order. It's too much. My brain is on fire.

But even if I can't see up, there are butterflies ahead of us, behind us, and to the right between us and the neighbor's house.

They move in thickening clusters. A cloud of them, black from this distance, take off in one direction, shift suddenly, dive together, pull up. They remind me of sparrow flocks in the fall, shifting and weaving, living smoke.

Closer to the ground, some flap at their own pace over the blacktop, dipping, rising. These also remind me of birds, but hawks, not sparrows, languidly circling on an air current, ever watchful for prey. They're all sizes of *too big*. Some are no more than eight or nine inches across, and some are big enough to remind me of kites.

The car is safe but temporary; we need to get into the house. The door is just a few feet away, locked. A butterfly flaps past the window on its way to a swelling swarm in the backyard. Keene cuts the engine and rotates in his seat to look at me.

"What do you think?" Keene asks. "We could try to pull into the barn."

The barn is what we call Mom's studio at the end of the driveway. It's a sort of big barn/garage hybrid that she had custom built when we moved in, so she could do her crafts in peace. It has running water, electricity, a toilet...and we could open the garage door and pull right inside the double-deep garage bay. There's even a loft with a couch in it, so we'd be relatively comfortable.

But it doesn't have food. If these...things are going to linger, we're going to need to be prepared to settle in.

I breathe deep. In through the nose. Out through the mouth. Like my therapist taught me. Think.

"It's gotta be the house," I say.

Jenny nods. "Yeah, just in case they don't go away fast," she says, echoing my own thoughts.

"One of us has to go first to unlock the door. The rest follow," I say.

"One at a time," Jenny adds. "I have a bad feeling motion is going to attract them."

"Can you manage Little if I get the door?" Keene asks.

"Yes."

"Did you take your pills today?"

I feel myself flush. "Not the time."

"Shur."

I think back, not sure. For all the other order I demand in my life, I suck at taking my pills. Mom is always on me about this, to move them to the bathroom, to take them at night before bed, or to the kitchen to take them with my coffee in the morning. Instead they sit on my dresser in their plastic prescription bottle. She bought me a day-of-the-week dispenser to make my life easier. It's still in the wrapper, $1.99 from Walmart. "Yes," I say.

"You're okay?"

For now, I think. "Yes."

He worries. I've frozen up before soccer games, once at the end of a swim meet, hiking. The panic comes without warning. Especially when I forget my pills. This would be the worst time to freeze.

There's no time to deal with the peculiarities of my daily existence right now. We need to get into the house. "I can do it," I reiterate, trying to sound confident. And I can, because Little is the world to me, to all of us, and I won't let anything happen to him.

Keene carefully picks the key to the house out from the bunch on the fob, holds it separate. He gives me and Little a final, frightened smile. Little can't see, because his face is still crushed into my shirt, and I wish I hadn't seen it either.

"Here I go." He opens the door slowly, looks both ways, ducks out, closes it behind him with a metallic click. He's up the three steps, opening the screen door, stooping. A butterfly bounces off the aluminum outer door, confused, and then the interior door is open and Keene disappears inside.

Nathan scrubs his face hard with both hands and slaps himself a few times on each cheek.

"Hold it together, bro," Jenny says lightly, then turns to me and Little. "Hey Little, want to give me a kiss for luck?"

His face emerges, red and damp, unhappy.

Jenny kisses his cheek and says, "Listen. We're going to get inside and close the whole house up tight. Right? No monsters are getting in. We're going to be like superheroes."

"Monster killers?" he whispers.

"For now, we're going to be monster escapers. Then we'll see what happens." She ruffles his hair, gives me a deep sigh, then turns to the car door. Her fingers twitch, counting: one twitch, a second, and third. The door opens, she slips out, door closes. Up the steps, Keene is waiting, opens the door. She's inside. Just us three left now.

Nathan unbuckles and squirms into the space between the driver's and passenger seats, pushing back so that he's nearly in the backseat with us. He moves his legs over into the driver's well, hung up momentarily on the steering wheel, cursing under his breath. Once he's in place, he pulls his backpack on, leaning forward to make room for it. "Do you want me to take Little?" he asks over his shoulder. "Because I will. If you want."

"We'll be fine."

"Here." He nudges the backpack off his shoulder, roots in it at an awkward angle, and produces a flannel shirt. "Put it over his head when you go. So he doesn't have to see."

"Good idea. Thanks."

He does that slapping thing to his face again, psyching himself up. "Here I go. One, two. Three."

On three he snaps open the driver's side door, gets out, closes it, then disappears suddenly from sight. I choke on panic. Did something bite him? Something under the car? I hold my breath, willing myself not to scream, because I might not be able to stop.

But then, he's up again, something clutched against his body, and he's running straight at the door, which opens to welcome him. In my mind, I play back what I saw, the grayish-brown mass in his arms, squirming.

"He saved Terrible Charlie!" I tell Little. I haven't given the cat a thought before now, even though he spends most days outside. He must have been hiding somewhere, made a dash for the car when we pulled in. Smart cat.

It's our turn. I say, "You heard what Nathan said, right? I'm going to put his shirt over your head, and I'm going to carry you."

"Piggyback?"

"No, front ways so I can see you. Can you climb onto my lap? Put your arms around my neck. Good. Now, your legs go around my waist, and you hold on." We maneuver to the door; position ourselves. I pull the flannel, green and gold and smelling of Nathan's cologne, over Little's head. He snuggles into my neck.

"You're getting to be a big boy," I say, feeling his weight. Carrying him is not usually an issue, even though he's so much bigger than he was as a baby, but the situation is not normal. "Do you want to count?"

"One," he whispers. "Two. Three!"

My fingers tug the handle, and I blindly push the door open. We're out of the car and onto the blacktop. I smack the car door closed with my hip and am scrambling up the steps when I see Jenny and Keene screaming and pointing.

Keene throws the screen door open, and Jenny peels Little from my arms, retreating. Nathan charges forward with something in his hand and with his other hand grabs my hair, yanking my head down hard. My mind processes in slow motion. He's got the egg pan I cooked breakfast in this morning. There's still yellow egg rind in it. He swings the pan, and it connects with a solid noise, like a baseball on a bat, and then Keene and Nathan are pulling me inside and closing the door.

"Is it off?" I scream, knowing. It was on me, there was one on me. I can't breathe.

"It's gone," Keene says, dropping to one knee. He checks me all over, looking for holes or bites or whatever. "Nathan clocked it a good one."

"My tennis game is strong," Nathan says, but he collapses against the cabinets. "Holy shit."

"It was on your backpack," Keene said. "Came off the car as soon as you stepped out, and was running up...never mind. It's gone now."

"I think I'm going to throw up," I say conversationally and gag.

Keene pats my hand and stands. At the sink, he fills a Mickey Mouse cup with water and hands it to me. "Here. Drink this. Chill for a minute."

"Nathan," I say, "I swear to God, when you got out of the car we thought something got you."

"One came at me. I ducked, then I fell over," he says. "Graceful, right? Anyway, who's under the car other than our friend Charles." He holds up one hand, showing a pretty good set of red scratches on his brown skin. "Lucky I like him. Right buddy?"

Charlie has made it as far as the food bowl, which is only nearly full, and he meows a complaint.

"Yeah, shut up you fat, awful thing," I mutter as I sip my water. It doesn't make me feel better.

Jenny comes back in from wherever she has been, Little still wrapped around her like a human boa constrictor.

"I'll take him," Keene says and reaches out. Little attaches to Keene, wrapping so tight that Keene says, "Hey, I need to breathe. Loosen that grip a little."

"I want Mommy!" The crying starts, frightened, earnest, his whole body shaking inside his striped T-shirt, all the way down to the toes of his Cookie Monster sneakers. "I want Mommy!"

"We all want Mommy," Keene says. "She'll be home soon." He carries our brother out of the room and down the hall to the den to be soothed by the television and his special blankie.

"He'll cry himself to sleep," Jenny says.

"I hope so."

"I might cry myself to sleep," she says. "I guess we should check the news."

"I'm going to try Mom again. You guys should try your families." We can find out the bad news anytime, but right now, like Little, I really want my mom.

6

Nathan smashed the killer bug with the smallest of our frying pans; the egg pan I'd scrambled breakfast in a lifetime ago now has a second life as a monster beater. As I press the phone to my ear, I drop the pan back into the sink and run water. The handle's loose, maybe from the impact. A dry, mechanical man's voice tells me over and over that the network is overwhelmed, to try again, try again, try again.

My therapist always reminds me to control what I can. My breathing, my chores, my bladder. These are the things I can manage. *Try again*, says the network. *Empty me*, says the dishwasher. *Empty me,* says my bladder.

The phone rings, and I snatch it off the counter, fingers damp from dish soap, and almost drop it.

"Shur!" Mom's voice, haggard, frightened. The line sounds distant, as if she's calling from a research station in the Arctic

Circle instead of an office building a few towns over. "Did you get Little? Where are you? Are you safe?"

"Mom!" I run into the den motioning wildly for Keene. "We're home, we have Little. Where are you? You're not outside, right? When are you going—"

"Stop, Shur. Stop. I'm inside at the office. We're safe for now, but I'm not coming home. Not soon. We're trapped."

"What do you mean?"

There's a beat of silence, and I know she's weighing what to say, not just because she'll scare me, but because she's afraid I'll crack like an egg and all my reason will run out. "Some idiot drove into the building and broke a bunch of windows. We locked ourselves in the cafeteria. One guy got bit. I'm fine, Shur, but I can't leave. There's no safe way to the car."

She's fading, fading in my ear, not her voice but my hearing, filled with buzzing and blood.

"Shur. Listen to me," she says. "I'm going to give you a job. Something to focus on."

"I'm not broken," I say, but only because that's what she wants to hear.

"Good. Good. Close the shades, and the drapes too. Lock all the doors. I want you to keep your phone on the charger, no matter what. And Little sleeps with you until I'm home. Repeat it back."

"Windows, doors, phone, Little."

"Good. Put Keene on."

Keene and my mother have a quick exchange that mostly involves him muttering "Yes" and "I know" and occasionally glancing at me. Finally Keene takes the phone off his ear, thumbs the screen, and is on speaker.

"Little?" Mom says.

"Mommy?" Little practically leaps from the couch. "Mommy, where are you? Did you see the monsters?"

"Yes, baby, Mommy saw the monsters. I'm at work right now, and I have to be here for a bit, but Shur and Keene are going to take care of you."

"And Nathan and Jenny!"

"Are they there too?"

"Nathan saved Charlie from the monsters. He was hiding under the car, and he gave Nathan a big old scratch right on the hand, but Nathan saved him anyway. He's a hero! Mommy, when are you coming home?"

"I don't know, baby. Right now, there are a lot of monsters outside. So it would be better if you stay in our house, and I stay where I am, and we all wait."

"For the monster hunters?"

"Yes, for the monster hunters," Mom agrees. The line is going bad, crackling and cutting out. "I love you, Little, but I have to go. Shur, take me off speaker."

I do. Keene sits and wraps his arm around Little, whose expression has brightened.

"What about Grandma?" I say at once, not giving Mom a chance to say anything else.

"All the families got an email from the manager of the independent living center. She says they're in complete lockdown, and they're fine. There's a nurse on staff and everything is closed up tight."

"So she's safe? Really? We shouldn't like...try to go get her?" I really don't want to leave the house, but what if Grandma needs us? What if Mom needs us? "Should we try to come get you?"

"No. You're staying put, and that's final. Shur, Grandma is okay. I'm okay. Listen," my mother says. "I know this is hard, and I know you're overthinking."

"Mind reader."

She laughs, not with joy. It's a hard noise, a verbal eye roll. "No, I just know my little girl. Daddy would be telling you the same thing: hunker down, and prepare for the worst. You and Keene are in charge of keeping everyone alive. Promise you'll do whatever it takes, and you won't..."

"Won't what? Fall into abject despair? Let my anxiety eat me alive?"

Silence at my humor attempt "Shur. I need you to hold it together. This is bad. But we can—"

She's gone. "Hello? Mom? Hello?" I look dumbly at the phone, but the connection is lost. I dial again right away, but the *try again* man is back.

Numbly, I follow her directions and plug the phone into a charger on the counter. I try to call her again. And again. And again. But I don't get through. My mother is gone.

After a tense lunch, I can't quite bring myself to leave Little alone in his room for a nap. What if something gets in, and I'm not there? What if he does something stupid, like opens the window? Every horror story I've never heard about a kid causing their own demise rushes to the front of my mind.

"Nap time is on the couch today!" I declare.

"I only sleep on the couch when I'm sick," Little says.

I'm in no mood, but I can't exactly give him a brain dump of my nightmares, so I say, "Yeah, but it's safer today if we all stay together. And Mommy says that tonight you sleep in my bed."

"Cool!" Little says. He yawns. It's been a lot for him, for all of us. "Can I have blankie and Billy Bear?"

The drapes are closed tight, creating an artificial dusk in the room. Little sings softly for a few minutes, soothing himself asleep. When his eyes finally close, I sit beside him on the couch and thumb the remote, turning the TV volume to its lowest audible setting. Finding a news channel isn't difficult: almost everything has cut over to live coverage of the butterflies. The others drift in, finding spots on the couch and recliner.

"We have confirmed sightings on every continent," the news anchor is saying. "Even the Arctic and Antarctic regions have not been spared from this event."

"Phil Huston looks like he's going to have a stroke," Nathan says of the anchor, a fixture on cable news, trusted by millions. "I don't think I've ever seen him sweat through his makeup before."

"We're getting word that President Barrymore is about to go live."

The news desk is replaced by an empty podium with the presidential seal on a low stage. A man steps forward, taps the microphone a few times. "We're almost ready. The President will be out shortly." He backs away and hurries off.

Everyone stands as President Barrymore, flanked by men in suits, enters from the wings. She looks the same as always, immaculate hair, flawless skin, meticulously cut business suit. Only her expression is different. Lucinda Barrymore smiles a lot. They call her Buddy Barrymore because of it, her perpetual happy smile, shaking hands, high-fiving. Not today. Today she's President Barrymore, no smile, no nonsense, and ready to lead.

"Ladies and gentlemen of the press, let me first assure your families at home that you are safe here. While I'm sure you didn't anticipate your daily briefing turning into an extended stay, let's do our best together to get what answers we do have out to the American public."

She looks directly into the camera. "My fellow Americans," she says. "We find ourselves this afternoon in grave and unprecedented danger. I have declared a national emergency and nationwide lockdown to last no fewer than thirty-six hours. For the families considering rushing to your children's schools or home to a loved one—please, I urge you to stay where you are.

"I will tell you what we know. At approximately 6:30 a.m. on the East Coast of the United States, the first verified sighting of an abnormally large butterfly was made. The CDC was contacted by the police shortly after, along with the National Parks Service. By 10:00 a.m. EST, hundreds of similar sightings and attacks were reported not just here, but around the world. As of the start of this press conference, we had confirmed sightings in twenty-two countries, with more pouring in. More alarming than their presence is the rate at which they continue to appear."

I fight the urge to rise from the couch and look outside. Keene's hand closes on mine.

Barrymore shakes her head at someone in the front row. "Sorry, Peter. I need to get through this before we take questions. We do not believe at this time that this is a coordinated biological attack, alien or terrestrial in nature. The current working theory is that the event has been triggered as a result of climate change, but we can't explain how, why, or why now. New species do not simply evolve overnight; our scientists believe this species may have been dormant for hundreds of millions or perhaps even billions, of years."

"Jesus Christ," Jenny mumbles.

"Of course we know now that they are not butterflies but, because of their resemblance, they have been assigned the scientific name *interfectorem papilionem*." She paused to give a rueful smile and added, "For those of you whose Latin might be a little rusty, that literally translates to *killer butterfly*. As many of us have witnessed, they range in size from roughly six inches across to more than two feet, and they primarily mimic the coloration of butterflies indigenous to the regions in which they have appeared. Initial testing shows they are, as my kids say, a mashup of reptile, insect, and crustacean. In short: Earthly in origin. In-depth testing is ongoing and will tell us more.

"Most alarming to my partners at both the NIH and CDC are their bites, because their saliva carries a previously unseen bacteria. If you are bitten, we urge you to immediately follow a protocol of deep cleansing and self-quarantine. Do not attempt travel to hospitals. I'll take some questions."

There's a clamor in the crowd, and Barrymore points to someone.

"Wouldn't the appearance of these things all at once, all over the world, imply that this was a coordinated attack of some sort, and not a biological event?"

Barrymore nods. "It's a terrific question. I'm going to give this one to Dr. Marla Shapes from the CDC. Dr. Shapes?"

A small, gray-haired woman steps to the podium and adusts

the microphone down. Her eyes squint out from thick, round glasses. "While it's true that we have limited information on this event's trigger, we're following Occam's Razor. There is no country in the world capable of such an attack as you're describing."

"What about aliens?"

"Aliens," Jenny huffs, indignant.

"The most likely scenario is that climate change has triggered something that made our current environment suitable for these creatures. Perhaps something with gas levels in the air, or relative humidity, or penetration of certain chemicals into the soil and permafrost. There are many repercussions we do not yet fully grasp, and this event seems to fall into that category."

"Even so," the reporter says, "those levels would likely be different everywhere. It's unlikely all these butterflies could show up at once without coordination."

Dr. Shapes gives a smile similar to the one Jenny gives me when I've asked a very stupid question. She says, "It's possible they've been waiting some time for the conditions in all environments to be just right before they emerge."

"What?" the reporter asks, sounding dumbfounded.

Another says, "Are you implying they're all one hive? Hivemind is at play?"

"I'm saying," Dr. Shapes says, "That we don't know what we don't know, but making assumptions about the science at this point helps nothing. We implore you to put the safety of yourselves and your community first while we work on this unprecedented problem."

From there, the questions continue, ranging from a "definition of deep cleaning" to "how many butterflies have been captured for study?" to "could this have been prevented?" Jenny turns off the television, leaving us in the quiet half-light. No one knows what to say. Ancient hive monstrosities? Unknown bacteria? Nationwide lockdown? We stay together, practically afraid to move.

Finally Jenny breaks the frightened silence. "Well, this just keeps getting better and better."

7

After the news conference, we're like zombies. We can't go out. We can't get through to anyone by phone or text. Email still sends, but the responses are slow or nonexistent. We go through all the motions of a normal night: dinner, bath time for the baby, Netflix, stories. Mom's absence hurts like a ripped-out tooth. Nathan's at the table where she should be; Keene's car is under the port in her spot. Everything is wrong.

I lay in bed listening to the sounds of video game guns from Keene's room for what seems like hours. Eventually, Keene gives up and goes to bed too. The house is quiet, and my brain is finally still. Jenny is passed out on the trundle bed, and Little is stuffed in beside me, sprawled out and taking up a ridiculous amount of space for someone so small. Charlie dozes at the end of the bed, legs tucked under, eyes closed.

In the dark, I can hear myself thinking sometimes in a way I can't during the day, like my brain speaks only at a very low whisper easily drowned out by every day ambient noises: talking, traffic, house sounds. Maybe light has its own noise. Maybe night is a kind of sensory deprivation chamber that makes me focus on that voice because there's nothing else to hear.

My therapist says it's the back of the brain, the part that does our actual thinking. She says that's the brain to listen to in the dark, because it's smarter than the front-brain voice, which likes to scream about the most irrational things:

What if I forgot to turn off the stove?

Or to lock the front door?

Oh God, what if Mom dies?

What if I do something that gets Little killed?

What if, what if, what if?

On nights when the front-brain wins, there is no sleep.

Light peeks around the edges of the pulled-down window shade, creeping in from the streetlamp. The bright spots on the wall and floor are occasionally interrupted by shadows, big ones, shapeless and restless. I am glad I cannot see their owners. I'm almost able to imagine those shadows are leaves whipping on an autumn wind.

I'm glad Jenny is here and not trapped at home with her mom and stepfather. Even before her mom got remarried, Jenny couldn't do anything right. At least her mom's constant criticism was bearable; it made Jenny work harder than anyone else, which earned her much love from our teachers. But her stepfather plays mind games, and her mother plays along. He accuses Jenny of stealing things from him, of being a drug addict, of all sorts of crazy, untrue shit. She's grounded about half the time, and they treat her like a maid, always screaming about how useless and ungrateful she is.

Jenny's had long talks with Mom about it. After one of those talks, Mom bought the trundle bed for Jenny as a Christmas present. A small sign that she's always welcome here, that this is her home if she wants it to be. Jenny cried when she pulled the paper off it. I wish she lived here all the time.

I'm not sure which is worse: not having a dad at all or having parents like Jenny's.

Even with all her problems, Jenny doesn't have anxiety. She's the smart one; the one with all the AP college credits and summer college courses, the science fair winner, the playwright, the chess player. She's pretty too, classically tall, blond, and willowy. When she wears glasses, which she really only needs to see the board from the back of class, the boys go crazy. Sexy nerd.

I'm not a genius like her, but I'm in honors classes and I mostly get As and Bs. While she's doing her summer biology camps, I'm at soccer camp or volleyball camp or swimming camp. I read. A lot. It's better for my brain to be busy, better still for my body to be busy too. Fewer chances to overthink when everything is in motion.

Tonight, I can hear the quiet voice.

My brain whispers, *We should be closing up the house. I mean, really closing it up. And…the power could go out. We have candles, but candles are a fire hazard, so we'll need to be very careful with them. And food. Once the power does go out, what will we do about food? We'll go through the canned stuff and the dried stuff fast if we have to feed all of us.*

It's calm, this voice—thoughtful, not the white wall of noise and drums that comes with my panic attacks. I'm ticking things off on mental fingers and, for once, it feels productive, not like a list of things I might have forgotten, but rather a list of to-do items. Things to do that can make a difference.

A routine for Little is going to be important—

The voice goes quiet, interrupted by a noise overhead. Stealthy. I hold my breath. Beside me, Charlie's yellow lamp eyes open a slit. We lie there, listening together. There it is again. Feet. Small feet moving, little paws and nails running inside the walls.

The screaming voice in my head warms up its vocal cords, stretches, prepares for an all-out onslaught, but the other voice, the calm one, shakes its head and silences it.

Squirrels and mice, it explains. *We didn't see any downtown because they went to ground. The attic is probably filled with hiding, cowering things right now. Birds, rats, chipmunks. This is good. If they think the house is safe, maybe it is. Animals have better instincts.*

My panic-self is not to be silenced, and it screams. *WHAT IF THEY AREN'T ALONE UP THERE. IF THE ANIMALS CAN GET IN, SO CAN THE MONSTERS.*

I sit bolt upright breathing hard. Charlie's eyes come all the way open.

They are too big to get in, says the quiet voice. *And they aren't inside, or the little things would be dead already.*

Oblivious, peaceful, Little sleeps on. On the trundle, Jenny drools into her pillow.

The mice are Charlie's domain. He doesn't tolerate them inside the house for long. But they do get down in through the walls sometimes. And if they can, what else can?

It's a long time before I fall asleep again.

We're all up too early. Even Charlie seems bothered, pacing back and forth through the house with his tail high and twitching, never settling in one spot for more than a few minutes at a time. His food bowl stands largely ignored. Jenny's laptop is open in front of her. Keene has his Algebra 2 book out. Usually, he never does homework until the last minute of the night before it's due, sometimes even the day of. Nathan stabs at his phone every few minutes redialing his mother's cell phone, refreshing his email.

Some part of me thought (hoped?) we'd wake up and find the world back to normal. Beyond the carport, the butterflies have thickened into a swarming tapestry of orange and black, swirling in a riot of wings. There are so many of them, even more than yesterday. They seem to prefer the wide-open lawn over the shade, so there are relatively few of them right outside the door. It's good to know, in case we need to make a break for the car for some reason. I imagine those wings brushing against me, the crab legs grabbing and tearing flesh. With a shudder, I banish the thought and drop the blinds down.

I need to keep my hands busy so I don't doomscroll myself right into a full-blown panic attack. I plug the phone in like Mom said, turning it screen down on the counter. I can still listen for her text tone. "Who wants breakfast?" I ask and am met by a bunch of mutters. Everyone is in their own head.

We're lucky in one thing: My mother's weird shopping habits are finally paying off. She buys in bulk, even though it's only the four of us. Toilet paper, paper towels, toothpaste and toothbrushes, soap, mouthwash, cat food, litter. Cans upon cans of beans, giant bags of rice. Flour, sugar, cake mix. The freezer is full of meat and frozen vegetables, the pantry with stacks of cans: soups, vegetables, beans. We won't go hungry fast, not even if the power goes out, but that's where my head is now: *when* the power goes out.

I scramble eggs with cheese for everyone, but they barely look up from their devices, engrossed in the doom outside

I fill the Instant Pot with eggs for hard boiling, and Keene says, "Take your pills today?"

"Yes," I lie. I'll take them. But not until after I get the eggs going.

"What are you doing? Why are you hard boiling so many eggs?"

"Idiot," Jenny says, glancing up. "She's prepping for the apocalypse."

"Is that really necessary?" Keene asks.

"Leave her alone, it's something to do," Jenny says. "Besides, don't you think it looks worse out there?"

Keene stares at her for a moment, then goes back to his math.

"Any news?" Nathan asks, hitting redial on his phone between bites.

"Looters hitting stores," Jenny says.

"Seriously?"

"Yeah, and they're getting bitten. Can you imagine, risking your life for a television?"

"It could be they're after food or medical stuff," Nathan says.

"Where does Mom keep the bread maker?"

"We have bread, Shur. We don't need to make any," Keene says.

"It was just a question."

"You're angling hard toward crazy," he says, closing the book. His pencil sticks out, a pink-topped bookmark.

"No one seems worried but me," I say. "Like, did anyone else hear the noises from the crawl space last night? That's not worrying you?"

They're quiet. Jenny even pushes down the lid to the laptop a little bit. "What noises?"

"In the middle of the night? Scratching. I think it was

probably birds or mice." I describe what I heard as best I can, adding, "I don't think it was...those things. But if regular stuff is finding its way inside..."

Nathan shudders.

Keene looks over at Little, who is shoveling eggs into his mouth, in a rush to get to *Frozen*. "Wait a few minutes," he says, and I get it, I probably shouldn't have said anything in front of Shawn anyway.

When the dishes are cleared and Little has been parked in front of the television, we four gather around the kitchen table. Jenny's laptop has been set aside, but Nathan continues to press redial on his phone, desperate to get through to his mother. Maybe if it rang and went to voicemail, he'd give up, but it doesn't. Even when he's tried my phone, and Keene's, and Jenny's, there's just *Network Busy* messages, or it disconnects without doing anything. I squeeze his free hand and he looks up, a little surprised, and squeezes back, giving me a grateful smile. "You'll get through," I say, hoping I sound encouraging and supportive.

"Yeah," he says.

Jenny says. "So I was thinking... Shur is probably right about the usual pests getting in and hiding, like mice and stuff. The butterflies seem to be happy outside...but humans might not be so polite. Looters might not just go after stores. Houses sitting empty? People are opportunists, after all."

"And not too smart," Keene adds.

"Maybe we can get a gun from your neighbor Bill," Nathan says.

"I don't see that happening," I say.

"We don't need a gun," Jenny says. "We can make it hard to get inside, so anyone who tries gives up and goes somewhere easier."

"We could push the furniture up against the downstairs windows," Nathan says.

"If someone trying to get in breaks the glass," Jenny says, "we're going to have those *things* in the house. We need to board up."

"And when the power goes out, we're going to have to deal with all sorts of new problems," I say.

"Who said anything about the power going out?" Keene snaps.

"She's not wrong," Nathan says. "Even if it's not something epically weird, like butterflies chewing through a power line, you know it's only a matter of time before some idiot decides to take a drive and hits a pole. It's not like the power people are going to be rushing out to fix it."

I want to add more. I've thought about all this already. But Keene's reaction tells me that he's going to chalk up my contribution to hysteria. For now, I keep my mouth shut.

"Yeah," Jenny says. "So, flashlights and candles. Batteries. Blankets, all that stuff. Do you guys know where your Mom keeps all that stuff?"

"Yeah...but also, Mom has plywood sheets in the barn," Keene says, and this is what he's been holding back. He shifts uncomfortably in his chair. "A whole bunch of them for her bird house projects. They're big enough to cover a window."

"But we'd have to go out and get them? Forget it!" I say. It comes out shrill and way louder than I intended.

Jenny says, "Let's figure out what we have inside before we freak. Shur, you start thinking about food and supplies. Keene and I will look at the windows and doors situation. Nathan..."

No one wants to make him get off his phone. He got an email from his sister saying she's closed up in her apartment at school with two of her roommates. No word from his Mom or Dad, though, and the phone barely leaves his hand for any reason. "And Nathan can keep an eye on Little," she finishes.

Keene and Jenny head for the dining room to start examining the windows there first, but I linger for a moment, feeling like Nathan might need a friend.

"Hey," I say. "Is there anything I can do?"

He shakes his head. "No. But...thanks for asking."

"I could warm up some Pop-Tarts? Tell you a bad joke?"

Nathan forces a smile. "I'm good."

"No you're not."

"No, I'm not."

"Sitting with Little isn't all glamour and shine," I say. "There's a lot of answering random questions about dinosaurs and imagining you're in a castle. But it is distracting, if nothing else. It'll be good for you to get your mind off this. And the phone will be right there with you."

Nathan rubs a hand down his cheek and stands. "Yeah, you're right. I need to do something besides just sit here. Is there anything special Little likes to do?"

"You want to be a hero? Play Candy Land with him."

"Oh, I could do that!" Nathan says, brightening.

"Watch out. He cheats," I warn.

Nathan starts to leave the room, then turns back. He gives me a quick peck on the top of the head, like Keene would. "Hey," he says. "Thanks for trying." Then he disappears into the den, calling, "Hey, kid, I hear you're a Candy Land champ!"

I'm glad if Nathan's stuck anywhere, it's with us. I'd hate to have to worry about him too.

8

When the sun dawns on the second full day, the raw excitement of everything that's happened so far is gone. Not that this has been fun in any way, but it has been undeniably all consuming. Every single thought has been about the butterflies since civics class ended in an uproar. About understanding them, escaping them, surviving them. But the *new* has worn off. Now, it's like being trapped inside during a nasty snowstorm that won't end. We can't go outside. We can't get away from each other, not really.

Keene is camped out in his room with Nathan, playing video games. Jenny's in her usual spot at the kitchen table with her laptop, doomscrolling for hours at a time. Only Little is in his glory, watching a Disney movie marathon and playing with every toy he owns, even some from the depths of his toy box that he's long since forgotten about.

I'm cleaning the kitchen. The laundry is running. The toilet in the bathroom is polished to a high sheen. Upstairs, my bed is neatly made, and Little's vast collection of bedtime stuffed animals have been carefully relocated to a wicker basket taken from Mom's room. I am trying to create order. It doesn't feel like I'm succeeding.

"Will you sit?" Jenny asks without so much as a glance up from her screen.

"I really can't."

Is it still morning outside? Noon? Night? We had breakfast together a hundred hours ago. I glance at the clock. Two hours ago. It's only 11:00 a.m. 11:00 a.m. How am I supposed to go on like this?

I want to watch the news, but dislodging Little from the television would take an act of God. Instead, I fiddle with Mom's smart device, a ten-inch screen parked on the counter so she can listen to the news or follow along with recipes as she cooks.

"—live from Florida's west coast, where Hurricane Elayne is creating chaos for Gulf residents caught between shelter-in-place and evacuation orders. Glen, what's the situation there?"

"Lester, I'm here at Home Depot in Sarasota and, as you can see, the leading edge of the storm is almost here. Winds have picked up considerably and, while it's not raining yet, this storm is expected to dump anywhere between six and twelve inches of rain on Sarasota County in the next few hours." Glen is decked out in a yellow raincoat and clutches his microphone like a life preserver. Behind him, Home Depot is an orange block against the darkening morning sky. "Usually Home Depot would be mobbed at a time like this, with locals buying last-minute supplies. As you can see, Lester, that's not the case with Elayne. The vast majority of businesses in this area are closed, and the locals are staying put."

"And the butterflies, Glen? How are they faring in this weather?"

"They seem to be keeping primarily to higher altitudes, Lester. That's the only blessing in this situation so far. Sir? Sir! Can we get you for one minute?"

Off camera, someone says, "What the hell is he doing out here?"

The man Glen has waved over appears to be in his midthirties, with orange-red hair and a thick smattering of freckles across his pasty white face. The screen is kind of small, but the guy doesn't look very healthy.

"Sir, what's your name?"

The man blinks twice and stares directly into the camera for a second, like he's not sure where to look. "My name is Emmanuel."

"Emmanuel, are you aware there's a shelter-in-place order? It's not safe to be outside."

"My name is Emmanuel," the man repeats. "I got bit."

"What?"

"I got bit right here on my arm. Yesterday. My name is Emmanuel."

"Yes," Glen says, glancing at a point above the camera, probably at some equally confused cameraman. "Emmanuel, do you have a fever? Do you need medical attention? Did you clean out the wound?"

"Got bit. Got bit right here on my arm. Yesterday. Need to get some screws for my storm shutters. They're flapping. They're flapping right here on my arm."

Jenny's standing behind me now. "What's up with that guy?"

"Lester, it appears we need to help our friend Emmanuel

here—" Glen's thought is cut off by a combination of gunfire and his own screaming.

The view goes through a wild arc as the camera drops. It hits the ground, bouncing, before settling on its side. A pair of men step in front of the camera with guns. Glen runs in a circle, head down and his arms covering the hood of his yellow raincoat, before disappearing.

Boom! Boom!

Emmanuel wanders into the shot, unbothered by whatever is happening. His mouth is still moving. We can't hear him, but the shapes seem to be *arm* and *Emmanuel* and *bit*.

"Glen!" Lester's professional nature has reached its limit as he shouts the reporter's name.

The camera is hoisted back up and points at Glen, who is on his haunches inside the news van.

"Lester, that was a close one. We do have security with us today, and they just shot an attacking butterfly out of the sky. We're going to deliver Emmanuel to the hospital now. Back to you in the studio."

The feed cuts to a commercial, and I thumb the power button. "That..."

"Was intense?" I finish Jenny's half-articulated thought.

"What was wrong with Emmanuel?" she asks.

I say, "Maybe he has an infection from being bitten." I think of Sandra-or-Sarah, the owner of the bakery, and her blood-soaked arm. "Glen asked if he'd cleaned the wound."

"Yeah. Like they said at the news conference," Jenny says. I can see the wheels turning in her head.

"What are you thinking?" I ask.

She shrugs. "It's just...you heard that guy. He wasn't making any sense. That would have to be one hell of a high fever for him to be so delirious."

"Great. So, if they don't eat you, the fever kills you anyway?"

"Don't worry about it," Jenny says, laying a hand on my arm. "We're safe in here. Clean a sink or something."

⸻

By dinner time, tempers are starting to grow short.

"Any news from your parents?" I ask Nathan, who stabs his potato with a little too much enthusiasm in response.

"Any from yours?" he retorts.

"There's was a huge accident in South Olmstead," Jenny answers. "It took out power for most of the town."

"That's where your mom works?" Nathan asks me, his annoyance changing to pity.

"Yeah, so she probably can't charge her phone or anything," I say. "I keep trying to call, but I only get the network busy message or voicemail."

"Sorry," he says.

"Me too," I answer. "But maybe your parents will call soon. I'm sure they're thinking about you all the time."

"I've never been so bored in my entire life," Keene says. "Seriously, I thought twelve uninterrupted hours of *Battle Station: Siege* was my dream."

"Doesn't help that the server went down," Nathan grumbles. "Me and you playing without the rest of the team isn't exactly the same."

"When is this going to end?" Keene asks. It's sort of a general, no-one-can-answer kind of question, but he's looking at Jenny.

"Well," she says, scratching a spot under her eye absently, "I guess that depends on the government, right? They write doomsday scenarios for everything."

"Like what?" Nathan asks.

"Like what?" Little echoes, although I'm 99% sure he has no idea what a doomsday scenario is. Nathan reaches over and ruffles his hair.

"Crazy stuff. Alien invasions. Pandemics, deadly plagues, planetwide natural disasters. If you've seen it in a movie, there's probably a plan for it."

"Sounds like bullshit to me," Keene says.

"You asked."

"I asked when it was going to be over," he corrects.

Jenny rolls her eyes. "Let's assume that the government planned for a very large plague of locusts. That's a thing that actually happens. Not here, but it happens in Africa. So, they would be readying planes with enormous amounts of pesticides and coordinating with other places where it's happening."

"Cool," Keene says, his voice sounding suddenly more chipper. "So, we could be back to school next week."

"They're just bugs," Jenny says authoritatively. "We've got a whole industry dedicated to pest control. Not to mention the Air Force has a whole fleet of planes that can be used to drop pesticides. Part of why they want us to shelter in place probably has to do with not wanting people outside breathing in deadly chemicals."

"That and the whole *the bugs will eat you thing*," I mutter, but everyone ignores me. I notice Jenny is not bringing up the topic of Emmanuel and infected bites. It's all positive; it's all going to be okay.

Outside, butterflies bounce off the siding and tick their crab claws against the windows. If I don't have my headphones on, I can hear them, and then all I can think about is how they're looking for a way in. Honestly, I don't think they're that smart. If they were, the windows would have been smashed long ago, and we'd be huddled the basement like Neanderthals in a cave hoping saber-tooth tigers don't find us.

Oh God.

After dinner, I decide Little needs a bath. I fill the tub and put him in it with bubble bath and all his floatie toys. He's tired. There are dark circles under his eyes, but he giggles and splashes all the same.

I doomscroll.

In Helsinki, Finland, the locals got creative with homemade flamethrowers and now half the city is on fire. CNN's anchor is nearly breathless as they air a cell phone video, saying, "That's the Uspenski Cathedral!" I'll take his word for it. There's not much to see but a flaming heap of brick and smoke.

The group at the school is doing okay, so far as I can tell. They're still mostly in the gym, where mats have been spread out and backpacks have been repurposed as pillows. Jocelyn Reed, who's on the soccer team with me, posted a story yesterday. "Hey, hey, hey!" Jos holds the phone high over her head, so we can see the masses of people behind her. Lots of people are pacing, many are lying on their mats, but most are clustered in groups. Jos continues, "Posting an update for my peeps in the outside world! Hope this uploads. Our Wi-Fi situation is crap." Her usually glossy hair is pulled up into a high ponytail, the skin under her eyes stained dark. "We're not living our best lives, but we are surviving. The cafeteria is stocked, and the power is still on. Mad props to Mrs. Covington, who's kind of in charge here now." Mrs. Covington is an English teacher. I'm curious as to what happened to the principal and vice principals that she'd be in charge, but Jos doesn't elaborate. Instead, she says, "We've boarded up a bunch of classrooms, and the bathrooms are still working. We can take showers. That's the good news. The bad is that a bunch of people were bitten. A few of them are okay. TJ! Show your arm to the camera!" She points the camera at a kid I don't know, who holds up a bandaged limb. "It's gross, but healing. But a few people got it worse, and they're quarantined, so I guess...I guess I don't know. Mom and Dad and Chrissy, if you're seeing this, I love you, and I'll see you soon." *#SurvivingTheSwarm #EffButterflies*

I don't at all like the "guess I don't know" about the quarantined. What does she mean? Why are some of them okay, but some of them aren't? I want to scream into her comments "tell me more!" But the rest of Jos's comments are things like "Stay safe" and "Luv u, gurl," so I stop myself from demanding answers and settle for a "thinking of you all" with some heart emojis.

A research station at the North Pole and a ship near the South Pole have posted nearly identical videos of butterflies, so not even really cold places are exempt from whatever this plague is. Their butterflies are bright blue with black stripes and are just as big as ours. At the South Pole, they've left a litter of dead penguins in the snow. But the North Pole video is highlighted by whoops of excitement from a team stranded at the Abisko Scientific Research Station. The video shows Arctic foxes hunting the butterflies, plucking them out of the sky, pinning them face down in the snow, and tearing off their wings, leaving the wormlike remains to squirm on the hard pack. The foxes really seem to be enjoying themselves, like it's a game. For their part, the butterflies seem to be adapting by flying higher or staying over a nearby lake.

"What are you doing?" Keene asks, standing in the doorway.

"Giving Stinky over there a bath."

"No," he says. "I mean what are *you* doing? You aren't doom-scrolling, are you?"

I shrug. "What else is there to do?"

"You know that's not good for you," Keene says.

"Thanks, Mom."

He sighs. "Did you take your pills?"

"Yes, Mom."

"Don't do that."

"Do what?"

"Dismiss me like that."

"Did you want something specific, Keene, or did you just come in here to take out your boredom on me? Because if you're that bored, you can take a turn with Little. Or doing the laundry. Or cooking. Or running the dishwasher."

"I had to pee. I'll use Mom's bathroom." He gives me one last scowl. "Don't doomscroll."

But what else am I supposed to do? Assume that all is well in the world, and Jenny's prediction of an air assault is coming true? We'll wake up tomorrow to a fog of pesticides and a litter of bug corpses?

Ms. Worst Case Scenario, that's me all right.

9

'm going to prep the basement," I say at breakfast.

"For what?" Keene asks.

"For...like...if a window breaks or something," I say. "If we have to hide somewhere safer." This is something that the calm, thoughtful, in-the-dark voice has been whispering.

"We can board up the windows," he says. "I told you. Mom has plywood in the barn."

"I don't want to argue about that." I push down my panic at the idea of him leaving the house. I think of bloody arms and gunshots outside of Home Depot. "But it never hurts to have a backup plan."

"She's right," Nathan says. "Plus, having the basement as a backup doesn't mean we can't still board up the windows."

"Thanks," I say to him, although I'm a little salty that the idea of going out to the barn to get plywood isn't off the table.

"Can I help?" he asks.

Keene rolls his eyes and rises. "I'm going back to the game." He dumps his plate in the sink for someone else (me) to wash and heads back through the den toward the stairs without another word.

"I'll keep an eye on Little," Jenny volunteers without getting up from the table. Little has long since cleared his frozen waffles and is back in front of the television.

"Where do we start?" Nathan asks, following me downstairs.

I don't have a plan so much as a vague sense that the basement might be our safest backup. We can't go to the barn. We can't easily get to Bill's house or back to the high school.

I bite my lip and survey the mess. We've accumulated stacks upon stacks of clear plastic storage boxes containing everything from old stuffed animals to clothing to holiday decorations. An entire rack of camping gear, including sleeping bags. A metal frame for an air mattress, piles of sports equipment. My brain tries to sort the useful from the useless. Baseball bats, good. Christmas tree, not so much.

"Hey!" I free a sideline Gatorade jug from a tangle of sports equipment, leftover from our town league soccer games back when Dad was the coach. Seeing it gives me a twinge of nostalgia. "Can you maybe wash this out and fill it with water? You'll have to use the bathtub. It doesn't fit in the kitchen sink...we used to fill it outside with a hose."

"Sure," Nathan says, taking the jug and heading back up.

Left alone, which is what I wanted, I start to move things. I empty one of the metal shelving units, dumping the contents into a corner. Now we can stack cans and stuff if we need to be down here. I clear the laundry table of clean clothes left for folding and put those on top of the dryer. Now we have a place to eat. It starts to come together in my mind—a safe haven. Half of me wants to go to ground. The other half wants to stand and fight. I tell them both to be quiet.

By the time Nathan returns with the jug, I've shoved enough stuff out of the way to make room for a tent. A tent feels like it could be safe. A cave within a cave within a house within a storm. But it doesn't have to go up tonight. Not yet.

"Wow," he says. "You were busy. Where do you want this?"

"Second shelf," I say, pointing at the rack.

"Can I ask you a question?" Nathan asks as he shoves the jug onto the wire rack.

"Sure."

"Is this what it's like for you all the time?"

"What do you mean?"

Nathan drops his gaze. "I mean, I feel like...stuck. Like I want to run, but there's nowhere to go. My brain won't stop turning. I can't make it shut up."

"Not all the time," I say. "But a lot, yeah."

"Oh."

"It helps to be busy," I say. "It helps me, anyway."

He smiles a sad "this is my life now" smile, and I feel for him, but everything is out of my control.

With the basement prep started, I turn to another thing I love: lists. I work around Jenny as she continues her vigil at the kitchen table, poring over news sites and forums and anything else that can give her even the most basic idea of what's going on out there.

I list all the nonperishables we have. Flour. Sugar. Salt and pepper, pancake mix, flavored powders for water, jars of pickles, cans of vegetables, boxes of pasta. Semiperishables. Bags of chips, boxes of cookies, cereal. Then everything else. Lunch meat. Bread. Frozen foods, eggs, an already-dwindling supply of fruit. Cheese, butter, milk. I should make a chart and hang it up in the pantry so I can keep track of what to use and what to save.

"Look at this," Jenny says, flagging me over. "This is like, holy shit." At first, I'm not sure what I'm seeing, but then I realize: It's a swarm eating something.

"God, that's not a person, is it?" I ask, nearly gagging.

"It's a zebra," she says.

Keene enters the kitchen and hears this last part. "What the hell?" he says, catching sight of the screen. "Enough!" He closes the laptop hard with one hand and snatches my cell phone off the table with the other. "You know better," he says to Jenny. "You of all people."

"It's not like it's not really happening," Jenny argues.

"*She* doesn't need to see it."

"*She* has a right to know," Jenny snaps.

"*She* is right here," I say. "Come on, you guys. I'm not that fragile."

They both look away. I know what that means. They think I am that fragile. But Jenny believes the best way to make me stronger is to expose me to the world, whereas Keene would stuff me into a box to keep me safe forever.

"I'm gonna go...somewhere else," Jenny says, picking up her laptop. She gives Keene a glare and disappears into the den.

I hold out my hand for my phone, but Keene places it face-down on the table. "Sit," he says.

I cross my arms instead. "You need to stop trying to manage me."

A strange combination of emotions flash across his face. Surprise, anger, then finally resignation. Like he's dealing with Little and needs to use his baby words. It pisses me off. Not only because Keene is treating me like some sort of broken thing, but also because this is his comfort zone — managing me instead of feeling things.

I stopped being depressed a long time ago, and now I'm a hot mess of anxiety. Anxiety seems called for in this situation. And I don't want to be managed. He's not in control of the situation outside any more than I am.

"You're pulling into your shell," Keene says.

"I'm not," I say.

"You can't. Mom said to watch you and make sure, and so I'm going to do that."

"Then actually watch, Keene," I say. "Jenny is doing all the same things I am. So is Nathan. So are you."

"For us, it's normal. For you, it's a warning sign."

"I love when you act like you know me better than I know me," I say, exasperated. "Mom said I should close up the house, plug in the phones, and keep Little with me. I did all that."

"What else did she say?" Keene asks, smug, crossing his own arms.

"She told me not to meltdown," I say. "And I'm not melting down, Keene. I'm not hiding in my room or sleeping all the time. Yeah, I took my pills today and changed my underwear. Is my brain crawling? Yes, it is, and you know what? That's fucking normal. If you need something to manage to make yourself feel better, Little's still in his pajamas. There are dirty plates in the den.

I stepped on Legos at least a dozen times this morning because his shit is all over the floor. Sooner or later, he's going to get bored and start noticing that things have gone sideways. Maybe you could use your super normal, well-adjusted brain to start planning for that!" My voice has gotten louder and louder, and I realize I'm shouting by the end of this little speech. Keene has gone pale, and there's no noise coming from the den. They've muted the television.

"I'm not trying to manage you," Keene says, and now his voice is dealing-with-an-angry-cat cautious, which makes me even angrier.

"Stop picking on me!" I say, struggling to keep my voice calm. "We are all in this together."

"Only one of us ended up in the hospital," he mutters.

"Yeah, that happened," I say. "It wasn't yesterday, and I've learned to deal with myself."

"Well, it doesn't show," he says, the cautious tone gone, replaced by anger. "I mean, Jesus, how many times a day can someone go to the bathroom? How many times has Mom had to talk you down from a panic attack in the last year?"

"That doesn't mean I'm broken," I scream. "It means I'm dealing with it! I'm a mess and I'm allowed to be, and who the hell are you to judge me, anyway? Not everyone got over Dad's death as easy as you did, Keene."

"I didn't get over it easy," he shouts back. "You having a complete mental breakdown doesn't prove you're mourning harder!"

"Jesus," I say. "Is that what you think? It's a competition?"

"Guys." Jenny and Nathan are standing in the kitchen doorway. "This is kind of awful," Nathan says.

Jenny nods in agreement. "Look," she says, as Keene opens his mouth. "Wait. Let me talk, okay? She's not having a breakdown, Keene. I promise. You're twins, I get it, but we're best friends. You know if she was falling apart, I'd say something to you, right?"

Keene glares, but he doesn't stop her.

Nathan says to me, "Dude, your brother loves you, and this situation...it kind of sucks."

"Not kind of," I say.

"Yeah, not kind of at all," Nathan agrees.

"We're used to things being a certain way," Jenny says. "Things fell apart for you guys a long time ago, and it's pretty normal that you'd be using your standard coping mechanisms to deal with it now."

"Oh, thanks, Dr. Jenny," Keene says, rolling his eyes.

"Knock it off," she says with some authority, and I can almost hear the future mom she might grow up to be. "I'm saying you're both right, and you're both wrong, and you both need to pull your shit together to take care of Little."

"But it's happening again," Keene shouts. He looks surprised at himself, and we're all startled.

"What?" I ask.

"It's...it's happening again," he says, more softly. "First Dad. Now Mom."

"Oh God," I say. I've been thinking about Mom too, but I've been studiously focused on the idea that she's safe and alive and called. Locked in a cafeteria. Has food and water. But Keene... "You think she's dead," I say.

Keene turns away fast, and I know he's crying.

Jenny and Nathan start forward in lockstep, but I shake my head and shoo them away.

"Keene," I whisper, putting a hand on his shoulder. "She's not dead."

"You don't know that." He puts his hand over mine. "She could be dead or alive. I hate it. I hate not knowing."

"She was safe when she called. She'll always come home for us."

"Dad didn't," he says.

I don't know what to say to that, exactly, but I take my hand back so I can lace my arms around his torso. I lay my head against his back. "If you need to manage me to feel better, I get it," I say. He's warm through his shirt. "But I'm not breaking, Keene. Mom said I have to hold it together for you and Little, so I'm going to. She's not dead until someone tells us she's dead, and I choose to believe she's alive."

We stay like that for a long time. Eventually, Keene turns and hugs me close. He stares down at me. "I'm sorry I shouted."

"Me too."

"Will you please, please stop doomscrolling?"

I nod. "I'll leave it to Jenny."

Keene kisses the top of my head and says, "I guess I should go get that monkey out of his pajamas and into a bath." He hesitates a moment. "I love you."

"Ditto, bro," I say, and I mean it more than anything I've ever said in my life.

10

My prediction about Little's boredom threshold starts to come true the very next day. As I come down the stairs with a load of laundry, he's arguing with Keene in the den.

"But when can we go outside?"

"When the monsters are gone."

"But when are they going to be gone? I want Mommy."

"I don't know, buddy," Keene says. "I want them to go away too."

"Then *make* them go away," Little demands. "Because I want to. Go. Out. Side!" He stomps his foot with each declaration, his tiny face screwed up in a scowl. "I want my friends. I want Ms. Caroline. I want Mommy!"

"Hey, buddy," I say, setting the laundry down. "How about we make some cookies?"

"I don't want to make cookies," Little says, dropping onto the floor. "I want to go on the swings."

"Well, we can't," I say. "But we can turn on another movie."

"I'm sick of TV! I'm sick of it, sick of it, sick of it!" There's a full-blown tantrum coming. I can feel it like the hint of a storm on a summer breeze.

"We could color," I say. "Or we could do some Legos, or I can show you how to do laundry, which is very important."

"I want to go outside."

"There are monsters outside," I say.

"Jenny said we were going to be monster hunters," Little says. "I want to be a monster hunter."

"It's too dangerous," I say. "It's safe inside because the monsters don't know how to get in. And, besides, Jenny said we were monster escapers, not monster hunters."

"But I'm bored!" Little screams.

"That's enough!" Keene roars, finally losing his patience. "Shawn, do you remember the monster when we were driving? Did you see how big its teeth were? Did you see its giant claws?"

Little's chin starts to wobble, but Keene isn't done.

"We saw a person get eaten up by those teeth, Shawn," Keene says, standing so he towers over our little brother. "It bit her right in the arm and there was real blood everywhere, and it *ate* her arm, Shawn. Her arm was *all gone*."

"Jesus, Keene!" I say.

Keene looks at me, then down at Little, and seems to realize the damage he's done, but it's too late to take it back. Little bursts into tears and runs to me, throwing himself into my legs as hard as he can. I scoop him up.

"I'm sorry," Keene says lamely.

I can't do anything but shake my head at him. Little is sobbing so hard, it's difficult to hold onto him. I carry him up the stairs and into my bedroom.

Jenny's on the trundle bed for a change of pace, still staring at her laptop. She glances up. "I heard shouting—hey! What happened?"

"Keene got a little too creative," I say.

"Hey, Little," Jenny says, climbing onto the bed with us. "Are you okay?"

He doesn't speak. His sobbing escalates to howls, as if someone is physically twisting at his insides. When he finally does manage a word, I'm not even surprised what it is.

"Mommy," he huffs out, and I feel like someone punched my heart.

"Oh, honey," I say, smoothing his hair. All we can do is wait for the storm to pass.

Eventually, Little's sobs turn to regular crying, and the crying tapers to hitched breathing. It's awhile before I realize he's cried himself to sleep.

"What happened?" Jenny asks again.

"He's bored. He kept asking to go outside, and Keene finally lost his shit."

Jenny blows air out. "I get it. Both sides. I'm bored too. And cranky. I guess there's no good way to explain that to a four-year-old."

"Can you stay with him for a while? I want to talk to Keene."

"Yeah."

I settle Little onto a pillow. His stuffies from the previous night are still scattered on the bed, and I put one next to him. Even asleep, he looks miserable. His face is red and puffy, and both cheeks are streaked with drying tears.

Before I head down to confront Keene, I sit on the top stair alone and close my eyes. In through the nose. Out through the mouth. Repeat. Repeat. How am I supposed to take Mom's place? This isn't like babysitting. She won't be home by 11:00 p.m. with leftovers. I can't even call her to find out what to do. It's on me to be the grown-up, to make sure that my brothers don't crack.

I don't know if I can do it.

I have to do it.

My heart sends a sick rush of adrenaline up into my throat. It's not like good adrenaline. It's sick adrenaline, the kind that comes with dread and too much unrelieved anticipation.

Did I take my pills?

I took my pills.

I stand and walk down the stairs. Keene is on the couch with his head in his hands, almost as miserable as Little. I sit next to him.

"You gonna read me the riot act?"

"Nope."

"I messed up."

"A little. He'll get over it."

"I get that he's bored, but why doesn't he understand? He can't go outside. Jesus, Shur, what if he went outside?"

I take Keene's hand in my own.

"You're all clammy," he says. "Are you okay?"

"Borderline panic attack," I admit. "Are you okay?"

"Do you think I'm okay? Did I sound okay?"

"Nope."

We're quiet again. Finally, Keene asks, "How do you live like this all the time?"

"I don't know, Keene. I just do."

Napping has done wonders for Little. The circles under his eyes are still dark, but he's babbling along a million miles a minute as he helps me and Jenny with dinner. She's teaching him about proper place settings. Mom would approve.

Nathan and Keene file in. While Little seems to mostly have forgotten the incident before his nap, Keene hasn't. He's watching Little like the kid might burst into tears and run screaming from him at any moment. His guilt is so thick, it practically radiates off him in waves. I squeeze his bicep and say, "Go help him in the bathroom so he doesn't flood us out."

"Are you sure?"

"Yes. Can you handle it?"

He sighs. "Yes." He disappears into the bathroom, and I hear him say, "How much soap does one person need? Are you washing an elephant?" Little's giggles drift out.

When we're all together and everyone's plates are full, I say, "So, I was thinking we probably need a little more structure around here."

"Oh God, you're the grown-up," Keene says.

"She's the best at worrying," Jenny says. "That's a very grown-up thing."

"You guys," Nathan says, giving me a sympathetic glance.

"Yeah, I guess I am," I agree, and Nathan gives me that beautiful smile. "Little is bored."

"I'm not bored!" Little says, stuffing a spoonful of peas into his mouth. "I'm eating."

"Close your mouth when you chew," Jenny says. "No one wants to see peas rolling out of your face and onto the table."

Little giggles but closes his mouth.

My mind wanders back to the feeling I had when I was sitting on the stairs, near panic, realizing this isn't going to just end. Some part of me thought disaster prep was enough. Some part of me thought doing a thousand loads of laundry would be enough. But now all of me knows this could be our life for a while. For a long, long while.

"Let's think of this as a family meeting," I say. "I can't be in charge. None of us can. We have to be a family and work together. You guys, I can't do it alone. I'm making food and doing the laundry, but we need...more."

Keene stares down at his peas, avoiding my eyes. He's not eating them. He rolls them from one end of the plate to the other, like he did when we were Little's age.

"So, what are you thinking?" Nathan asks. "We treat this like pioneer times and set up our own school?"

I half smile. "I wasn't going there, but I like it."

Jenny says, "Regular bed times during the week. Baths or showers every day."

"For as long as the power is on," I say. It slips out of my mouth before I can stop it.

"You're so sure it's going to get worse," Keene says. He's still pushing those peas around. What I really don't like is that he's not questioning it. It's not a sarcastic statement at all. It sounds resigned.

"I'm not the Oracle at Delphi," I say. "But nothing seems to be stopping these things, and I've seen about a million disaster movies."

Jenny lays her fork down and says, "I didn't want to say

anything before, but I guess now's the time. I was checking the news this morning. The government tried to get some crop dusters up in the air. To poison the butterflies from above."

"That's great!" Nathan says, practically bouncing. "Finally!"

"It's not, though. They couldn't get the planes off the ground. The butterflies are so thick, they got into the engines. Even the propeller planes couldn't take off. There's no way to get the planes into the air. I'm guessing Plan B was a lot like Plan A, but with fire instead of poison. But either way, they needed the planes to work..."

"So there's no plan?" Keene asks, finally looking up.

"I guess the plan is probably to spray insecticide on the ground or to use flamethrowers."

"That didn't work out so well for Helsinki," I say.

"That's not the only place on fire," Jenny says, trailing off. She's watching Little, who is stuffing as many peas into his cheeks as humanly possible, so that he resembles a chipmunk. At least someone is enjoying dinner.

"How long?" I ask. I'm trying for casual, but it comes out as a whisper, like my throat doesn't really want any part in asking the worst question. "How long until there's a new plan?"

They all look at Jenny then, Keene, Nathan, even Little. It's the question no one wanted to ask, and no one really wants the answer.

She shakes her head. "No one knows. If it was isolated, other countries could send help. But everyone is in the same boat. We're outnumbered."

"But they'll figure it out, right?" Nathan asks. "You said before..." He trails off as Jenny pushes away from the table. She stands at the sink with her back to us. "You said before they have plans for everything. What did you call it? Doomsday scenarios. They have to have a backup plan, right?"

"Jenny?" I say.

But when Jenny turns back, she's pale and her eyes are filling with tears. She says, "Nathan, the plans didn't work. Maybe they'll come up with something eventually, but...but the plans didn't work." And more softly, "They were supposed to work."

"What do you mean, eventually?" Nathan asks. "What does that mean, Jenny?"

"It means I don't know, Nathan!" She isn't quite shouting, but there's a note of hysteria creeping into her tone that's genuinely upsetting. "It means I don't know. No one knows. It means someday. Next week, next month, next year. Never. I don't know."

After that, no one is really very hungry.

11

Today is first day of "school" for Little. Nathan and Jenny are taking a turn at teaching him. They have a whole day laid out (with some input from me and Keene). So far, they've practiced ABCs, have sung about roughly thirty animals on Old MacDonald's farm, and have finger-painted several masterpieces currently drying on the refrigerator. Right now, they're playing hide-and-seek while I organize our supplies.

The sense of "doing something" is soothing, even if it doesn't actually change anything. I've emptied a half dozen of Mom's large, plastic storage containers into garbage bags so I can use the containers themselves. One sits on the counter behind me as I consider the enormous pile of candles on the table.

I don't think I ever really fully grasped just how many jar candles we have. There are dozens in every color, scent, and seasonal variant. Birthday Cake, Maple Syrup, Winter Breeze, Cotton Candy, Fresh Laundry. Who comes up with these things? I've organized the candles by size, with the biggest jars at one end of the table, then the middle-sized ones, the smaller ones, then votives and, finally, birthday candles. We are not going to run out of candles any time soon, so at least we have light, even if it does come with weird smells.

Matches too. Mom has a huge can of paper matchbooks, plus the longer ones to light the fireplace. There are three stick lighters (although one is nearly empty) and three old regular plastic lighters. That's good—it means we won't have to learn to make fire with rocks and sticks any time soon.

"Come out, come out wherever you are!" Jenny calls from the next room, and I smile. She and Nathan are so good with Little. He'll sleep really well tonight, I think.

I put a jar candle in the bathroom and set aside two more for the upstairs bathrooms, along with some matches. Each room will get one jar candle for starters, so we have them placed when the power goes off. The rest will go into the storage bin, and the storage bin will go into the pantry for easy access.

When I'm done, I mark off the chart and move onto my next chore.

"Little? Come out, come out wherever you are! You win, buddy!"

He's really kicking their ass at this game.

Blankets. By the calendar, summer isn't over yet, and with all the windows closed up, it's been a bit warm in the house, even with ceiling fans running. But we don't know how long this is going to go on. This scares me almost as much as the potential to run out of food. Creating a food plan is my next chore, and that's a big one, almost as big as Keene's job of creating a defense plan for the windows and an escape plan if we need to get out. I can't even bring myself to think about outside, so that one's all on him. I can control inside. Thinking about outside makes my heart beat too fast, so I turn my attention to the blanket on the back out of the couch. It smells like sweat and something sour. Probably milk. Into the wash it goes.

Outside, the whine of an engine breaks the quiet.

Mom!

I rush to the window, pulling back the drape, shoving the shade aside a tiny bit, and startle back with my heart in my throat. There's a butterfly right there, hanging on the screen. Can it see me? I don't think so. Up close like this, it's even more terrifying and awful. Its torso is like the leg of a tarantula, covered in bristles. The split where its mouth opens is a closed seam. As it shifts, I get a glimpse of teeth.

But a car!

I see it, and my heart sinks with disappointment. It's a black pickup truck with tinted windows, driving along at a crawl. The butterfly on the window screen launches itself toward the street, attracted by the sound. Dozens more gravitate in the same direction, a thick cloud of wings beating. As I watch the truck's progress, sound starts to blast from speakers mounted to the roof of the cab. "The Star-Spangled Banner."

Jesus, what a weirdo.

Or maybe I'm being judgmental because it would never occur to me to drive around an empty neighborhood in the middle of a global disaster blasting the national anthem. It's possible the driver has good intentions. Maybe he's trying to remind us that America still stands. That we'll be free again.

"Little! Come out! You win!"

Is that like the third time they've called for him? He usually hides in really obvious places, like directly behind the couch you're sitting on while counting or under the kitchen table.

I pick up the blanket and carry it to the kitchen, draping it over a chair.

Nathan rushes in. "We can't find Little," he says.

"What? How far could he have gotten?"

"Shur, we've checked everywhere. Like every closet, under every single bed. We can't find him."

As if in slow motion, I turn to look at the back door.

The latch is open.

I can't breathe. I can't breathe. *I can't. I can't. I can't. I can't.*

"Get Keene," I wheeze through a closing throat. "Get Keene right now."

If he went outside...

You were in here the whole time.

No I wasn't. I was in the basement getting the containers for at least ten minutes. Keene is upstairs. They were supposed to be watching him.

The latch is unlocked.

It could have been unlocked before. Do you remember locking it?

I don't remember locking it. I don't. But I always lock it. Do I always lock it? I always try to remember to lock it, then I agonize about whether I remembered to lock it. But did I this time? Did someone else open the door to look outside?

"What's going on?" Keene asks as he comes in, trailed by Jenny.

"We can't find Little," Nathan repeats. "We were playing hide-and-seek. He's..."

"The door is unlocked," I whisper.

"He wouldn't have," Keene says. "Not after the other night. He wouldn't have, would he?"

In through the nose, out through the mouth. Repeat. Repeat.

"We have to go out and look," Jenny says definitively. "It's my fault. I'll go."

"I'll go with you," Nathan says.

"No one is going anywhere yet," I say. Logic. Think logically. "Not until we recheck the house."

"But he could be out there!" Keene says.

I shake my head hard. "Not until we check. If he's out there... Well, we can't risk going out unless there's a reason."

Because if he's out there...

I can't finish that thought. I'll start screaming.

"No," I say. "He's not. He's not out there. He's inside." I stride past them, nearly pushing Jenny out of the way, stopping at the bottom of the stairs. "Little! Game is over! Everyone got bored because you're so good at hiding!"

No answer.

I breathe. Breathe. Breathe. Up the stairs. One at a time, not galloping like I want to. "Little," I say in the hallway. "Where you at, buddy?"

I think I hear something down at the end of the hall. Maybe. "Little?" I follow the sound, not sure if it's real or just the ringing in my ears. Vaguely, I'm aware of Keene behind me.

"Little?"

"I hear something," Keene says.

"Me too. Mom's room."

The door to her room is closed up tight, as it has been most of this time. It's her sanctum, and we've avoided going in there as much as possible so far. We're not allowed in without permission, and old habits die hard. But...

One shade is up, and sunlight streams into the room, sending dust motes dancing across the white bedspread. For a moment, my heart aches with unexpected force. It's all her: her smell, her personality, her jeans hanging from the back of a chair like she'll be back tonight to throw them on.

That shade was down. I closed them all.

Keene rushes to the window. "Closed. Locked."

Of course. There's no way Little could have reached the latch. "Little?"

Again, that tiny sound. A snuffle. Frightened crying. We follow it together to the bathroom door.

I push it open. "Little? It's Shur."

There he is, in the shower, his knees wrapped to his chin. "I looked outside," he says. "I looked and the monsters saw me, so I had to hide."

It's Keene who leans down to pluck him up from the corner of the shower. Little clings to him with one arm and both legs, popping his thumb into his mouth. "I don't want to go outside anymore, Keene," he whispers into our brother's ear.

12

After that, it's nothing and nothing and nothing for days. It's not the worst kind of waiting, this calm between storms. The worst kind is when something really bad is probably going to happen, and you know it's coming, but you have to sit there and wait anyway. Like when my Dad got in his accident but didn't die right away. That's the worst.

That's what broke me. Knowing the worst was likely to happen but waiting for it and waiting for it. Having false hope when he didn't die right away. Thinking that maybe a miracle would happen. Knowing it probably wouldn't. Where do you put that kind of anticipation? It was too big for my brain. Even when the end came, the anxiety never left.

But this is different. There's nothing to do, so I take my turn teaching Little. We read picture books and count to a hundred. We play with Play-Doh (and we have to be reminded that, while Play-Doh technically can be eaten, it is not actually food). We have lunch without fresh vegetables because we're out, and we're hoarding the frozen and canned vegetables. We color.

There's no more talk of visiting the barn to get plywood and supplies, because the butterflies are politely staying on their side of the walls.

The power goes out twice. The first time, it blinks a few times. Off, on again, off for ten seconds, on, off, then it stays on. The second time, it's off for more than a minute, and I think, *this is it; this is what we've been waiting for.* I feel the strangest sensation of relief, like waiting for this one thing is over. Then, there's a click and the refrigerator whines to life behind me.

Jenny is on the Internet all the time, except when she's eating, asleep, or taking a turn with Little. She knows more than she's saying. The rest of us could go look ourselves, of course. We all have phones. But I don't want to look. My whole world is in this house right now, safe behind our walls.

Everyone goes to sleep at 9:00 p.m.; everyone wakes up at 7:00 a.m. Charlie's litter box gets emptied. We develop an entire routine to throw our bags of garbage out onto the front porch without letting anything in or getting attacked. We save cardboard in case we need to burn it.

I try to read, but my brain wants nothing to do with it. Half of me is still listening for Mom's car or the sound of breaking glass. I don't sleep well. I mostly remember to take my pills and can tell when I don't because my mind crawls and swarms like the butterflies on our siding.

Nothing and nothing.

And then something. Something bad.

"Guys," Nathan calls from the dining room.

We don't use the dining room, and it's gotten dusty since the house got locked up. Nathan is at the window that looks out on the porch and the street beyond. The curtains are pushed back and the shade is up, which is unusual. The room is flooded with midday light, and I think I should dust before Mom gets back. Outside, the butterflies are still doing their thing, swarming and hunting, crawling on every surface.

But that's not what Nathan called us for.

"That's the truck from the other day," I say. "The music I heard was coming from that."

All four of us crowd around the window to stare.

The truck moves slowly down the center of the street. Limp flags hang from either side in the quiet, windless day. One might be the U.S. flag.

Without warning, "The Star-Spangled Banner" begins to blast from the speakers at a volume appropriate for a football stadium. Jenny lets out a yelp of surprise, and Nathan physically jumps.

This time, four people are standing in the back of the truck, covered head-to-toe in black. Ski masks, heavy jackets, combat pants, black gloves. I can't see their feet, but I'm sure they're wearing combat boots. Every inch of skin is covered. Butterflies hover over them, confused. Can they smell them under the clothing? Are they confused by the motion?

As we watch, they simultaneously raise guns, big, black weapons of war, and fire erupts into the sky.

I scream and drop, scrambling on all fours into the den. The gunfire mixes with the music, creating a cacophony that's woken Little from his nap. He's sitting up, rubbing his eyes, confused when I snatch him up. I run, hunched, into the kitchen, throwing the door to the basement open with a solid, hard yank that's so overzealous, I already know my arm will hurt later. We're down the stairs into the basement, and he's so startled, he hasn't even had time to begin to cry.

The others follow fast, thundering down the stairs seconds later. We sit huddled in a group on the cold floor, listening, holding our breath. Far above, the music, muffled, moves slowly, too slowly. Pops, like corn in the microwave, over and over. Pause. They must be reloading. New clips. It resumes. How long are they out there? Time stands still while we wait for the onslaught to pass. The music fades; the gunfire becomes faint. Then it stops, or at least moves out of range.

Keene is clutching my left bicep so tight I think it'll probably bruise in the shape of his long fingers. His other arm is around my right shoulder, and Little, wide-eyed with confusion and alarm, has his face pressed against my chest. Jenny is the first up. She paces to the bottom of the stairs, then back, opens her mouth as if to ask a question, snaps it shut. Paces again. Seems to make a decision. She says, "I'll go look. You guys stay here, okay?"

She takes the stairs by twos. To everyone else, it probably seems like she's in a rush, but this is Jenny—Jenny doesn't do things in half measures. The more scared she is, the more she commits. The door opens, the door closes. She's gone for a while, long enough for Little to cork his mouth with his thumb and start to doze off.

When she comes back, her intertwined hands wring at each other, worried. "There's a bullet hole upstairs. Through the window in your room, Shur, and into the wall over your bed. The window didn't break, but it's cracked all around the hole."

It's exposed, a weak point. And they could come back, spraying the neighborhood with lead again. We're lucky it's just one hole, I think. It probably isn't. It's probably just one that hit the window. I wonder if the outside of the house is covered in holes, a hundred little punctures. How many butterfly corpses are in the street?

This sort of settles things though. The argument for going to the barn is decided, regardless of my objections, because Jenny is right: The butterflies aren't the only thing we need to keep out.

Eventually, enough time passes for us to feel confident the gunfire is over for the time being. Gathered in the kitchen, an argument almost immediately begins over who will make the voyage to the barn, and who will stay behind.

"Me and Jenny," Nathan says, even as Keene starts to object. He holds up his hand, for once not relentlessly redialing his mother's number. The gunfire seems to have activated something in Nathan, like he realizes we're in danger too, not just his mom and dad. "You two need to be here for Little."

Keene says, "It should be me and you, not you and Jenny."

"No way," Jenny says. "That's your macho, testosterone, caveman instincts talking."

No one is suggesting I go, maybe because I'm standing by the table with my arms crossed, pouting. I can't help it. I still don't want anyone to go, even if I know it's the right thing to do for our safety.

Keene is gearing up to be a total dick to Jenny, I can see it. They get along sometimes, but then they get into these pissing matches. Before he can really tear into her, which won't help, I say, "You need to be in the basement to help unload the car."

"But I know where shit is in the barn!"

"Yeah," I say. "So make a map or whatever." Selfish, on my part. I don't want him out there, with the Butterfly Militia on the loose, let alone the butterflies themselves.

Jenny's eyes are narrowed, and she's itching for a fight. But she catches my expression and changes tack. "No one is happy about this, Keene. You want to be the one to go outside, I get it, but the same reasons you want to go out are the reasons you should stay in. You want to protect your family."

"Whatever. You get bitten, you stay in the barn."

"That's cold," Nathan says.

"Those are the terms. You still want to be a hero for some nails and batteries?" He's straightening, making himself taller, but that doesn't work on Jenny.

"So you're in charge now?" she asks, crossing her arms, ready for combat.

"It's my house."

"It's our house," I interrupt. "Knock it off, both of you."

They turn away from each other, petulant, and I close my eyes. Deep breath. Everyone wants to run face-first into the slimy jaws of insect death, but no one seems capable of talking like we're adults. Because we're not. We're really, really not.

Jenny waits a second for Keene to flare back up, but when he doesn't, she says, "Do we have any walkie-talkies?"

"No," I say.

"Yes," Keene says at the same time. "You know, those stupid Elmo things Mom got Little for Christmas?"

"I forgot about those."

"Do they have any range?" Nathan asks. "They're toys, right?"

"They should work between here and the barn," Keene says. "They're not going to work a mile away or anything."

"Can you find them?" Jenny asks. "It'll be best if we can keep in touch and with the phones..."

"I can, but, for the record, I still think you going instead of me is shitty idea," Keene says angrily.

Jenny starts to respond, but Nathan touches her arm and motions to the den. I think it's about privacy for me and Keene, not because they have anything profound to discuss.

"They're trying to help," I say, pulling out a chair to sit.

"It's going to get them dead," Keene says. He's leaning against the sink, looking out the window. There must not be much to see under the carport except his beater and butterflies.

"Give them a little credit. Butterflies were one thing. Gunfire is a whole other story."

He's silent for a long time before he asks, "What are you thinking about?"

Keene hears things in my voice other people cannot. Even Jenny. Sometimes I can lie to him, like about my pills, but not when he's really listening. "I'm wondering what Dad would do," I say, honestly, "if he was here."

"Yeah. Me too."

I don't want to be thinking about Dad, but being surrounded by death (and Mom being absent) has bubbled him right up to the surface of my brain. If he had lived, would be here protecting us? Or would he be on one of trips? What would he think of this barn pilgrimage? My heart twinges, and I shove his memory away.

"I really hate bugs," Keene says.

"I know."

After another long pause, he says, "When they go, they should wrap themselves in blankets. To keep the butterflies from biting them." That's as close as he's going to get to accepting not going himself, to sending his best friend and my best friend out to either success or death, no in-between.

In the kitchen, planning started without me while I tended to a freaked-out Little and mostly ambivalent Charlie. Someone has laid out three pieces of paper, sections of a hand-drawn map.

They bring me up to speed. The plan seems pretty straightforward: Jenny and Nathan get into the barn, load the car, close the barn, come back. Keene opens the hatchway when they arrive, then the three of them unload the car while I wait upstairs for the all clear.

I'm stuck on the details, as is Keene.

Nathan will get into the barn through the side door, then he'll raise the garage door manually from inside because it's much faster than waiting for the automatic opener. He'll drop it closed as soon as Jenny gets the car in.

"But what if they follow you into barn?" I ask.

"Some will follow us into the barn," Jenny says. "But probably not a lot of them. Look, it's like a gnat swarm, right? A few of them always drift away to investigate when something interesting goes by, but the swarm stays where it is until there's a reason to move. We'll deal with any that follow us in, but I think it'll be just a few."

"Unless it's like an angry swarm of bees," Keene says, crossing his arms and giving Jenny his most disgusted look.

"Yeah, well if it's like a bee swarm, clearly we're not getting out of the car. We'll abort the mission and drive back to the carport."

"'Just a few' is still too many," I say. "It'll only take one to kill you."

She looks to Nathan for support, but he just shrugs.

"Okay, you get the stuff and leave the barn. Then we…" Keene says. He knows the plan as well as she does, but he's picking at it. Looking for flaws.

Jenny lets out an exasperated sigh. "Then we park the car alongide the hatch. You open up the first side of the hatch, using the tarp like an umbrella. You and Nathan drape the car doors and the hatch, while I get out and grab the cement blocks. We'll use those to pin the tarp to the top of the car so we're basically working under a tent while we get the plywood out."

"What if the tarp falls?" I ask.

"We'll still have our blankets on until we're closed up and sure none got in," Nathan says.

"And you'll know when it's all clear because we'll give you the secret knock," Jenny adds.

"Why the knock, though?" I ask Jenny. "I mean, you could just tell me you're okay. Won't I have the walkie-talkie by then? It seems kind of…I don't know, silly." Childish is what I mean. Like it's a game she's not taking seriously enough.

"Because if someone gets bit, we might panic and come running up the stairs. Your first instinct would be to open the door and help us, letting God-knows-what into the house. I know it sounds stupid, but it's a safeguard. No one is going to use that knock in a panic. You need to keep us in until you know for sure it's safe. And if it's not safe..." If it all goes wrong, then I'm supposed to nail the door shut. Keep them locked down there forever.

I shudder at the thought of my friends and brother trapped in the basement with a swarm of butterflies.

"Hey," Nathan says. "It won't come to that. It's going to be fine, you'll see."

"We're ready," Jenny says.

Nathan pulls me into an embrace, kissing the top of my head. He's shot up so many inches since last year, when he was barely taller than me. "Listen," he says. "You know that mac and cheese your mom makes?"

"Yeah?"

"Can you figure it out? Because it would be awesome to have that for dinner after this. I'm gonna be really hungry."

It startles a smile out of me. "You're so sure of yourself."

"Jenny's got a plan. What's not to be sure of? Plus, mac and cheese? I will find a way to survive for that. Can you put chicken in it?"

"I'll do my best," I say. Tears of fear are rising, but I push them back, still forcing a smile. Nathan's hand drops to mine and catches, swinging back and forth for a moment. My heart speeds up. He lets go and gets out of the way so Jenny can say her goodbye-for-nows, leaving the lingering feel of his warm skin on my palm.

Jenny comes around the table and hugs me tight. She whispers in my ear, "I think Nathan likes you."

"Shut up."

"Don't worry, I'll bring him back," she whispers, her breath tickling my ear.

Keene says to Jenny, "Don't die, loser." They exchange a look as meaningful in its own way as my hand intertwined with Nathan's. It's time.

———

Jeans and long sleeves are inadequate armor against nasty, jagged teeth. For an added layer of protection, Keene cuts eye holes in some of Mom's old quilts and throws them over Jenny and Nathan. Jenny's brushes the kitchen tile. Nathan has a full foot of exposure. As long as the butterflies don't attack from the ground up, they should be fine to get to the car without a bite. We hope.

While they perform this final prep, I stare out the back door windows and take stock of the situation. Few butterflies have found their way under the carport, presumably preferring the ability to soar out in the open. A handful of the bugs flap at the edges on either end. One perches on the car's trunk, flexing its wings open and closed. That one worries me. Also, I cannot see what might be on the siding, and that worries me too.

Nathan takes the frying pan he saved me with. It's under his blanket. Jenny has a meat cleaver. I'm not sure if either is practical without the range to swing or stab, but I don't say this.

"Why are you dressed like ghosts?"

Little stands in the kitchen door with his sippy cup trailed by Charlie, who twines between Keene's legs.

"They're just messing around," I say.

"Can I have more juice? Can I be a ghost too? Is it snack time?"

"Sure. We'll make you a ghost costume later. Let me have your cup," I say. "Do you want to watch a movie?"

"We do projects in the afternoon on school days."

Everyone stands stock-still, as if caught doing something naughty. I refill the cup and take Little by the hand. "Come on," I say. "You've earned a day off, and you can watch any movie you want."

Little pulls his hand from mine and dashes off toward the den.

I want to make deep, meaningful eye contact to tell Jenny and Nathan I love them, to be careful, not to do anything stupid, or anything I wouldn't do, or anything dangerous. I want to stop them.

But instead, I follow Little out, feeling helpless.

13

They're out the door in a whisper of fabric, everyone holding their breath as if any little sound or movement might attract the butterflies.

Keene snaps the screen door shut behind them. That thin barrier is protection enough, for now at least, against things with teeth. We stand holding hands as they squat/walk to the car, Jenny to the front driver's side, Nathan in the back seat behind her. The blankets sweep the ground, limiting access for creepy crawlies to fly up and under. Jenny opens the driver's door an inch. It gives a squeaky whine I never really noticed before. I wince, tighten my grip on Keene's hand. They're inside and the doors click closed.

"We're in and safe, over," Jenny's voice says. She waves from the front seat, blanket around her shoulders like a quilted cape.

This is when it really starts—feeling helpless. Being helpless. At the mercy of the universe, and the judgment of Jenny and Nathan to make the right decisions, to follow the right instincts in the right moments. I pull my hand out of Keene's and begin to pace back and forth in front of the sink, biting at the skin beside my thumbnail.

The car creeps toward the barn and Mom's ample supply of crafting material. It has a workshop at the back, a huge bench, and tools that would make a construction worker proud.

That's Mom's thing—craft projects. She took up crafting with a fevered intensity after Dad passed. Bat houses, seasonal wreaths, hand-beaten metal jewelry, quilts—if you can find it on Pinterest, Mom has done it. I asked her why once, when I was jealous of the long hours she spent alone in the barn, and she said, "It's creation, Shur. I need it to undo the destruction."

She didn't have anyone, not the way she needed, so if she wanted to make bird houses out of repurposed license plates, that was her right. I stopped feeling jealous after that and felt sad instead.

"We're here," Jenny says, her voice crackling with static and sounding like she's three miles away.

"You're supposed to say 'over' so I know you're done talking," Keene gripes.

"So are you, over," Jenny says.

"I hate you. What's the situation? Over."

Nathan says, "Remember we did exponentials with bunnies in math? It's like that, but with monsters."

In the background, Jenny says, "Over."

"Oh yeah, over. Wait, no, not over. We're going to put the radio down for a sec while we open the door. You're sure the side door is unlocked, right? Over?"

"Mom has literally never locked it. Hell, we have to remind her to lock the house. Over."

"Radio silence for now. Wish us luck or pray or whatever. Over."

Quiet rules the kitchen. The walkies are so stupid, Elmo's red, happy plastic Muppet face staring up at us, ready for adventure. These walkies are for little kids playing hide-and-seek in closets and under beds, not for big kids trying to save their family.

"Can you see anything?" I ask Keene.

"Sort of." He's closed the door again and presses his face right up against the glass. "Sort of a shitty angle, but I think I can see the...yeah. The garage is open. She's driving inside." He pauses. "Okay, it's closed."

"Should I go upstairs and look?"

"What the hell are you going to see? A closed garage door? A shit ton of butterflies? Just chill."

I don't go upstairs. I pace some more, chew my finger some more. I'm not a finger-chewer usually. About six months after Dad died, I spent a week in a special hospital. I couldn't stop crying, and I couldn't concentrate on anything. I wasn't sleeping, and I wasn't eating. Even with all that, I wasn't in the worst shape there. My roommate bit her nails down to the quick, so her fingers bled. I'm not like that. It's just a piece of loose skin, a convenient thing to worry at. It pulls loose, hard and deep, and a drop of blood falls into my mouth. I spit the blood and skin away.

"You guys there, over?" Jenny's voice, breathless.

"We're here. What's going on? Are you guys okay? Over? What took so long?"

"It takes a second to battle bugs, Riordan," she says, and the sass in her voice says volumes more than the words themselves.

"They're way more aggressive," Nathan adds. He sounds breathless too. Scared, exhilarated. "Over."

"Any bites?" Keene asks.

"No, but you're going to need a new egg pan. I knocked the handle right off this one, over."

Keene gives me a bright smile, over bright, a performance for me. "Did you find the batteries, over?"

"We're looking now," Jenny says. "Consulting your map. Radio silence again for a few. Get ready for the next part. Over."

Keene hands me the walkie, striding away from the door toward the basement. "We're up."

"Keene, I really don't like this plan."

"We're good. We've got this."

"We? I'm not part of it. I'm up here with the baby while the rest of you are...you know, doing the dangerous stuff. I should be in the basement with you."

Keene drops a hand on my shoulder, but his eyes are already half gone, onto the next task. I want to shake him back into this moment. "Anyway, come down and help me prep the tarp quick," he says. "One of us has to stay up, and you're the best with Little. If anything happens to us, he needs someone to protect him."

There's not much to do in the basement. We've already prepped it all except the tarp. It's sitting in a neat square on a step inside the hatchway, next to a pair of cement blocks leftover from some yard project and a blanket with eye holes to cover Keene. He takes the concrete steps up to the closed hatch doors, frees the latch, and comes back down to me.

"Listen," Keene says. "I love you."

"You what? I didn't quite hear that," I say. My eyes sting with tears and he pulls me into a tight hug.

"You want to keep me safe. I want to keep you safe. It's an

infinite loop of safety. Trust me. I don't want to die any more than you want me to die. I will be fine. Help me with this."

Together, we unfold the tarp, shaking it out. Gray dust rises from the creases. Once it's fully extended, he drags it up the concrete steps where it fills the hatch space like blue plastic water.

"When did we last use this?" he asks, but we both know. He's just making small talk to distract me.

"Last summer. When we camped in the yard with Little."

"Oh yeah, Charlie slept on my bladder. That was great."

"Keene?" The walkie bursts to life in my hand.

"It's Shur. Are you guys okay?" And then, as an afterthought, "Over?"

"We're good. Keene was right about the plywood. It's perfect, but big. Tell Keene to throw on some work gloves if he has any. The splinters are no joke. We have tools and a shit ton of batteries. An air compressor. Your Mom isn't fucking around out here, that's for sure. We're out of here in two minutes, over."

Over. That "over" means it's time for me to leave my friends to fate.

The two minutes pass. Distantly, we hear the car coming back toward the house. Then nothing. Then a double-pound on the hatch doors. They're back.

I give Keene one last hug, then a kiss on the cheek for good luck before beelining it back up the stairs.

I close the door and lock it, sealing Keene in the basement. Blissfully oblivious, Little is swinging around the den with an imaginary blond braid singing about letting go of the past, kept company by Terrible Charlie. I am completely alone in my paralytic state, Elmo's stupid face in front of me between the saltshaker and the butter no one remembered to put away.

I imagine the worst. Dive-bombed as they get out of the car or as Keene pushes the door up on its screaming metal hinges. Bitten with razor teeth before they can get the tarp over the top of the car or crushed by falling plywood sheets.

It feels like I'm waiting forever, trapped in a moment. Are they out of the car? Have they made it downstairs? What about the tarp? Is it over the car? Did it stay in place? Someone tell me something!

The walkie squawks static and I jump, bumping my knee on the underside of the table hard enough to bruise.

"Shur? You there?"

"I'm here. Over."

"Yeah," Jenny says. "I'm in the basement and the guys are securing the tarp. The butterflies are thick, but they're more focused on the sunny spots, so we might have a little bit of time. I found one of those big red rubber bands in the garage. I'm gonna try to use it to keep the Talk button pressed...you won't be able to talk back once we do. Over."

Rustling, banging, then, "Hey, can you hear me?" Then silence. "She's not answering, I think it worked. Alright, let's do this. Shur, whatever you do, don't panic. I'll knock on the basement door when we're under control."

"Be careful," I say, knowing she can't hear me.

"Don't worry, we'll be careful," Jenny says. Best-friend telepathy.

"Bricks are in place. The tarp seems secure enough for now. I'm watching to make sure nothing gets through." Her voice is upbeat and chipper. She could be at a ball game waiting for her favorite player to come to bat, instead of in a basement waiting to be attacked by something that shouldn't even exist.

"Here come the tools. Ow! Watch my foot, jackass!" Mumbled response, probably from my brother.

"They're going back for the plywood sheets. We really had to jam them in."

I stare down at the walkie on the table, unable to be heard, heart doing triple-speed jumping jacks. How can she be so cavalier? Excited, even? "Here they come with the first piece. Man, they really had to tug. Your brother's losing his shit, I think they might have torn the fabric on the ceiling in his car. What? No, you shut up."

I can't hear the back and forth, and this bothers me in a way I can't begin to describe. It's a cousin of jealousy. Over being left out, over not having enough information. It's listening to one side of a really important phone call, and the person holding the phone isn't telling you what you need to know.

There's a scream and a thunk. The walkie goes dead.

I'm up, knocking the chair, sending the butter teetering on the table's edge, and to the basement door as fast as I can move. In a split second, I have a hand on the locking mechanism, ready to charge downstairs.

From the next room, Elsa really does not want to build a snowman.

The music. It stops me in my tracks. I'm not even sure which one this is, the original, one of the sequels? Made for television?

It doesn't matter, it's the thought of Little that makes me rest my head against the white-painted wood instead of ripping it open, listening to the chaos unfold below. I have one job.

A rush of feet on the stairs. Pounding. Will it be pleading screams for freedom and help? Or something more mundane, like the knock we agreed on?

Knock knock. Pause. Knock knock knock.

I twist the knob and throw the door open. Jenny nearly tumbles into me, sweating, exhilarated, almost crying. Behind her, Nathan stands on the steps, rubbing both arms like he's cold.

"Where's Keene?" I nearly scream it. He should be the first one up.

"Stop your damn panicking, I'm right here. The tarp fell and one got in. Jenny killed it." His tone is grudging, but impressed.

"I couldn't hear you!"

Jenny holds up the twin to my Elmo. "I dropped it. The batteries popped out. It's fine."

Nathan comes the rest of the way up the stairs, nudging Jenny aside. He puts his long arms around me and pulls me close. I feel warm, fuzzy. Different. I didn't realize how much I'd worried about him. About all of them, but about him. I'm glad he's alive, even if he does smell like a giant boy armpit.

"About that mac and cheese," he says, and it startles a laugh free that I didn't know was in there.

14

'm exhausted. Emotionally spent. Maybe physically spent, too, from all that pacing and adrenaline. While the others enthusiastically replay the horrors of the basement more like it was a championship soccer game than a near-death experience, I concentrate. Instant Pot. Macaroni. Dwindling milk supply. Enough frozen butter to bake a thousand cakes, a quantity of garlic powder appropriate to fend off a small vampire army.

"I think we should raise a toast," Keene says. He's rummaging around in the liquor cabinet above the fridge. He pulls down an unopened bottle of tequila and strips the plastic off a wooden cork.

"To what, not being eaten?" Nathan asks.

"That's not enough?" Jenny says.

"To surviving," Keene says. He pulls out shot glasses. There are only three, so he improvises and puts a Mickey Mouse juice glass out beside the others. He hands one to each of us. I sniff. It smells like heat.

"We need salt and limes to do this right," Jenny says.

"We have salt, no limes," Keene says. The saltshaker gets passed around our small circle. I mimic the others as they lick the space between their thumbs and forefingers and dust the spit with salt, very unhygienic.

"To family," Keene says and raises his stubby glass. "Even weird ones like this."

"Especially weird ones like this," Jenny agrees and knocks it back, wincing. She sucks on the salt.

I sip the tequila, and Keene reaches over, tipping it up. It floods my mouth and I choke, sputtering it down, and lick the salt from my hand. An eruption of heat and coughing rips my throat, and Jenny pounds my back, laughing. "You're such a douche," she says to Keene.

"You can't sip tequila."

"Of course you can."

While I continue to cough, wheezing at the inhaled alcohol, Jenny shakes salt into the empty shot glass, and then refills it. She sets it on the table. "Watch me."

I give Keene a watery-eyed, dark glare.

"You had to drink," he says.

"Why?"

"Because!" Nathan says. "You should have seen Jenny! She took a hammer to that thing. Bam! And she didn't just hit it. She *threw* the hammer. *WHAM!*"

I jump and turn away. They're enjoying a rite of passage, the warriors returned from battle, and I, the maiden, left behind, am choking on tequila.

"Like a ninja or something," Nathan says, but his voice is questioning now, like he realizes maybe he said something wrong.

I can't bring myself to talk about it. "Well, the mac and cheese is going, and it's Little's favorite, and no one died or got bit." Forcing a smile, I add, "Let's celebrate!" Nathan's face relaxes into a grin, but Jenny and Keene exchange a look. They know my smile is fake. I hate when they gang up on me.

"Thanks," Nathan says. He throws his arms around me again, brings me in tight, and smiles down into my face. "I'm really glad you weren't there to see it. That sounds bad. I mean, I'm glad you and Little were safe. So...thanks for being cool about it."

Heat rises in my face, and I am hyperaware of his body against mine. When did he stop being just an extension of Keene and start being so hot? "Maybe you should take a shower," I say. "All of you. To get the butterfly off."

Nathan raises his arm and sniffs, recoils. "Oof, sorry. No one should be subjected to that. I'll head up. Bro, can I use your Mom's shower?"

"Just check the skylight first, make sure nothing got in," Keene says, eyebrow arched. I look away fast, my face warm from tequila-choke and boy-proximity. "It's double thick, but, well, whatever."

"This is where we are now," Jenny says, sipping her tequila. "Checking the skylight for monsters before we get soap in our eyes." She winks at me, and I scowl back, not ready to forgive them all yet for almost dying.

Jenny and I go upstairs to find clothes, not that she doesn't know my wardrobe as well as I do. She closes my bedroom door behind us and says, "Spill."

"What?" I say, refusing to make eye contact.

"Come on, Shur. It's me. I know something is wrong. Something other than"—she points vaguely in the direction of the window and the giant, mutant butterflies just beyond—"that."

"Jesus!" I say, hoping to distract her. "Look at that." *That* is the bullet hole through my window. It's a solid puncture. Cracked, white glass spiders away toward the outer edges of the pane. "How did the glass not break?"

"Oh, lots of factors," she says absently. "Velocity, angle, wind speed, whatever. Just be glad it didn't shatter, or we'd have a room full of bugs. Anyway, what is your problem? Is it the booze? You think your mom is going to be mad?"

"No, Jenny. Come on. Mom isn't going to care. It's that you could have died, and you're all acting like it was a prank or something."

Jenny laughs. "This wasn't life and death. Life and death is those idiots with the guns."

I'm silent and getting angrier.

"Now you're mad because you think I'm being dismissive."

"You *are* being dismissive."

"Fine, maybe I am," Jenny says. "That was a lot to get through, and to come back to you pouting—"

"I'm not pouting!" I shout, not meaning to.

"Then what would you call it?"

"You know what, Jenny? Turns out I'm bad at watching the people I care about maybe live or maybe die when I have no say over it." I rise and stalk to my closet. "Here're your stupid sweatpants from last time. I washed them. Help yourself to underwear or whatever else you need." I make to leave the room, tears close to the surface.

Jenny jumps up and grabs me by the shoulders, looking down

into my face. Then she pulls me into a crushing hug. "You were scared," she says. "I get it. I'm sorry."

At last she lets me go, and I pretend like the tears haven't leaked down the side of my face and that my nose isn't turning a bright, ugly red. "I wouldn't let just anyone wear my underwear," I say, and she barks out laughter, making me smile.

"I know," she says, "and trust me, I wouldn't even consider wearing anyone else's. Come on. Sit down. We haven't had five minutes alone since this started, unless you count whispering over Little at night."

She's wearing my sweatshirt, the one she always borrows when she's here. It's oversized and gray, with a logo so faded from time and washing, it's indecipherable.

I let her lead me by one hand to the bed. She drops and I sit beside her. Over our heads, the bullet's passage is marked by a dark, ominous hole.

"Are you worried about your Mom?" I ask.

"No. Yes. It's complicated."

"Because of your step monster."

"Yeah, him. And my mom's still my mom, but you know how things are."

I do. "Do you want to go home?"

She laughs, and it's bitter. "No. If I'm going to be trapped somewhere, I wouldn't want it to be in that house. Not with *him*." We're quiet for a moment, and I can feel her rage and hurt rising, can see it in her expression and the way she crosses her arms against her chest. "Anyway," she says. "What about Nathan?"

"What about him?"

"He's...huggy."

"It's new. I don't know what it is."

"Do you like him?"

"I've never given him a thought. He's always just been Keene's friend."

"He's not skinny and short anymore," Jenny says. "And he sure seems to have given you a thought or two."

"It's the end of the world," I say.

"First, no it isn't," Jenny says. "It's a biological or ecological or some other sort of logical disaster. Second, if it is the end of the world, this is your chance to not die a virgin."

"Shut up. I hate you."

"No you don't," she says.

"Maybe I do."

"But you don't."

I sigh. "I'm not losing my virginity just because the world is ending." Honestly, I'll probably never lose it, because I'm so paranoid about pregnancy, I'd lose my damn mind.

"You're such a killjoy."

"That's my actual job," I say. "Killing joy. You kill monsters; I kill your buzz. It all evens out."

"Seriously, though. Studies show that crises bring people closer together," Jenny says.

I lifted an eyebrow. "By 'studies,' do you mean disaster movies you've seen?"

"Exactly. And movies never lie. If we're trapped in here indefinitely, it's probably going to be a good opportunity for you to, you know, hang out and do a jigsaw puzzle together."

"A jigsaw puzzle. Is that a hint about sex? Pieces fitting together?"

"No," she says, "but that's brilliant, so consider that what I meant."

"What are you going to be doing, while I'm doing jigsaw puzzles? Becoming best friends with Keene?"

"No," she says. "Ew. Your brother will never not be icky. I'm trying to figure out what's really happening out there."

"So you're doing research? Are you writing a paper on this already?"

"Maybe," she laughs. "Maybe I'll start a blog. Anyway, are we good? You know I can't stand when you're mad at me."

I shrug and try to sound nonchalant, but I couldn't be more serious. "You guys can't do that to me again. It was Dad's accident all over. Totally outside of my control. If one of you had died..."

"It wasn't going to happen. We were safe."

"Taking precautions doesn't mean you were safe. And if you died, I'm not sure I could have handled it."

"Brain explosion."

I nod.

She puts an arm around my shoulders and doesn't say anything. She was there through all of it, of course, had been around before the accident, in its immediate aftermath, and for everything that followed. Visited me at the hospital. Sat up with me in the middle of the night when my anxiety spiked. Still makes me playlists, draws me baths, and makes sure I take my pills.

But that doesn't mean she understands what it feels like to be in my head.

Next time, I decide, I will not be the one to be left behind. I will be the one to go. I need that kind of control over my life. Even if everyone else thinks I'm made of glass.

15

After the others get cleaned up, we make it a priority to cover the windows before the sun goes down. There's only enough plywood for downstairs: two over the windows in the den, three in the dining room, and a chunk over the back door's glass. That's okay, a least for now—keeping the doors upstairs closed seems like enough—the butterflies don't seem interested in attacking the glass, and someone would have to be really motivated to both get through the swarm and climb up to the second floor to break in.

Little follows us, trying to help and desperately wanting to hit something with a hammer. Despite a nap and so little activity, he's coma-level tired right after dinner. We've decided to sleep communally in the den. Upstairs feels breached by the gunshot, even if nothing bigger than a bullet has gotten in.

Sleepy as he is, Little still isn't a fan of this new arrangement. "I want to sleep in my big boy bed."

"I know," I say. "But we're going to have another sleepover tonight. This time it's with everyone! Me and you and Jenny and Keene and Nathan. And even your stuffies."

"What about my blanket?" His eyes are thick with sleep.

"It's waiting for you."

"Did the monsters eat my room?"

"Nope. And tomorrow we can go look at it, but tonight things are kind of scary, and so we're going to all stay together so we can be less scared."

He looks down at his feet. "I bet Mommy is scared."

I give him a smile and chuck his chin up with my finger so he sees it. "Hey. Mommy is very, very strong. She's not afraid of anything. Not monsters or dragons or anything. But she's super smart too. She knows it's not safe to come home yet. Even if it makes us sad."

"I am sad."

"Me too, buddy. I'm super sad, and I miss Mommy so much. And I know I'm not Mommy, but I'm going to do the best I can for you, okay? Me and Keene and Nathan and Jenny. We're all going to do our best."

"And Charlie."

"Oh my goodness, how did I forget Terrible Charlie?"

I put him in the center of the pull-out couch. It's queen-sized, fine for me and Keene with Little stuck between us. Terrible Charlie will no doubt stand guard, probably on my chest. Nathan will sleep on the recliner, and Jenny has her trundle bed, brought down from upstairs, crammed up against the wall. Close quarters, but everyone is accounted for.

I tuck Little's regular quilt around him and give him blankie, along with Billy Bear.

"Shur, will Mommy be home soon?"

"I hope so."

"Is Daddy watching her? Mommy says Daddy is in Heaven, and that's why I've never meeted him, and she said angels are in Heaven, like Mr. Gibbons from church who used to give me chewy candies, but then he died in the summer, and now Mommy says he's in Heaven. And she says angels watch over us and protect us. Garden angels."

"Guardian," I say.

"Yeah. So Daddy is Mommy's garden angel?"

"I don't know, Little," I say. "I sure hope so though, because that would make Mommy really happy to have Daddy looking out for her. Now, my tiny little buddy, you need to get some sleep."

I kiss his forehead and smooth his light hair. Little's coloring is like mine and Dad's, less like Keene's and Mom's. I get up to turn off the overhead light and plug in the night-light. By the time I return, not even a whole minute later, he's already drifting off to sleep.

I sit bolt upright in the dark as a piercing wail directly from my left tears me from an already fitful sleep.

"What the fuck?" Keene grumbles. I fumble for the lamp and the room is bathed in entirely too bright light.

"I'm wet!" Little cries.

"Oh for the love of..." Keene starts, but stops himself before he can make things worse.

"It's fine, honey, accidents happen," I tell Little.

"I peed like a baby!" he shrieks, the dismay and humiliation so thick, my heart tears for him. The acrid smell of urine rises from the blankets. I scoot to the side of the bed, then lift him out, setting him gently down on the floor. The crotch of his pajama bottoms is darker than the surrounding cloth, and he sobs in despair.

"I'll clean him," Keene says. "You grab some clothes?"

"Are you going throw him in the shower?" I say.

"I'm just going to wipe him down and get him back in bed," Keene says. "It's the middle of the damn night."

"I'll strip the sheets," Jenny volunteers, kicking off her blankets.

Upstairs, the hall window is uncovered, but closed. I gather clean things for Little from his room and hurry back out, pausing at the linen cabinet for a fresh set of sheets. I don't want to hear noises from the crawlspace or scratches on the siding. But I hear both. I imagine the butterflies out there in the dark, crawling. Tapping on the glass with clawed legs. *Knock knock.* I take a towel too, to put under Little while he sleeps, just in case.

Downstairs, Jenny has the bed stripped down to the mattress. "You're lucky," she says. "There was a mattress protector. Would have been a long night trying to avoid the pee spot."

"Poor kid is a mess."

"Yeah, well, it's not like the rest of us are handling it like champs. Nathan started the laundry." She wiggles her eyebrows up and down, like men doing laundry is the sexiest thing in the universe. I hand her the clean sheets without a word and leave to check the situation in the kitchen.

Little's sobs have been replaced with chattering about something that happened once at day care. Keene takes the fresh clothes from me. His expression is so exhausted and run down that I want to laugh and cry. "You guys need me?"

"We'll be out as soon as the Human Bladder here tries to pee again."

"I don't have to go now," Little says.

"You're trying anyway," Keene says, and I close the door on the argument.

Jenny has the fitted sheet half on. I take the other side, and together we tug it into place. I settle the towel down across Little's spot as she picks up the top sheet.

"I didn't tell you what I found on the Internet while you were doing your basement thing," she says.

"What's that? More theories on where those things are from?"

"Lots of that, actually. Creatures from below! The thing from the center of the Earth! Aliens among us!"

"Not sure it matters."

"There are worse things. They're saying there are quarantine wards popping up all over the place. The bites are really bad."

"Bad how?"

"Well..." Jenny says. "Are you sure you want to hear?"

"Nothing you can tell me can be worse than the stuff I make up in my head, Jenny."

"The bites mess with your mind. First you start talking like that guy we saw on TV, Emmanuel, like your brain can't quite make sense of language. This nurse at some hospital wrote a thread about how bizarre it's gotten there. He said the local National Guard showed up and put all the bite victims into one wing, then blocked it off. With guns and everything. Only government doctors are allowed in."

"Why?"

"I don't know. Maybe they're super infectious to other people? If the bites were just deadly to the victims, then there wouldn't be a reason to guard the patients with guns. So, it has to be something really bad."

"All done!" Keene says, following Little into the room. Little scrambles up on to the bed.

We settle back into our respective sleeping spots, but I lay awake long after the lamp is off. Real or imaginary, the rustling, creeping noise from upstairs lingers in my ears. How many are out there? And how many ways can they kill us?

Around dawn, when gray light seeps in to frame the kitchen doorway, I give up on sleep. Our part of the house is still and dark, masked by the boards nailed over the window. I leave Little beside Keene in a tangle of sheets and blankets.

Terrible Charlie trails me, always hopeful a meal will be forthcoming. He twines between my legs and makes cat noises as I turn on the coffee maker. As I do, a car pulls into the car port.

All sleeplessness gone I rush to the back door, yanking it open so I can see who it is. The engine cuts on a red pickup truck.

Not Mom. Bill from across the street. At least it's an adult, even if it's not the one I really want to see. It takes him a minute to climb out of the truck, a rucksack over one shoulder and a gun in his hand. His grizzled face is set into a grim expression of disgust. I open the door and he rushes in. I check him for bugs.

"What are you doing here?"

"Checking on you. Bring it in." Bill is a hugger. He's not really here for us so much as he's here on behalf of Mom. He adores her. We're just kind of a bonus.

I don't love hugging, especially not semi-strangers, but he seems to need it more than I do. He smells of smoked wood and Old Spice. His shirt sleeves are pushed up, exposing his faded tattoos, and some newer ones. Dates of his dog's birth and death alongside a pair of paw prints. An American flag. A faded Confederate flag, which always gets my mother's hackles up. A skull with roses in the eye sockets.

"Your mom didn't make it home."

"She got trapped at work."

"You guys want to come to my house? The wife and I talked about it. We can make it work."

"Maybe? Not yet." Bill's house is smaller than ours, and they have a lot of animals. "Did you bring the chickens in?"

"They're terrorizing the cats. How are you set for food?"

"I mean...as good as we can be? Lots of dry food and canned stuff, but we're not touching that until the power goes out. You want a cup of coffee?"

"Sure." He sits at the table, sets his bag down beside him. "Saw the holes in your house."

"Those guys in the truck didn't seem to care much what they hit."

"They come back, they're in for a surprise," he says in a way I don't much like. It's mild, but matter-of-fact. If they come back, there's going to be return fire.

"Do you know them?" I ask.

He shrugs. "Dumb-ass kid from the top of the street. Huge

guy without the brains God gave a rock. I see him and his friends up at the range. Don't treat the guns with respect. Don't worry about them, I've got that covered." The scowl under his scruff makes me nervous.

Maybe he senses my unease, because the topic changes suddenly. "Just you and Keene here? Where's the little one?"

"We picked him up from day care before things got too out of control. It's us and a few friends."

"Good. Hate to think of you guys alone. It's one messed-up situation. Brought you some stuff." He tugs the bag open and pulls out a couple of boxes. "Milk."

"Boxed milk? I didn't even know that was a thing."

"It's emergency food." He adds a couple of large cardboard canisters. "Instant eggs, freeze-dried chicken, freeze-dried berries."

"You just have this stuff?"

"We could survive two years over there. Longer if we rationed. Even longer if Mona would let me eat the damn chickens."

"I thought you didn't like hurting animals?"

"All this has me rethinking a few things." He sips his coffee. "You got water set aside? Know how to light that gas stove of yours? Power's gonna go soon. I can feel it in my bones."

"City water, Bill. The power shouldn't affect it." I don't mention the Gatorade container or my own paranoia. "And yeah. Mom showed us how to light the burners. I've got one of those long lighters she uses to light the grill."

He nods. "Good to be overprepared. You never know what bullshit might happen. Fill some bottles with water, just in case. A bathtub, if you can spare one. You know you can drink from the toilet tank if you need to? Unless your mom puts bleach in it. Don't be drinking that."

"You think it's going to be that bad?" I ask, paranoia spiking now that it has validation and company. "How long is this going to go on?"

"Now, see, that's the million-dollar question. You're smart, like your mom. The news isn't saying. Maybe it'll come down to basic biology. I was never much good with science, but even I can tell you, butterflies don't last long."

"Jenny said there were quarantine wards being guarded by the military."

"I heard that too. Why would the Army need to guard sick people?"

I don't have an answer. "Why do you think?"

He shrugs. "Ever seen an animal with rabies?"

"No."

"Good for you. Hope you never do. But maybe it's like that. Maybe it makes them sick."

"That's some zombie shit, Bill."

"Yep." He drains his coffee and stands. "Listen, you want to come over, you send me a signal. You got candles?"

"A zillion."

"Good. You get yourself in trouble or change your minds about coming over to our place, you put a candle out on the front porch. I'll see the light at night, and I'll come get you."

He pulls two last things from his bag and sets them on the table. They're knives, big ones, in sheathes. "Thought about bringing you guns, but you don't have any safety training, and your mom would kill me if anything happened. Plus, it's not good to have a gun in the house with no safe, what with your little guy around. Keep these close. They'll do in a pinch. I saw the windows boarded up when I drove over. What did you use?"

"Plywood. We only have enough for downstairs, though."

"Do as many as you can. Use whatever you can find. Those guys will probably be back."

16

'm thinking about what Bill said. It spins around my head like the view from the metal merry-go-round at the park at full speed. Dad used to grab it and run hard, and Keene and I would scream, "Faster! Faster!" The passing landscape was a dizzying blur, nausea-inducing, exhilarating. They'll be back, Bill said. Board the windows, hoard water. Light a candle. Should we have gone with him?

I scrape a pancake onto Little's plate, and he slathers margarine on it with a butter knife. I don't stop him; it'll only go to waste when the power goes out anyway.

"So, I was thinking," Jenny starts, but a strange sound interrupts.

It's not a strange sound so much as unexpected, unheard recently. The vibrating of a phone. *Bzzzz. Bzzzz. Bzzzz.* We all stare at each other, one person to the next, and then Nathan snatches it up. It's his. A picture of his mom lights up the screen, her head thrown back, laughing, arm around his older sister. He pokes the speaker button so we can all hear.

"Mommy?" he says, and he's suddenly a scared child no older than Little. I'm frozen in place with a pan in one hand, spatula in the other. We're silent and still. Even Little is spellbound, butter knife stopped midswipe.

"Son? You better come home. You better come home now, son. You better. You better come home."

"Mom? What's going on? Is Dad there? Are you at home? Tell me what's happening."

"Son, you better come home now. You better come home. It's time to come home now, son." That's all she says, over and over, a mantra. Like she's swaying and praying, stuck on repeat. It's hypnotic, hollow. "Son. Son."

"Mom!" He's starting to panic. "Mom, where's Dad? Where are you?"

"Dad is gone, you better come home, son. It's time to come home. You better come now."

Little looks confused, head cocked to one side, and he says, "How come she can't say anything else, Shur?"

I resist the urge to clamp a hand over my mouth, Emmanuel's pale, freckle-speckled face rising in my mind. *They're flapping. They're flapping right here on my arm.*

She starts to scream. It's a sudden, soul-piercing scream, maybe fear or pain, and ends as abruptly as it started. Then she shouts: "NOW!"

Nathan drops the phone to the wooden table top as if he's been burned, and Little drops the knife, his lower lip trembling dangerously. I want to move but just stand there stupidly with the pan and spatula, the burner still lit on the stove behind me. "Son!" She rages. I flinch. "I said it's time to come home to your mama! I said NOW! I said— "

There are three beeps in rapid succession. Disconnection. The line is dead.

We stay perfectly still until Jenny touches my arm, then points at the stove. The open flame. Like a zombie, I walk to it, put the pan down, pour in more mix. A new batch.

"She...maybe I should..."

"Maybe you should stay here for a while," Jenny says calmly. "She didn't say where she is, right? Maybe she was still at work. Wasn't she at work?" She works hard to avoid my eyes, because Nathan will see dark knowledge pass between us.

"Yeah," he says.

I pour a cup of coffee, hand it to him. He probably doesn't need caffeine, but what else can I do? I squeeze his shoulder.

"Jenny's right," Keene says. "Let's think this through."

"She needs me," Nathan says. "You heard her."

That's the problem: We *heard* her. Her weird, repetitive speech, like her brain was a vinyl record skipping on a bad scratch.

"I should go."

"Bruh," Keene says. "No. Not right now, not like this. Look out the window, see all those bugs? Twice as bad as yesterday and getting worse. Let's wait. She might call back."

Keene distracts Nathan by making him help with the rest of the downstairs security. When Jenny rises, Keene shakes his head behind Nathan's back, and she sinks back down into the chair, understanding this is best friend time. Maybe "best friend losing a parent" time, even. My heart aches for Nathan, but my mind chews over that phone call, the weirdness of it. *Rabies*, Bill had said. *Messes with your language*, Jenny had said. *They're flapping right here on my arm*, whispers my memory of Emmanuel.

Jenny opens her laptop while I clear the dishes and load them into the dishwasher. I set it to run, even though it's far from full.

"What are you doing?" I ask.

"Trying to figure out what it means."

"What what means?"

Jenny stares at me, hands still on the keyboard. "His mom's speech."

"We know what it means."

"We know it probably means she's infected from a bite. Yeah. But...does it mean she's...gonna die?" The end comes out super quiet, and we both look around to make sure Nathan didn't hear that. He's nowhere to be seen. "Maybe her body can fight it off."

"Maybe," I say, but I don't think either of us believe it.

I decide to make myself useful and do as much laundry as I can. No need to start the apocalypse with dirty sheets. I brave Keene's room and the lingering boy stench—armpit, socks, body spray. I try not to look at his sheets as I strip them, or at his hamper as I lug it to the door. The floor is covered in empty water bottles and clothes. I collect the clothes, leave the bottles, and move on to my own room.

I watch the window warily while filling the hamper with sheets and Jenny's discarded dirties. Then Mom's room, which feels sad, but also optimistic, won't she want clean sheets and clothes when she gets home? Finally, Little's stuff, which is always covered in something sticky or muddy.

When last night's sheets are in the dryer and the first load is in the washer, I retrieve a very reluctant and crabby Little from the den, interrupting the showing of *Moana 2*. He forgives me in the tub, splashing happily with his toys, hair in a silly shampoo mohawk. From a perch on the closed toilet seat, I surf. The news mentions quarantine wards, but not with a lot of specificity. Only noting they exist. Little splashes me with soapy water. I try not to doomscroll too much, deliberately staying away from social media because I know it'll send me down a rabbit hole of wacky origin theories and conspiracies.

When he is dry, warm, and in front of the television with Terrible Charlie, I check the dryer, which is not done. I return to the kitchen and start emptying the now-clean dishes, still hot and steaming, from the dishwasher.

"Jesus, sit already," Jenny says. "You're making me tired just watching you."

"I have to keep busy."

"Yeah, I get that. But you're making me nervous."

I sit. Stand. Pour a cup of coffee, sit again. Jiggle my leg up and down. "What's the latest?"

"Let me put it this way. How does tequila go with coffee?"

"Sounds like it would taste like ass," I say.

"Yeah," she agrees, glum. "Too bad. I think I found the most disgusting thing on the Internet. You want to see?"

"Is it porn? Because no."

"Oh, you are *so* optimistic. No. It's way worse."

"Come on, I don't want worse. I want better! Better. Help is coming? This is all a nightmare?"

She shakes her head. "Sorry. You don't have to watch, but I really think you should. After Nathan's mother...well."

"Well what?"

"I found something really bad. Something I don't think we ought to show Nathan and, really, you have to promise me you won't..."

"What? I'm not going to go batshit, if that's what you mean."

"Because I don't want a lecture from Keene."

"I promise!"

"Fine. Then watch," she says. "But also, sorry in advance?" She turns the screen so it's facing me and scoots around to the corner of the table so we can watch together. The screen is frozen on a single frame. A still picture, a video waiting to play. I already want to barf before I hit the space bar. It's a body part, an arm or maybe a leg, hard to tell from the camera angle and lack of context, and it takes up most of the screen. The skin is waxy brown, not like a natural skin tone, but like fruit left out in the sun, starting to rot. It might feel wet to the touch.

I give Jenny a side-eye. "Really?"

"Oh, it gets much worse, trust me." She picks up her coffee and tips it in my direction as if making a gruesome toast.

I hit the space bar, and the picture jumps to life on a cell phone video, bad lighting, bad sound. Jumpy, like the person is on the move.

"When was this recorded?" I ask.

"Two days after all this started," Jenny says.

"Okay, my dudes and ladies," a male voice says. Late teens,

accented, Spanish maybe? I'm not great with accents. "I'm in my basement alone, quarantining. My parents want to take me to the hospital, but I shut that down right quick. Everything you heard about the wards? I heard that shit too. I nailed the door shut from this side, so they can't get in. I love my folks, right? So sue me. But do it fast because I'm here to tell you that some bad shit is going down inside me, for reals."

He pauses. "Miguel in West Texas, hey, amigo. Danica in Mass, yeah, I'm sorry too." It had been a live stream, recorded. Comments flash by on the screen, almost too fast to read. He's got a following. The livestream is spotty. The video glitches at times, freezing in place as he talks. The sound stutters.

"Let me just..." The phone settles against something solid and the picture stops shaking. A moment later, his face appears as he reverses the camera. "That's better. My rig, the view you all are used to, is upstairs in my office. I'm improvising. Lighting down here is for shit, right? So, as I was saying, this is probably going to be my final show because I gotta be honest, I don't think I'm gonna be alive a whole lot longer. I got bit by one of those things and I feel like ass. Worse than ass. I never felt like this before, and I had COVID. That's how bad.

"I'm hoping you all will share this video, so I'm gonna introduce myself for those who maybe have never seen the channel before. Like and subscribe!" He shakes his head, frowning. "My name is Joe Arroz, and my channel is BLOX & Crafts with Joe. Usually, I talk about games. Not today.

"I've been lucky in life. Well, up until now. Making a living, supporting my parents on something I love doing. The American dream! First generation born in this country, baby! Second to die here, looks like. My grandma, God bless her, passed two years ago at ninety-two. God spared her from this nightmare."

Joe's a little older than I thought at first glance. There's a slash of hair on his upper lip. Handsome in a narrow, wiry way. Perfect teeth, great cheekbones. Pale and sweating. Sick.

"About a year ago, some of you will remember I moved my moms and pops in with me, because Dad has cancer. So, if you get through this and the world doesn't end, can one of you check in on them?" He pauses, reads the screen. "Thanks Dan. No, don't risk it now, they're all set. They're good for a few days at least. Thanks Ella, he's in remission. Dad's a fighter."

He takes a deep breath, blows it out, turning his face away from the screen for a second like he's bracing himself. "Here's the hard part, right? We were on our way back from Dad's checkup when we ran into what y'all have been seeing out there, those crazy monsters. That was the very first day, before we knew they were dangerous, before we knew not to go outside. Feels like years ago. What was it really, two days? Three? Hard to tell day from night down here. We went into the doctor's office—nothing but blue skies and seagulls. Came out? Well, you know, you all saw. Butterflies everywhere."

Joe takes a swig from a can before he continues. "We got home and into the garage fine, but one bit me. I'm going to show you and tell you all the truth because I'm not seeing anything on the news saying what happens. Rumors everywhere, but the big shows are only talking about looters and fires. Not what happens to you. That's why I want you to record this. Share it. Put it in front of as many people as you can before it's too late. I saw some idiots out there shooting cell phone videos. Like this is fun, some big joke." His laugh is bitter. It morphs into a wet cough, and he takes a moment to recover.

"Ben from Paris, let me read that out loud. Ben says Paris is in full lockdown, not even police on the streets, just the Army? What's that word? Gendarmerie? Oh, he says it's like militarized police. With flamethrowers, trying to fry these things. Stay safe, Ben. Drink lots of vino. Myself, I will be getting drunk directly." He holds up the can of beer, jiggles it lightly, then shows us a bottle of vodka. "No way I plan to go out sober," he says. "Recording going? Good, good. Let's hope they don't cut me off before I finish. For the love of all that's holy in this weird-ass universe, if you get bitten, record it. Upload it, share it. But do *not* get bit on purpose, friends. This," he jiggles his arm, "is a death sentence."

"Look away now if you're squeamish. Here we go. Three, two, one." On one, Joe holds his arm up to the camera. I cringe, coffee rising. The still picture had not done justice to the damage. The waxy, brownish sheen covers the skin all around the bite, which is gruesome. The rot is spreading in tendril-like stains up his arm.

"I made a mistake. I ripped it off. The thing landed and bit and I freaked the fuck out like any normal person. I grabbed it and tore it off my arm and stomped it but good. It took a chunk with it."

The wound is a raw, fleshy mess, oozing. Exposed muscle. Red and maroon against jagged skin. "I never wanted to see my insides like this. I'm a live biology class, y'all. Science for the masses, and you probably thought I was going to be reviewing the new *Halo* today." He gives a halfhearted laugh, then picks up a Sharpie and uncaps it with his mouth, spitting the cap away off camera. "You see where the bite is. Watch." He draws a dark line around the brown and the tendrils, showing how far it's spread. It's almost to his shoulder. "I'm rotting from the inside out. I've got maybe a few days, best guess, not that I plan to wait."

"Anyway, that's not the worst of it. The scary part, the *really* scary part, is that I've been having some really weird thoughts—the violent kind. They feel like they don't even belong in my head." He pauses for a swig directly from the vodka bottle.

"Something is happening to me. I think that bitch dropped something into my blood, some bacteria or virus. Hell, maybe it laid eggs." He pauses to read the screen. "Jenna from Austin wants to know if I've been speaking weird? I saw those videos too. I'm not there yet, but it's getting harder to form coherent thoughts. Feels like my brain is caught in the spin cycle, so that's probably coming soon.

"Anyway, for the safety of my parents, I'm locked away down here. Secure. They can't get in, I made sure of it. And more important, I can't get out. I'm going to leave the stream running for as long as I can so you can watch. If you want to stay with me, I could really use the company. Tell me about your games, your fears, your dreams. We can do this together, anything you want to talk about. You've been like family."

I stop the video. "How long does this go on?"

"Another hour. He started talking like Emmanuel. Saying the same thing over and over again, shouting for his mom on repeat. Then he had a seizure and knocked over the phone."

"Did he at least get drunk?"

"Not as drunk as he wanted."

I don't want my coffee anymore. I think of Mom, locked in her cafeteria. I hope they're safe. She said someone there was bit.

"It doesn't seem real," Jenny says. "I mean, it's real. I get it. I can look out the window and see monsters in the yard. But...it's like a horror movie."

"Surreal."

"Yeah. Surreal. Are you...scared?" she asks.

"Are you kidding? Have we met? I'm always scared. Are you? You seem so chill."

"Dude, I'm frozen in place. Why do you think I've been on the Internet all this time? You're functioning. You're doing stuff, planning. Even with your anxiety."

"Because of," I say. "It's sort of my thing. Besides, that's bullshit. You went to the garage. You helped put up boards."

"Yeah and as soon as that was done, I started drinking and watching videos. Like I'm going to hit the site that tells me, 'Good news, it was all a joke, let's go get ice cream.' Shur, it's like I can't move."

I squeeze her shoulder. "It is real. It's not going to just end, and that's the way it is."

"Gee, thanks."

"Come help me with stuff."

"What stuff?"

"Food prep. Laundry. Setting up the basement. Getting candles and flashlights into all the rooms so when the power goes out, we're ready. Someone needs to get some videos and music onto a device and keep it charged."

"I can do that," Jenny says. She blinks hard a few times.

"Hey!" I say. I pull her to me, hugging her. She sobs into me.

"I do hope my mom is safe," she says. "I am worried. She's a nightmare, but she's still my mom, you know?"

"I hope your mom is okay, and maybe your stepfather will get eaten," I say, and Jenny laughs through her tears. "But outside, so he's not a problem for your mom."

"Shur, I'm really scared."

"Me too." We stay like that until she calms, wiping her face with the palms of her hands.

17

Jenny's red-rimmed eyes have stopped streaming by the time the boys return. She's back in front of her computer, this time making a list of to-do items. Once she has a project, Jenny goes into methodical mode, which is a good place for her right now, in my opinion. Comfort zone.

"We're going to have to improvise," Keene says. He glances at Jenny, then gives me a raised eyebrow. I shake my head slightly. *Don't worry about it.* He shrugs. "We've got all the downstairs windows secured, but upstairs windows?"

"Keep those rooms closed," I say.

"We might have to."

Little crosses the kitchen, ignoring all of us, and heads to the bathroom. I ruffle his hair fondly as he passes, jealous of how oblivious he is.

Keene picks up one of Bill's giant knives. "Think he'll try to cook one?"

It startles a laugh out of me.

"What?" Jenny asks, turning toward us.

Keene's eyes sparkle. I realize he's trying to distract her, to make her smile.

"Bill says he can cook anything," I say.

"He can. Crab, rabbit, venison. I've seen him BBQ an entire duck," Keene says. "He builds his own...what are those things, Shur?"

"What, the smokers?"

"Yeah, those. Builds them for cheap and sells them. He has a waiting list."

"I thought he did construction," Nathan says.

"That's his day job," I say. "His real love is cooking. Award-winning BBQ and soups."

"Stop," Jenny says. "You can't be serious. He can't cook those things."

"He can certainly try," Keene says.

"They're full of writhing bacteria and parasites!"

Keene says, "That's why you *cook* them, Jenny. To the proper temperature. What the hell, didn't you learn that in Culinary?"

"Tell me, Keene," she says. "What exactly is the proper temperature for lizard, insect, shellfish hybrids?"

"I think it's in the Bible that you can't eat lizard, crab, insect hybrids," Nathan offers. "Leviticus."

"Oh, you're keeping kosher now?" I ask.

The banter is relief from that awful video, from Nathan's creepy phone call. It feels almost normal. Almost. It's forced, all of us trying, all of us playing our parts, putting on our appropriate faces, saying our lines at the right moment. A performance for us, by us.

Little, done with his peeing, comes back out and closes the bathroom door behind him. "Can I watch *Mulan*?"

Above us, glass shatters. We hear it, smashing and splintering, followed by a thump and the sound of a struggle.

We leave Jenny with Little, who grabs onto her like a drowning man to a buoy. He's screaming, short, electric bursts of fear. Jenny isn't much better. The residual pink in her face has faded to bloodless gray.

It's easy to track the noise. We creep, the three of us, up the stairs: Keene in the lead, then Nathan, then me. The hallway is light. I think, *Towels. We can use towels, double thick. Not as good as wood, but it's hard to punch through layers of fabric. That'll at least provide some protection.* I push the thought away. Focus. Focus. We don't have far to go. A battle is happening in the first room at the top of the stairs. The room where the window was already weakened by a bullet hole.

My room.

A seizure of flapping comes from within, something ricocheting off every surface. It sounds big. We huddle around the door.

"Shit," Keene says. "We should have duct taped that bullet hole."

"Do we just leave it?" Nathan asks.

"What is *it*?" I say. "We can't just let something run loose in the house without knowing what it is."

"I didn't say to let it run loose. It's inside. Contained."

"If the window is broken," Keene says, "more stuff could get in. We're going to have to deal with that."

"Why? It's behind a door." Nathan is looking from me to Keene like we're speaking in tongues.

While we argue, the frantic motion from within stops.

Keene reaches forward and puts his hand on the knob. Nathan grabs his wrist, gripping, and they have a brief staring contest before Nathan drops his hand and his gaze. Keene opens the door an inch, peeps through the gap. The room is ablaze through that crack, a solid strip of sun. He closes it again.

"Well?" I say.

"It's a bird and a butterfly. All tangled up. They crashed through the window."

"I don't think duct tape was going to stop that, Keene," I say.

"A bird is making all that racket?" Nathan asks.

He shakes his head, as if he doesn't quite know what to make of whatever he just witnessed. "It's a big bird. A turkey vulture, I think. I didn't get a great look, but it's ugly."

"Is it dead?" I ask.

"No. It's definitely breathing."

"What about the butterfly?"

"Couldn't tell."

"What do we do?" Nathan asks. "Let them both die, come back later?"

"The window is broken," Keene repeats. "So. I think we should kill it. Kill them both. Burn the bodies, close up the room."

"I want to see what we're up against," I say.

Keene steps out of the way, and Nathan throws his hands up in the air. "Jesus, you two have no sense of self-preservation."

Which is the most ironic thing anyone has ever said to me,

queen of paranoia. The door knob is cool under my hand. It's my room, but it's like I'm trespassing in a strange place. I open the door a crack, just enough to see.

Unfiltered sun, dust dancing everywhere. The bird and butterfly have come to rest beside my bed, fetched up against the bottom in a tangle of wings and feathers. Everything is coated in red and brown, blood and...whatever else the bird and butterfly might be leaking. It's on the walls, the ceiling, and in a thick streak across the carpet, ending where they lie.

I run to the bathroom and toss up my pancakes. When I come back out, Nathan's parked on the top step, and Keene is leaning on the wall beside the bedroom door.

"Want to sit this one out?"

"I'm not sitting anything out. We're in it together."

"Good," says Keene. "Let's get this thing done." He pushes upright, retreats to his own bird-free room, and comes back with an aluminum baseball bat and a golf putter. He hands the putter to Nathan, who takes it reluctantly.

"What's first?" Nathan asks. "Window or monsters?"

"I don't even know," Keene says looking at me. "Can you stand guard over the butterfly and bird while we put something over the window?"

"What are you going to put over it?"

"The mattress?"

"They're between the window and the bed," I point out.

"Shit," Keene says, tapping the bat on the floor. "Monsters first then?"

"No fucking way," Nathan says. "So more fly in? Hell, they could be coming in right now."

"How about this," I say. "Let's nail up the shower curtain quick to block the window."

"Something could fly into it," Nathan says. "A shower curtain isn't going to stop much."

"I'm not expecting it to be a permanent barrier. Just block the hole until we can put something stronger over it."

"What about a door?" Nathan counters. "We could take one off its hinges and prop it against the window. That would cover it."

"It could fall over," I say. "If something hits it hard enough. So it's the same problem."

Keene holds up a hand. "Okay. Shower curtain first. A stop gap. We'll nail it up, get rid of the bird and the butterfly, then we'll figure out how to secure a door over the window as a more permanent solution. Good?" He looks from Nathan to me and back. "Okay, Shur, get the curtain. Nathan, can you grab the nails and a hammer?"

Grudgingly, Nathan heads down the stairs.

The bathroom still stinks like my puke, so I rush to pull down the frilly cloth curtain and the plastic liner behind it.

We meet back by the door. Keene hands me his bat and takes the curtains. He turns to Nathan. "Ready bro?"

"No."

"Okay, let's do it."

Keene pushes the door open all the way, spilling warm yellow light into the hall. There's glass everywhere, an explosion of it, glittering like diamonds in the carpet. And red. On my open chemistry book, on one white Converse All Star. In a heap, a weird pile of brown and orange and black and red. Feathers, bones. Wings. Blood. The bird's eye opens and rolls wildly, settling on me. Staring.

The butterfly is still, wings spread. One twitches.

"Make sure they stay put, Shur," Keene says, rushing across the room to the window. The curtains flap on the breeze.

The bug and bird show no other signs of life, no fight. My palms are sweaty on the bat's grip, and I keep it raised, resting against my shoulder, ready to be swung down like an axe at the first aggressive movement.

The boys nail the shower curtain into place, top, bottom, one nail on each side. It's rudimentary, but at least there's no longer a huge hole in the wall anything can come through.

Keene returns to my side and takes the bat. "Is it alive?" he asks, looking at the butterfly.

Nathan slowly extends the putter from arm's length and gives it a hard poke. In response, the butterfly scutters sideways a few inches closer to door, away from the bird. Keene and I both jump, and Nathan takes a step backwards.

"That's a yes."

"Should I kill it?" Keene asks, jiggling the bat.

"Not with that," I say.

"Why not?"

"You could get guts everywhere. And...like...wing dust. What if the bacteria is airborne too? We should put it inside something," I say.

"Like one of the plastic storage bins in the basement?" Nathan says. "There were some with lids that latched. So even if it's alive, it can't get out."

"Good idea," Keene says. "You get one and we'll take the door off Little's room to block the window."

Nathan nods.

"How are we going to secure the door?" I ask.

"I don't know yet. We'll have to nail something across it. Like a belt or...something. A couple of blankets." He leads the way to the hallway, grabbing the hammer as he goes. "Hey, get a crochet needle from Mom's room."

"You making a sweater?"

"I need to knock the pins loose from the hinges so we can take the door down." He looks at my raised eyebrow and says, "Just trust me."

"Fine."

Mom's room is quiet and serene. Her yarn basket is by the bed. She sometimes crochets before sleep while she watches the news. I pick one of the bigger hooks from the basket and bring it to Keene. He slides places it under the pin in the top hinge and taps the crochet needle's bottom with the hammer. The pin pops up a bit. He continues until it's free.

"Where'd you learn that?" I ask.

"Dad," he says. "Bet he didn't guess I'd be taking off a door to use as a protective barrier against monsters though."

Nathan comes back with a container at about the same time we're setting the door against the wall near the window. "Is this big enough?" he asks. The bin is better than two feet long, almost the same size as the butterfly.

"It'll fit, I think, but it's going to be a tight squeeze," Keene says. He takes the bin from Nathan and hands me the lid. "What do you think?"

"Lower it over the thing like a dome."

"You guys are crazy," Nathan says.

"You got a better idea?" Keene snaps.

"No."

"Then stand guard. If it tries to get us, beat it to death."

"Maybe we should put on masks," I say. "In case he does have to beat it to death."

Keene is already moving in on the butterfly, ignoring me. He squats and lowers the bin gingerly. It's like the claw machine, trying to catch a stuffed animal perfectly in the center, except this animal is stuffed with turkey vulture meat and will eat him if he misses. No pressure. The plastic edge catches a wing, and the thing contracts, making itself smaller, sealing its fate. With the impromptu cage in place, Keene straightens and wipes his palms on the legs of his pants. "Now we've just got to get the lid on," he says.

"Oh man," Nathan says, flexing his grip on the putter.

Lid in hand, I kneel beside the box. Keene lifts the corner a tiny bit and I wedge the lid under.

"Now...push it under the butterfly."

"What if it doesn't move?"

"It'll move," Keene says with confidence I don't feel.

I push the lid slowly, maneuvering it under the butterfly's bulk. As Keene predicted, the butterfly moves, bothered by the contact. Encouraged, I shove the lid forward. The butterfly shifts its weight, seems to pick itself up, and settles heavily on plastic cover.

"It's on the lid," I say. I keep pushing until the lid reaches the edge of the box.

Keene adjusts the box until it's lined up to close, then pushes down. There's a click as the edges connect. I slide my fingers under the plastic, lifting the box enough to pop the latch in place, while

Keene does the same on the other side. That done, we flip the entire box over. The butterfly scrambles and thrashes inside, stuck on its back. It kicks at the lid, but the latches hold.

Trapped, the butterfly vibrates its orange and black wings. They brush the plastic. Its prison is too tight for it to do much in the way of stretching, but a black crab leg pokes out, feeling the smooth surface. It probes, pushing in a slow circle, its form made slightly foggy by the semiopaque plastic.

"Do you think it smells us?" I ask.

"I don't know," Keene says. "Oh shit." He rises, carefully, steady, picking up the bat as he goes, all focus on the window. A butterfly leg, pitch black, is poking through the gap between the shower curtain and the wall. It probes up and down, a claw at the end opening and closing. Keene brings up the bat, ready to strike.

"Fuck off!" Nathan screams, startling me and Keene as he bashes at the leg with his putter. It retracts fast, followed by the flutter of wings.

"Oh my God," Keene says, putting a hand over his heart.

We stand there looking at each other. Keene has gone pale. "I'm...going to put this in Mom's room," he says, picking up the bin. He disappears down the hall.

"I guess we should put the door over the window," Nathan says. "That thing spooked him, huh?"

"Not you," I say. "You went full tilt at it."

"Oh, I was spooked," he says. "That's what it looks like when I get startled."

"Remind me not to jump scare you," I say.

We lift the door together and settle it against the window,

watching for rogue butterfly legs and keeping half an eye on the inert bird.

I tug down the curtains and fold the first one in half, then in half again. "Here, nail this on that side." He does so, then hands the hammer and a bunch of nails to me. I nail the cloth into the wall, then put a few nails into the wood through the cloth across the door. We do it again with the second curtain, higher up.

"You really think that'll hold?" he asks.

I shrug. "I guess if something hit it hard enough, it might come loose, but nothing's going to come crawling inside by chance."

Nathan nods toward the bird. "So how do you want to take this thing out of the house?"

"Kill it, then throw it out."

"Now?"

"There's not going to be a better time," I say. "Do you want to do the honors?"

"No, but I will. Maybe we should cover it with a coat or a sheet or something? You're probably right about the blood having gross stuff in it."

"Yeah." The blanket from my bed is downstairs, and the sheets have been stripped from the bed. "I know," I say. I cross to the closet, throw it open, pushing aside my regular clothes, looking for the stuff hidden behind everything else. There it is, the semiformal dress I wore to the Sadie Hawkins dance freshman year, ugly as ever. The important part is that it has lots and lots of fabric.

"Here."

Nathan isn't looking at me anymore. The turkey vulture is

struggling to its feet, maybe disturbed by all the talking or sensing our murderous intent. Either way, it's got its head down aggressively, rear end up, ready to charge.

Turkey vultures are naturally hideous creatures. Red, wrinkly heads. Short, sharp beaks. This is a small one, maybe two feet, which is still a big bird. Its eyes are a strange, milky white. It screams and extends its wings. I also scream and grab onto Nathan, who lets out a strangled squawk.

"I don't think it's going to work," I whisper.

It bobs its head left and right. Is it like Joe Arroz, suffocating on violent nightmare thoughts? Does it feel parasites wriggling inside, or is it simply pissed at being trapped in a human cave with a huge wound in its chest?

Nathan pulls the dress from my arms and takes a step forward. Immediately, the thing lunges.

"Don't," I cry.

He backs up.

"New plan," I say.

"I can catch it," Nathan says.

"It's going to peck you, or worse. We'll lock it in here like you said before."

I grab my soccer bag from the desk chair, dump out the contents, and start loading it with crap from the dresser. Underwear. Sweatpants. Socks, a couple of sweatshirts. My laptop. A spare charger. The bird continues to bob its head furiously at Nathan. I think it's saying, "Fuck off and let me die in peace, this is my room now."

"Let's go." I pull at Nathan's sleeve, and we begin to back out.

The vulture charges. Not thinking, I punt it. Hard. As hard

as I've ever taken a goal kick. The vulture sees it coming and tries to fly but is launched farther and harder as a result of its own momentum. It screams and hits the wall, plummeting to the bed. A dark red smear of blood marks its point of impact.

So much for that mattress, my brain helpfully supplies, sour.

I slam the door, and we stand in the hallway together, breathing hard.

"You turned that thing into Thanksgiving dinner," he says.

"With parasite stuffing?"

"We talked about proper cooking temperature," Nathan says, and we both start to giggle, on the edge of hysteria.

18

The butterfly lasts another hour. We sit together, Keene and I, watching it circle around and around its plastic prison. The shades are down and the curtains pulled tight in my mother's white-washed room. A cacophony of flapping comes from outside. How much of this noise is my imagination, I can't say. I have wings on the brain, bird wings, butterfly wings. And scratching. Clawed, armored legs scrape and slide across the window screen, across the siding. Sometimes they thump hard, maybe landing or squabbling.

We're side by side on the bed. Overhead, the fan spins lazily on its lowest setting. It's too warm in the room, but I still have a chill. I could turn off the fan, but I'm hypnotized by the circling. Circling fan, circling butterfly, circling cycle of endless days. It's magical in a terrible, boring, eternal way. Like watching the minute hand refuse to budge in a slow class. The butterfly pauses, feels for an edge it never finds, moves again.

The next pause turns into a hard stop. It's perfectly still. Light pricks through the curtains, dappling the wings, illuminating its orange spots. It's almost beautiful. It gives a last shudder, twitches, spasms. Then is still again. Forever.

It'll stay entombed in its plastic coffin. An exhibit from the Time of Monsters.

"We need to get rid of that bird," Keene says.

"Yeah."

The bird is screaming and murderous, bouncing off the walls of my room. We dare not open the door, not even to peek. In my mind's eye, the room is covered in blood and brown goo, parasites. The stench of death and rot. I don't think I'll ever be able to sleep in there again.

I say, "I wish Mom was here."

"Me too," Keene says.

We stare at the dead bug for a long, long time.

"What about that thing? What do we do with it?" Keene says.

"Leave it for now. We can always burn it."

"You were brave," he says and squeezes my hand.

"You too."

"We should cover the rest of these windows," I say and tell him my idea about the towels and blankets. "Maybe you guys can take care of that."

"What are you going to do?"

"Laundry," I say. "Cleaning. What I always do. Are you holding it together?"

"I honestly don't know," Keene says. "It's so surreal, but hyperreal at the same time. My mind..."

"Isn't built for it?"

"Yeah."

"No one's is."

He squeezes my hand again. "I guess not."

We're brought back downstairs by angry shouting. Little is back in front of the television, probably forming permanent butt callouses and ADHD from too much screen time. His thumb is corked in his mouth again, with special blankie in the same hand, pressed close to his face. Terrible Charlie squishes against his side, legs tucked, eyes closed. He does not seem concerned with the argument raging in the kitchen.

Jenny and Nathan are clearly in the middle of something. He's pacing back and forth with his backpack on, and she's red faced, standing between him and the basement door.

"What's going on?" I ask.

"Dipshit here is trying to leave."

"What?"

"You heard my mom," Nathan says. "You saw that thing upstairs. If I'm leaving, this is when it has to happen. I can probably get home pretty quick, check the parents, make sure they're...fine."

"You can't go," I say. Jenny's eyes are wide with alarm, and she obviously has not said anything about the course of a bite infection.

"Of course I can. I just need to be careful, like we were on the way to the barn."

"Nathan," Keene tries. "Be real."

Outside, beyond the carport, the butterflies mass in ever-thickening streams.

"You can't stop me," Nathan says, petulant.

"You couldn't even take that bird, Nathan," Keene says, his voice carefully casual. He opens the fridge, looks inside. I see his anger in the yellow light from within. The door blocks Nathan's view of Keene's emotion. He closes the door again without taking anything out. "Besides, how are you getting there, on foot?"

"I'll take your car."

"You're not taking my car. What if we need it?"

"I'll be right back."

Keene shakes his head. "No. Absolutely fucking not."

"You're not my father," Nathan roars.

"You're acting like a complete numb-nuts!" Jenny screams. She storms to the back door, throws it open so that we can see the butterflies on the other side of the screen. As if sensing, or probably smelling, us, one lands on the screen, then another, claws clacking. Then a third. They crawl all over each other, mismatched puzzles pieces trying to fit in the limited space. The biggest has a body maybe two feet long, and it fans its enormous wings, trying to dislodge its competitors.

"Jen," I whisper.

She closes it. "That's what you're rushing into, Nathan."

"Nathan," I say, "Your mother is gone."

There's a sharp intake of breath from Keene, and Jenny's face drains of color. I'm thinking of Joe Arroz, of his mangled arm and sweaty face. It's not hard to imagine how he must have sounded toward the end. Crazy. They have closed wards. People locked up. People who probably sound like his mother.

"You bitch," he says. It's almost mild. "Does this make you

happy? Your father's dead, so this makes us even? Welcome to the club?"

I feel slapped in the face. It's so cold, so unexpected, so angry. We've never had an argument, not ever. All the warm feeling from before, the potential that something might be starting between us, is suddenly absurd and tainted. Gone.

"Are you kidding?" Jenny snaps, wading into the fray. "Are you fucking kidding, saying that to her? To them? Fuck you, Nathan. Take the keys and leave."

We stand there, no one daring to move. To breathe. Jenny breaks first, putting her arms around my shoulders as my chest starts to hitch.

"I SAID LEAVE!" She screams it at Nathan, the level of rage in her voice new even to me. She shakes with the force of it, spit flying. She turns and snatches the keys from the key hook and throws them at him, hard. They hit his chest and bounce off, dropping to the floor.

Nathan stares down at them for a long moment, then leaves them. He opens the basement door and disappears down into the cellar, slamming the door hard behind him.

Jenny turns and hugs me tight. I cry into her shoulder, dampening the thin cloth with tears and spit. All of it spills out: the fear of losing someone else, admitting Nathan's mother is most likely dead, the thing in the box upstairs, losing my room to a half-mauled bird. My missing mother. The ever-present specter of my father.

"Hey," Keene says, his voice soft. "Are you okay?"

"Are you?" I ask, my voice muffled by Jenny's shirt.

"No." He says to Jenny, "Thanks. For trying to stop him."

"You don't think he'll go out through the hatch?" Jenny asks.

I stiffen. I hadn't even thought of that.

"No," Keene says. "He left the keys. He's out of his mind, but not that far gone that he'd try to walk. He just needs time."

19

Anyone would protect their little brother, especially a baby like Shawn, from monsters. It's our job as older siblings, implied with the sit-down by your parents: You're going to be promoted to Big from Only! A new baby is coming, it's in Mommy's tummy.

We didn't have any of that.

Our father, Sean, Big Sean, was a salesman for a very successful international computer software company. He was good at his job, very good. Mom didn't have to work. She liked being a stay-at-home Mom.

We lived in a fat McMansion up on the other side of town, in the same neighborhood as Nathan's family. The houses had manicured green lawns, in-ground swimming pools, elaborate decks for yard parties.

Dad worked from home, so he was around a lot, a steady, constant presence in his office down the hall. He made snacks when we got off the bus. He drove us to sports practices, and he rarely missed games. We were a tight family, the four of us.

One day he went out for milk and eggs and never came home.

It was summertime, closing in on September, when the air is hot and still, but somehow there's a hint of chill in the evening that wasn't there two or three weeks earlier. We always worried when he traveled for work, long weeks away at conferences or at client sites. That day, he was out getting milk and eggs. A twenty-minute trip, tops.

He hit a tree. The police couldn't figure out why. He wasn't drunk, and there were no swerve marks on the road. His phone was in his back pocket, so he wasn't texting. Their best guess was there was a bee in the car and he got distracted. There was no one to blame but God and the universe.

My anxiety had always been there, even before. Keene was a carefree wild child, taking the hills in the neighborhood on his bike at full speed, constantly falling off his skateboard and getting back up laughing (always covered in scabs and bruises), climbing trees with no regard to what would happen if he fell. I was the cautious one, always dwelling on consequences. I rode the bike brakes. If I tried the skateboard, I wore all the safety equipment and panicked if the board went too fast. The only interest I had in trees was reading at their base, and only if I could guarantee I wouldn't be consumed by ants. I always fretted about the worst happening, and my parents thought it was endearing. I'd grow out of it, they said.

Instead, the worst did happen. And I'll never grow out of it. I was right all along to be anxious.

Dad didn't die right away, so there were lots and lots of hours

spent waiting for the tide to break one way or the other: death
or recovery. In those hours, probably sitting in the uncomfortable vinyl seat beside his bed, staring at the breathing tubes, the
ruins of his face, his greasy, unwashed hair, Mom decided that she
might like to have another child.

We heard all this later.

"I'm pregnant," she said, a year after his death.

I asked, "Who's the father?" Because that is the sort of
common sense, rude thing you ask when you're a kid. Are we
going to have a new father too? Is a new person going to be hanging around?

"Your father is the father," she told us.

"How?" Keene asked. We were doing math in our heads, with
our limited imagination on the topic of pregnancies. We knew it
took nine months for a baby to cook, and Dad had been dead for
a year. Mom was not even showing.

"I had a procedure. Some of your Dad's sperm was saved." She
said it so matter-of-factly, it could have been anything. *I bought
popcorn. We're replacing the old SUV with a Subaru. I had a procedure with your dead father's saved sperm.*

Keene and I exchanged a look, a shared twin look, and I saw
he was thinking something very similar. *What are we supposed to
say?*

"Well, can we name it?" Keene asked. Mom brightened
immediately.

"Maybe."

"Is it a girl or a boy?" I asked, following his lead.

"I don't know yet."

"Are we going to find out?" I asked. "Before it comes out?

Because we have to paint a room. And I don't like when people are going to have a baby and they paint the room yellow or white or green." I was thinking of Dad's office. Would the baby sleep there?

"Actually," she said, "I have one more important thing to tell you."

That's when we found out about the farmhouse. It was being restored for us, gutted, rebuilt from the ground up. Dad had left lots of money, lots of insurance. She didn't want to be in our house anymore, with Dad's empty office, a huge lawn she now had a service tend because Dad's mower was terminally in the shed, and closet full of his clothes she couldn't bear to part with. She wanted new. New furniture, new house, new car, new baby.

She showed us what it would look like, this new home, and asked what we wanted in it, and she cried at first when we cried because we didn't want to leave the only home we'd ever known. We wanted Dad to come back. We didn't want a new baby, or a new house, or a shed without Dad's lawnmower. And she didn't want to live in a place haunted by memories.

I overheard her sobbing to my grandmother in the kitchen, upset at us.

Grandma, ever stern, always straightforward, said, "You can't partner with kids, and you're expecting too much of them. They're little, yet. They miss their Dad. They're not going to buy into your plans. You just need to drag them along."

"The therapist says it would be good for Shur."

"She's not going to get that, Ellen. She's misses her Dad and is afraid of losing everything else. You're taking away her home."

"I'm taking her out of a place that makes her miserable!"

My grandmother sighed, loud. I couldn't see her, but I could picture it. I'd gone stiff when they started talking about me and my problems. The hospital stay and extended out-patient period were still fresh. I had weekly therapy visits and pills to combat my constant anxiety. Things were at least bearable now. Why would she risk it?

Grandma said, "You can't rush her grieving. You're dealing with it in your way, she'll deal with it in hers. But, for the record, you're right. This is a mausoleum. It's time to sell it and make something new."

I didn't want something new, but the words stuck with me, and I talked about them with the therapist. She said I should try to be optimistic, or at least not pessimistic. Neutral at worst, hopeful at best. I landed somewhere in between. Cautiously optimistic.

And then he was born, Shawn. Little Shawn, not Sean like Dad, more like a sequel than a junior. He would never know our father, and we felt bad for him because of that. He squirmed and kicked, smiled at us, took a bottle from us. I'd stare at him in his crib in his blue room in our new house. We didn't forget Dad. His riding mower was in the barn. Keene and I took turns mowing. Mom got a job when she was ready, although I don't think she needed to. Shawn went to day care. He asked about Dad sometimes, how come other kids had one while he didn't. We told him stories.

In time, we came to see it Mom's way. Little was a miracle, a way of dragging Dad along with us into the future, another chance. We didn't hold that over Little, only celebrated him as a way of not having to let go of Dad completely. A new life where a life had been stolen. A life stolen back.

So keeping Little safe isn't only about him. It's about Mom

too, and Dad's memory. It's about looking death in the face and saying, "You took one. You can't have them both."

———

Nathan doesn't come back upstairs to sleep. He's moving things around in the basement, maybe making a nest or throwing a tantrum. We leave him alone. If he doesn't come up to rejoin our tiny society by morning, I'll check on him. He was mean, but he's still our friend, and it came from a place of pain. I know enough not to try to pet Terrible Charlie when he's feeling sick, and I know enough not to poke a person when they're hurting.

I reheat a bowl of macaroni and cheese and bring it halfway down the stairs with a glass of milk, leaving it there so he doesn't have to talk to me. A boy has to eat. I call down, "Can you move the laundry? Please? Thanks." I try to say it nicely. I don't want to disturb him, but we need clean towels. There are so few left after nailing most of them to the windows, along with every broken-down cardboard box we could find.

While Little defaults to the couch and *Frozen*, dragging a reluctant and upset Keene along with him, I pace the kitchen. By now, I must be wearing a groove in the laminate. Jenny's eyes flick up now and then from the laptop, where she's following whatever the latest developments are.

It's all very tense.

What would Mom do? She'd pour a glass of wine and make dinner. There's an open bottle of something red in the fridge, still mostly full. I pull the cork and sniff. It smells sharp. I pour it. It tastes thick and meaty. I sip it diligently, hoping it will, by virtue of being Mom's and therefore a grown-up thing, bring me great wisdom. Make me smarter, older, whatever it is that makes you an adult. Being an adult has never seemed so far away.

I preheat the oven and chop potatoes. Like an adult. I sip wine and contemplate the potatoes. Mom would douse them in olive oil and toss them with the expensive salt. And a spice. Rosemary, maybe. Or thyme. I have no idea what the difference is. I sniff them. The rosemary smells nice. I add them both. We have frozen chicken breasts, super thin, in the freezer. I drop them into the sink and run hot water over the package, poking it every so often to see if it's thawed. The wine is improving with time. I think maybe I'm losing my mind. Is this what it is to be a mother? One kid pitching a fit in the basement, two more pouting in the den, one at the computer with her headphones on, none of them doing anything productive at all to contribute to the family? Parenthood is making sure your kids have vitamins, minerals, and aren't eaten by monsters or shot by randos? Why on Earth had my mother signed up for a third kid? And why, without Dad to help?

The thin chicken thaws fast. We have gobs of frozen vegetables. Cheesy broccoli, Little's favorite. I make two packs because there are four of us, and the power will go out soon, so we might as well use it up. Who knows if frozen cheesy broccoli will even exist in a post-butterfly world? Who knows if a world will even exist in a post-butterfly world? I finish the glass and pour another. Wine hangovers, that's an adult thing too. I have that to look forward to. Mom always sucks down bottle after bottle of water the day after she has too much wine. Maybe I should drink some now. Get a head start.

I put a pan on the stove and mix various flavors of

breadcrumbs. I beat an egg in a bowl, and my tears drop in, so I stir those too. Efficient. Had I really thought maybe there was something between me and Nathan? Has he secretly been judging me all this time, thinking my reaction is overwrought? I dredge the chicken in flour and egg and breadcrumbs. I fry it in the oil.

I am definitely losing my mind. Definitely. I should drink more wine.

Jenny pulls off her headset and unplugs it, so I can see it too. I don't really want to, but she doesn't ask, just angles it my way, then gets up to pour herself a glass of meaty wine. She gives it a dirty look but keeps drinking.

"Are you crying?"

"Onions," I lie.

"As long as you're fine, watch this."

"Oh, come on, Jen," I say, but she's already pressing play. The oven beeps. Temperature reached. Naturally, I have forgotten to wait for the potatoes to finish before cooking the chicken, so now the chicken will be cold. Typical. I put the potatoes in and cover the chicken with foil while Jen watches me bustle back and forth.

"Sit."

"I'm cooking dinner."

"Sit your ass down, you need to see this," Jenny commands. She leads me to the seat, more or less pushes me onto it, then rewinds the video.

Our old friend Lester the reporter has aged ten years in two days. His suit is crisp, neat, clean. His glasses are spotless and modern. But his face is haggard and done. It's in his eyes and the tension around his mouth. Like he wants to cry.

"I don't want to know."

"We have to be prepared," Jenny says. "You know that."

Things are not going well in Helsinki, and it's not just the fires. That's what it's all about, Lester's sad face and wilting posture. He's gone live as we bicker. There's a man in a parka in a dark hotel room. Behind him, the windows are covered. There are other people with him, shapes, huddled together.

"We're lucky it's September, not December," the man is saying. "We're cold. But it could be much worse. The real threat is from the infected. We carried as much food, water, and other supplies as we could, Lester, but there's no electricity. We won't be able to broadcast much longer. I wanted the viewers at home to see this."

He guides the camera guy to the window and pushes the shades apart. The camera takes a second to focus through the glass, a little, jumping blur of reality, and then a city on fire in the distance resolves.

"Helsinki is gone," the man says, and his voice breaks. The entire skyline glows orange, a long, unbroken inferno.

"About the infected," Lester says, trying to pull the man back to him, away from the window.

The man swipes his face with a gloved hand. "They came into the hotel. A half dozen at first. Violent. We barricaded the stairs so they couldn't get to us."

"Are they zombies?"

The man shakes his head. "They're people. They're just people! But they're rotting from the inside. The smell, Lester. I can't..."

I slam the laptop shut. I don't want to hear more. I don't want to see more.

We stare at each other.

"Is there going to be anything left?" I ask finally.

"What do you mean? Of course there is."

"How can you be so sure?" I ask. "It was burning. The whole thing was burning down."

She shrugs. "Civilizations have fallen before, but humanity always gets back up. Rome. Europe during every single plague. The Ottomans."

"Roanoke? The Mayans?"

Keene escorts Little into the kitchen by hand, oblivious to the discussion. His eyes are distant and far away. When he finally glances up, he says, "Are you drunk? Oh God, tell me you weren't drinking red wine. You know that makes Mom all sappy and sentimental. And sad. Not a good choice. I smell food. Is it ready?"

The chicken is cold. I nuke it. The potatoes are too hot to eat, and the cheese sauce on the broccoli tastes vaguely like plastic. We sit around the table, the four of us, Nathan somewhere below and Terrible Charlie parked on my left foot. I'm not hungry, but I am drunk. I drop most of my chicken for Charlie to eat.

I think about the infected, my thoughts drifting inevitably to Nathan's mom. Is that what she is now, something to hide from? Something so dangerous, you barricade yourself in the dark? Maybe it's time to think about reinforcing the basement, so we have a place to hide. Or leaving and going to Bill's house. Outside, the sun is setting, and the sound of wings is louder than ever, impossible to ignore or to pretend it's something else, like wind through the trees. There are so many of them.

20

I wake up hungover. It could be morning, the middle of the night, afternoon, any time. It's so dark in the den. My mouth is dry and tastes like the inside of a garbage can. I'm not getting back to sleep. My brain is muzzy and exhausted, but the sleeping part is currently broken. I roll and grope for my phone. The screen says 6:00 a.m. Can't keep my circadian rhythms down.

The kitchen is quiet and dim, so I switch the light on over the sink to give myself enough light to make coffee. I drink a huge glass of water while I wait, then another with a couple Tylenol from the bottle on top of the fridge. Little might sleep for another hour, two with luck, crushed up against Keene. Charlie, on the other hand, strolls into the kitchen, tail high and flicking, and mewls at me. He rubs his bulk against my legs. I empty half a can of wet food into his bowl, mix it with a bunch of dry, and check his supply in the cabinet. Still good. Part of Mom's bulk-buying plan.

As Charlie chows, I stand by the back door. He throws me

a side-eye and meows, disapproving. Too close to danger. "I'm fine," I say. Just listening for monsters, hungover, talking to a cat. Everything is perfect, Charlie. Everything is fine. I can hear them out there, their sail-flap wings. Is it wet out, I wonder? Raining? Sunny? Miserable, windy, perfect, still? And the scratching, always with that nasty sound of clawed things, bone on glass. I burp, and it burns like stomach lining. I rummage in the bathroom until I find a cannister of Tums and toss a handful into my mouth. Now it tastes like garbage and chalk.

Helsinki is bright in my mind, unshakeable, fiery orange on a grayish horizon. The news crew, their Finnish hosts. Fugitives from insanity, holed up together in a hotel room. Come to investigate the local butterfly infestation, stay for the violent infected! Stay forever and ever.

Helsinki is on fire. My brain is on fire. How long has it been since I took my pills?

Oh God, my pills.

My bag is next to the kitchen door, the bag I dumped everything into when we gave up my room, my sanctuary, to that slavering bird beast. I dump it all out onto the table, a spill of underwear, phone chargers, a lip gloss that's probably been in there since time immemorial. No pills. No matter how many times I comb through the pile, putting things back in the bag one at a time, no orange plastic bottle, no tiny orange pills. My favorite water bottle, a novel for English class, but no pills. I ignored that Days of the Week container Mom bought because I am nearly a grown-up. I do not need such childish reminders.

Except she was right. Damn it.

"Shur?"

I jump and let out a squeak.

"Sorry," Nathan says from the basement doorway. "I thought you'd have heard me come up."

"Lost in my head," I say. My heart is jackhammering too fast to focus on being mad at him for yesterday. Plus, I'm not even sure I still am.

"So, I should apologize," he says.

I hold up a hand. "We can talk about it later. Right now, I have a big problem, and I really need help," I say.

"What's wrong?" He comes forward to the table, gripping one of the chairs with both hands, all concern. And it's that kind of concern when you know you've screwed up and you're super anxious to make things right. I know it well; I wear it often enough.

"I forgot my pills upstairs in my room with that turkey vulture, and it's super possible I'm starting to have withdrawal."

"Oh! Shit!"

"Yeah."

"I can get them for you."

"Can we do it together? I don't think anyone should go in there alone, just in case it attacks."

"Yeah." His face breaks into a relieved grin. I'm not angry and I'm asking for his help. Knight in Shining Armor Duty has called him to the castle.

Nathan knows all about the pills. He's been around the family long enough to have witnessed the before, during, and after of my father's life and his death's impact.

"Maybe we should take the big knives," he says.

"Definitely."

"I don't know how to use them."

"Me neither, but if it comes at me, I'm going to stab and hope for the best."

"Or scream and run."

That surprises a snort of laughter out of me. I'm glad we're friends again.

He holds one of the knives in one hand, brings it up in front of his face, and twists it in the light. "This is like...something out of *Aliens*."

I'm glad he didn't make a zombie movie reference.

We creep through the still-dark den and up the stairs to the second floor, letting everyone else stay asleep and peaceful, or as peaceful as they are in sleep given the circumstances. I flick on the light at the top of the stairs. The doom at the back of my mind whispers, *the light worked this time...this time...*

Nathan presses his ear against the door.

"Anything?"

"Nothing. Maybe it died."

"Maybe."

"Do we have a plan?" he asks.

"We go in fast, I grab the pills, we run out."

"That's not really a plan. How about I open the door and see if I can spot it first? Then, when we know where it is, I'll go in first and point the knife at it, you can get the pills, and we'll back out."

"That is a much better plan," I admit.

"Good." He puts a hand on the knob, slaps his face with the other, free hand.

"You always do that," I say.

"Yeah, it's a stupid superstition," he says.

"I don't judge," I say. I really don't. I've seen much weirder nervous ticks than that in my time.

He opens the door a quarter inch and presses his face into the crack. "I don't...oh." The *oh* comes out slightly strangled, like he's choking on it.

"What?"

He pushes the door the rest of the way open, and I see.

I guess I'm expecting to be witness to a rotting corpse, but that's not it, not at all. That would be better. The bird is gone. Not gone, exactly, but transformed. In the corner, closest to the window, a brown, fibrous sack throbs against the molding, cemented to the wall by thick, organic strands. It pulses. Is it breathing? Is that a heartbeat? The room stinks like mud and rot. Earthy, bad. Damp.

"Get your pills," Nathan whispers.

It takes every ounce of willpower to reach the dresser, watching the thing as I go. They said on the news that the infected in Helsinki were people. No mention of anything like this. My hand closes around the bottle, and I back up to the door, still watching the brown sack like it might burst open at any moment, spilling its contents into the room. Into us.

Nathan creeps up on the sack, standing entirely too close to it.

"What are you doing?" I ask. "Get away from it."

"I just want a closer look..." He prods it with his foot.

"Nathan, have you lost your damn mind? Come on!" I close the space between us in two steps and grab him by the shirt, hauling him toward the door.

In the hallway, the closed door doesn't seem like enough of a barrier between us and that...thing.

After I take my pills with another monstrous glass of water, I set them on the counter and open the Days of the Week container. I meticulously put the pills into their individual compartments, and then set the container in the cabinet next to the coffee. Away from Little's prying fingers, but in a place where I will not forget them again. I try not to wonder if the ninety-day supply, already half-empty, is enough. Nathan watches, fidgeting the whole time, arms crossed, uncrossed, crossed again. Shifting. Maybe he needs some pills too.

"I just wanted to see if it was...like...solid," Nathan says after I'm silent for several minutes.

"What if it wasn't? What if your foot went right into it?" I hiss, trying to convey my alarm without waking up everyone in the house. "What if something came out of it?"

"It didn't happen," he says.

"It could have."

Nathan sighs. "Okay. I'll be more careful. I promise. Anyway...I set up the basement. I couldn't sleep. I knew you wanted it done, so I kind of...you know. As a good will gesture? Do you want to see?"

"Sure," I say, accepting this peace offering.

He leads the way down the stairs and says, "When I volunteered to help with the basement before, I thought it was a nice thing to do for you. To show support? Now I'm thinking you've been right all the time, about prepping. Hearing my Mom... We might need the basement for real." Whether he means to protect us from people or butterflies, he does not elaborate.

The basement is a transformed space. Nathan has set up our old tent, pinning the ropes in place with a bunch of heavy boxes. An air mattress is inflated inside it, and he's rolled out a few sleeping bags. Next to the tent, which takes up a solid quarter of the basement, he's made another bed out of Little's gymnastic tumble mats. He's gotten resourceful, unearthing Mom's collection of semidiscarded quilts and afghans made by various relatives over the years, which can never be thrown away or donated. The laundry table has been set up with folding chairs, and the green camp stove is on it. Jar candles are scattered here and there as would-be light sources.

"This is the *best* part," Nathan says, and he sounds nervous and proud. "I mean, there is not a best part because really I hope we never have to use any of this, but I set up a private area. It took me forever to get the clothesline to stay up." He guides me to the other side of the stairs, where he has repurposed the tarp as a curtain.

I say, "So it's for changing?"

"No! Look, I found the camp toilet. So, if we need to...we can go." He's even set up one of Charlie's old litter boxes.

"That's actually kind of awesome," I say.

"Yeah. It's my way of saying I'm sorry."

"You didn't need to apologize."

"I do. I was...am...upset about my mother, and I probably would have gone out if you hadn't said what you said."

"I could have been kinder."

"I don't think anything else would have gotten through," Nathan says. "I needed to hear it. So thanks, and I'm sorry."

"I hope she's safe," I say.

"Yeah." We both know she's not, and by the way his eyes angle up toward the ceiling, it's not a stretch to think he's got his mind on that cocoon.

21

RedBlip, that rumor center of the Internet, is alive with theories on parasites, cocoons, and manifestations in humans. The Internet is failing, though. I don't mean failing to provide us with theories or even at an infrastructure level, but rather failing to exist site by site. Instagram is gone. Mastadon is alive with crazies screaming into the void about the failure of this administration to predict the coming of monsters, and at the previous administration for not having built out a Monster Containment Playbook for the Oval Office. Screaming at each other for being alternately liberal snowflakes and right-wing fascists. More moderate voices in the middle point out that butterflies seem to enjoy the taste of both rednecks and snow-flakes equally.

And the theories...oh the theories. Each more batshit than the one before.

That the government unleashed these things by accident

from a top secret underground lab. Which government? China, Russia, the United States...even Luxembourg is accused.

That these things are from space and rode in on a meteor shower that passed by two months ago, throwing spores into the atmosphere that eventually drifted down, hatching in a coordinated biological attack ahead of an alien colonization that will follow when we're all wiped out.

That a rich billionaire in a doomsday cult hidden inside a mountain fortress in the Rockies with his followers had the butterflies bred in a lab so he could repopulate the world with his own descendants and position himself as God to the survivors.

That this is a simulation, and nothing is really happening.

That this is the apocalypse, and the faithful will be raptured soon.

That this is the apocalypse, but God has forsaken us.

The most popular theory, endorsed by the CDC and most foreign governments, is that the butterflies follow a similar gestation and hatching pattern to cicadas. Their eggs are microscopic, laid in the ground; they stayed dormant until global warming brought the Earth's temperature up to the threshold for hatching. The nymphs emerged and matured at a rate unheard of in animals or insects—almost like bamboo. No one grew them in a sinister lab—they've been here all along, waiting.

Facebook is offline. Google works, but half the results go to nonresponsive servers. Disney+, YouTube, Amazon, all down. Netflix still works, rolling along like nothing in the world can stop it. TikTok has a new viral dance for the apocalypse set to some old song called "The End of the World as We Know It." I don't have the energy to watch, forget learning it.

I read over Keene's shoulder as he scrolls the forums dedicated to cocoon-related horrors. The titles are all things like "*KILL IT WITH FIRE*" and "*Sayonara, Tokyo Prefecture*" and "*If Raid Doesn't Work, Try Fire.*" Every time he reloads, a dozen more responses fill the screen.

Jenny and Nathan are looking up the effects in humans. There's no hiding what's happening to his mom from Nathan now, but he's taking it about as well as can be expected.

"Here," Keene mutters. He stops and opens up a thread titled "*Hatching a Creeper.*" I read, eyes skimming over a story about a neighbor's chicken getting into a garage after it was bitten. Like we did with the vulture, the owners of the house left it there, expecting it to die, only to find a big, gross cocoon nestled against their car tire. The prevailing advice is to burn it.

Jenny says, "It works different in mammals. No cocoon. The parasites or bacteria or whatever get into their brain."

Keene is onto another post, and he waves at the screen. "This is nasty. Some of these animals start to transform. Like, into a hybrid of the butterflies and whatever they were before."

"Birds, right? They used to be dinosaurs. Maybe they're genetically closer to whatever these things are," Jenny says.

"Nature is fucked," Keene says. "Look at this picture."

I do not look at the picture. I get up and pour a glass of water. My hangover is beginning to dissipate thanks to water, coffee, and half a bag of potato chips. I'm craving grease. Maybe I'll make a burger, but definitely not if I have to look at a hybrid chicken butterfly monster.

"So we can't just leave it up there to hatch," Nathan says, stating the obvious. Keene can't take his eyes away from whatever monster is on his screen.

"We'll put it in a box or something and throw it outside. Or burn it in the fireplace," Keene says.

"It's stuck on there pretty good," Nathan says. "We'll probably have to cut it loose."

"How do you know that?" Keene says, his eyes narrowing.

"Because he gave it a poke with his foot," I say, ratting Nathan out.

"Dumbass," Keene says.

Nathan shrugs. "It didn't budge. Felt solid to me."

Jenny says, "Cocoon silk is like glue. He's right, we probably will have to cut it loose."

"What if it breaks?" I ask.

"Cocoons are durable," Jenny says. "We can use one of Bill's big knives to cut it free. Let's go look," she tells Keene. "Since we're the only ones who haven't seen it." She pushes out the chair to stand.

Several things happen next, in rapid succession.

On the periphery of my attention is an engine, not distant. Just as the front of my mind acknowledges it and immediately goes into overdrive at the possibilities, there's a second sound, this time the *tat tat tat tat* of gunfire, driving everyone to the floor again. Except me—I am running into the den where Little is leaning against the couch on the floor, watching some sort of morning cartoon with police dogs. Of any place in the room, this is probably the safest, with the couch forming an additional barrier. I scoop him and run, hunched, back into the kitchen where the others already have the basement door open.

As I'm handing Little off to Keene, there's another gunshot, louder and nearer than the first volley, quickly followed by the sound of an engine accelerating, the squeal of tires, and a tremendous crash that shakes the entire house.

The power snaps off at the same time we hear the crash. We're plunged into darkness. I fumble for my pocket and my phone.

"Did they hit us?" Keene screams.

Silence. Well, not silence, wings, wings everywhere, louder and agitated, but no more gunshots, no more engine.

I find the flashlight function, hands vibrating like they've been electrified. Bluish light bathes the kitchen, throwing Keene's frightened face into sharp relief.

"I don't think so," I whisper.

Jenny, already halfway into the basement, pushes back up and past Keene. "Downstairs, now," she commands him. "You and Nathan and the baby. Shur and I will look."

"Do *not* go outside!" Keene's becoming increasingly shrill with fright.

I put a hand on his arm. "We're not going outside. Little needs you. Light the candles. Show him the toilet and pretend like everything is fine." Charlie shoots between us and down the stairs. He doesn't need to be told shit's gone south. Again.

Jenny and I rush to the second floor. "Let's try Keene's room," I suggest.

The window in his room has been secured with his curtains, doubled up to thicken the barrier. "We'll have to pry it down," Jenny says. "I'll get the hammer."

"Just cut it," I say. I rummage around Keene's desk for a pair of scissors and come up with a pocketknife instead. "Here. Cut it loose. We'll put another one up."

She takes the knife and sighs hard, like I've asked her to do something impossible. Maybe she doesn't want to see whatever there is to see out there.

"You want me to do it?"

"No." She saws at the cloth along the nails until it flaps to one side. The room fills with grayish morning light, thick with the movement of restless shadows. So many wings.

That's the thing I really register first, the wings. The sheer number of butterflies out there, drowning out the sky, a writhing screen. Artificial night. It's raining too. It takes a moment to realize the splats against the glass are water and, somewhere overhead, visible through breaks in the living orange and black fog, comes silvery slices of sky.

It's hard to miss what happened, even with the moving tapestry obstructing the vista. The house on the other side of the street, the one next to Bill's, has a black pickup truck parked in its living room. The gray power pole that used to stand to the right of their empty driveway is on the front lawn, spitting yellow sparks into the damp air. There's a small *bang*! I think maybe a bug tried to investigate and got too close.

They come back, they're in for a surprise. That's what Bill said. I think of the louder, closer gun shot. Had he waited until they were just clear of our houses and fired into the truck? The butterfly curtain parts for a second, and I see a wheel still spinning, like the motor is on and in drive, and someone is stuck but good on the gas pedal.

"Holy shit," Jenny whispers. "Do you think anyone was home?"

I shake my head. "Their car isn't in the driveway."

"Look," Jenny says. "The house...someone's coming out."

It's impossible to tell if it's a woman or man. He or she is stumbling out of the hole where the front of the house used to be, dressed all in black. One pant leg is torn nearly off.

"No," Jenny moans. "No, go back."

I can't even form words. My tongue is too big in my mouth.

The person doesn't go back. He staggers from the jagged hole, maybe concussed. He's all the way to the lawn, too far to make it back, when the butterflies notice him.

It's one at first, then three, then a whole swarm. His arms flail, and howls of pain carry across the street, growing increasingly high pitched as he tries to run, slams into the truck's protruding back end, tumbles backwards. Then he's still. We can't see the shape of him at all, but the butterflies on him are a living, writhing death shroud. I turn away.

Together, we move down the stairs, too shocked to immediately go to the basement. We knew it was bad. We didn't realize...

"Everything okay?" Keene's voice floats up the stairs.

"Yeah," Jenny calls back. "Yeah, it's all clear!" Her voice is fake chipper. To me, she says, "Maybe we keep that to ourselves."

"We should start talking about moving to the basement," I say. "If those things get in..."

"Or the people," she starts, but leaves the thought at that.

"Yeah. We need to start thinking about what happens next."

22

The basement is timeless. Both small windows have been blocked with stacks of paver bricks, leftover from Mom's garden project last year. Nothing is getting in that way, at least not easily. That includes light.

"Safe in here" is what I'm choosing to expend all my mental energy on right this second, because I am at the edge of a full-blown anxiety attack. I have not had one in at least two years. Panic attacks, yes, plenty of those. But I thought the "I can't breathe, my heart is going to explode, I can't think, can't function" anxiety attacks were behind me. Until now.

I want to curl into a ball and rock and cry and maybe scream. I want it all to be over. And my meds are not quite right yet, not balanced, so it really is up to me to try and get control over my mind before I go spilling over the edge.

The screamer in my brain has plenty to say right now, but I need the middle-of-the-night voice. The logical side.

She says, *Obviously you want to break down now! Your little family group was safe. There was power, and even if the world was falling apart, even if something got into the house, it was manageable. But Swarms eating the living? Guns? Infected crazies? That's some hot shit. That's what the guy in Helsinki was afraid of. Human monsters.*

I can almost picture her. Older than me, wiser. Glass of wine in one hand. Smart. Cynical.

We're ready for this. You know what anxiety is? Hypervigilance.

That's what the therapist says. I'm always on high alert. Always ready for disaster.

Well, it's worked for you so far. Jenny is freezing up. Nathan tried to leave against all evidence pointing to that being the shittiest of shit ideas in the vast human history of shitty ideas. Like it or not, you're going to have to be the voice of reason here, kid, because you're the only one equipped to function when everything is on fire. You're a pro. So that's why you can't freak. Have a panic attack if you want. Cry. Go into a bathroom and scream. Whatever. But you cannot freak out if you want to keep these people alive, because they are not up to handling this.

———

Jenny has her laptop charged and ready to go with a selection of Disney movies scraped off the Internet. It won't last long. The battery will wear down super fast.

The basement is a sea of strange, mixed scents: basement damp, rose petal candles, and dryer sheets. Candlelight flickers and dances on exposed pink and brown insulation. No one wants to go upstairs.

I'm going to have to go up eventually, soon even, to pack up stuff from the fridge. We'll need to eat the things that will go bad first, save the dry goods for later. I eye the small camp stove. Is it even safe to use that in here with no ventilation? Will I need to cook upstairs on the stove?

I can spend time upstairs in bursts while everyone else stays safe down here.

We need to find a way to secure the basement from this side.

I wish we'd gone to Bill's.

We're hiding like the squirrels, like the birds. The small things that could wiggle through cracks into the attic, into holes in the ground.

The four of them are packed inside the tent, three not-adults and a baby. Inside, blue light trades place with white, now bright, now subtle, warming their faces. Keene hates *Frozen* with the passion reserved for a movie you didn't want to see the first time and now have seen at least three hundred times, and songs you never wanted to hear but know by heart. His face is rapt, arm wrapped around Little so tight, I'm surprised the baby doesn't complain. But I don't feel safe down here. Inside the tent is too restrictive, too hard to escape from fast if something or someone came down the stairs without warning.

The music plays, the candle wicks waver, and I pace.

Finally, exhaustion hits, crashes really, and threatens to knock me straight off my feet. I retreat to the makeshift bed Nathan set up next to the now-silent furnace and useless water heater. The pile of gymnastics mats smells plasticky beneath me, but it is so good to be lying down that I don't even care. I close my eyes and hear the music, but it fades in and out as my brain settles.

When I awaken, it's very quiet in the basement, almost eerily so. Everyone is asleep. My sleep was deep and dark. Restful. A defensive sleep. I push the blanket aside. It's cool in the basement, probably a good fifteen degrees cooler than upstairs, and we'll need Little's warmer clothes if we're really going to stay down here. It's time to head upstairs, while Little is not awake to freak out.

Plus, it's been way too long since anyone checked on the cocoon. We should have dealt with it, and we would have if it hadn't been for this latest turn of events.

I sneak up the stairs in bare feet. At the top, I pause to listen. Did anyone get inside? On this side of the door, I can hear nothing. The house has no heartbeat, no hum of electricity, no thrum of the fridge. It sounds abandoned.

The kitchen is as we left it. Dishes in the sink. My phone on the table, Charlie's food bowl half full. We'll need to move that to the basement, along with his food. I am planning for a new life, one spent underground. It's hard to believe we were in class not that long ago. Mom was drinking coffee right here at a counter I can barely see but for a few rogue sunbeams peeking through the space above the covered window above the sink.

This place might not have been my first choice, but it's our home now—our home with Little and Mom and Keene and Charlie, and even Jenny and Nathan. It's ours, and what's ours is precious. I don't want to go underground in the basement cave. I want to fight.

The second floor is more of the same, eerie quiet. Before, there had always been street sounds, house sounds, a sense of nearby humanity. Bill in his house, the hum of electricity. Now, far below me, my family sleeps, tucked away in a hole. Across the street, maybe Bill is still alive, and in the house next to that, maybe a lot of people are bitten, dying, dead.

But I'm not alone on this floor. There's the cocoon. The upstairs is silent, silent. I linger outside my bedroom door, listening. No movement. Nothing I can register. I will check the cocoon last, before I go back downstairs. I just need to work up to it.

I slip into Little's room to get some of his warmer clothes. I collect a few shirts and pants, socks and footie pajamas. I will stop in our bathroom for his toothbrush.

Closing the door behind me, I start back toward the stairs. *The vulture is quiet, but is the butterfly still dead? The* thought creeps up on me, and I can't shake it. Setting the bag down next to Little's door, I pad down the hallway to Mom's room. I crack the door enough to peek in, needing confirmation that the butterfly is still a corpse. The bin is resting right where we left it on top of the dresser, sun catching the top through the towels on these windows, glinting.

It's empty.

My heart rears up in my chest like it's trying to leave, one tremendous *KICK* and then begins to gallop. Is the monster loose in the room? I pull the door closed hard and rest my head against it, breathing hard. I have to go back in. If it's loose...

It could get us.

The nearest room is Keene's. I slip inside and grab the first thing I see, which is his bedside lamp. It has a little heft to it. Ideally, it would be a shotgun. Is it enough?

Reason is starting to settle in as I replay the scene in my mind, that quick glimpse. The lid wasn't on the floor. It wasn't even askew. Unless it thoughtfully replaced the lid after crawling out, that makes no sense. And it doesn't feel like we're talking about a super smart species here: one of them attacked a windshield wiper in front of me.

Lamp in hand, I return to the room and crack the door again. No change to the box. I slide inside as quietly as I can, lamp raised like a baseball bat.

The bin is undisturbed and right where we left it. And it's not entirely empty, I see, as I creep closer, stealthy, eyes wide and wary, heart so loud as to give away every move. It's not empty.

I set down the lamp beside the box and bend to see better through the plastic. It's filled with dust and the remains of black exoskeletal legs. It's not escaped, it's...gone. Rotted, decayed, efficient. No wonder we've never seen these things before. They don't turn into fossils: They turn into dirt.

My heart takes it down a notch, even as my mind turns over this new information. Feeling lighter, like at least one thing doesn't have to be worried about anymore, at least one room isn't completely off limits, I step back into the hallway and right into a scene straight out of a horror movie.

My bedroom door is open, exposing a black slice of dark. Little is backing slowly away from that gap, backing up, backing into the hallway. Terrible Charlie is beside him, hissing, hairy ears flat against his massive Maine Coon head. So many teeth showing. Spit flying.

Something in my room is alive.

23

ittle turns at my noise and flat out runs to me.

I don't think. I grab him and shove him along, half carrying, half plowing him toward Mom's bedroom. Door open. "Hide!" I whisper-hiss.

Door slammed in his pale, frightened face.

I should go in too, but I can't leave Charlie. He's still spitting at the opening, and whatever is in my room needs to stay in there. His fur stands on end, back arched. I need to get that door shut. I sprint back up the hallway and reach for the doorknob, but it's already too late. Something is coming out. Something is loose.

That's it for Charlie. He howls and charges directly up my body, digging in, nearly pulling me over with his frenzied terror. He's huge and has chosen his path badly. I stumble backwards, trying hard to stay upright, wondering if I can make it back to Mom's room before the thing, whatever it is, gets us. The shape, given an extra few seconds by Charlie's panic, now has the advantage and has come forward. The thing is between me and the stairs.

"Help!" My voice comes out as a weak whisper, and I barely hear myself over Charlie's screaming. He's gotten as far as my shoulders and has dug in on either side, a terrified, shrieking backpack. I wouldn't be able to get him off without help, so I don't even bother. I scream again and this time my voice carries down the stairs. I hope it gets as far as the basement. I scream again and again. Charlie and I really duet, belting it out.

I continue backing up blindly, feeling behind me with one hand, sweat pouring down my face, teeth chattering so violently, my jaw already hurts. The hallway is suddenly funhouse long. Two bedroom doors on each side, another at the far end, the stairs at the other. Between the bedrooms is a linen closet and, across from it, a narrow coat closet. I can't fit into either one, not with a cat on my back. I ease open the smaller closet and snatch up the first thing my hand falls on: a dead handheld vacuum. The battery has not worked in years, but it has a heft to it. Maybe I can use it as a weapon.

"Shut it!" I yowl back at Charlie, who digs in harder. There are punctures everywhere, through my skin, through my clothes.

And here it comes. It is no longer a turkey vulture, definitely not a butterfly, but some sort of horrifying mashup. A little kid's monster drawing. Bald. No more feathers, just raw, brownish meat, slimy, swollen. Bloated and bruised. The noise from Charlie is worse. Hoarse.

The thing fully emerges from my bedroom. It has a spare leg, kind of exoskeletal, like the butterfly's, but ringed in scales, like a bird's. The leg is in the wrong place, jutting out of its torso. It drags itself along. The beak is gone, leaving a gaping hole. One eye stares dead at the ceiling, but the other is bright, interested. Aimed at me. Sizing me up, I think. Trying to determine if I am a threat or if I am food. That eye does not blink. The pupil gets larger and smaller, larger and smaller.

A second leg unfolds from its torso, then a third, so that it starts to seem less like a bird and more like a spider. The thing scuttles sideways, closer to the door, then back, as if trying its new legs out. I inch backwards. The bathroom door is closed, Keene's room too. If I can reach one of those rooms, I might be able to get in. Unless it's fast.

It scuttles forward again, like a crab on a beach. Another leg. That's four. It's decided that I'm food. Or that Charlie is, and I'm in the way. Its motions are clipped. Scuttle, scuttle. Pause. Head tilt.

Mom's room is my best bet, I decide. I can open the door, back in. Kick the thing before if it gets too close.

Downstairs, people are shouting my name. The turkey vulture does not look in that direction. It only has eyes for me and Charlie.

Backwards another few inches. Death grip on the Dyson. Charlie's death grip on me.

It's hunting. I don't know how I can say that for sure, but its movements are subtly more sure now. Not scuttling. Creeping. Preparing.

I hold my breath.

It charges.

The vulture launches at my legs with unnatural speed. I swing down with the Dyson, trying to bash it, but it latches onto the vacuum's attachment with one crazy leg and yanks the device loose from my grip. I take a few unsteady steps backwards to recover, gaining some ground. Another mouth has opened, like the butterfly's in its torso, between all those legs, and it tries to stuff the vacuum into this orifice. Realizes it's not food. Drops it and charges again.

I'm aware that the shouting is closer, is almost here, is coming. Not fast enough. The bedroom door is behind me. My hand is on the knob, but the thing is too close. If I open the door, it'll get in. If I don't, it'll get me. I square up, making myself bigger, reminding myself not to kick into the torso if I want to keep my foot. I'll have to fight.

With a strangled cry, Keene is on the thing, hitting it with something. It rebounds against the wall to my right, and then Keene is at it again, even as it scrambles upright. It backs away, hissing. It knows we are a real threat. Predator, not food. The wild eye snaps at me and Charlie as Keene, bat in hand, gets between us.

A dark blur rears up behind the monster and arcs down hard, hard, a motion driven by hatred and rage and fear. A long, long knife. The thing is impaled, the hilt of the knife driven right down through its entire body, through the carpet, into the sub-flooring. It screams and wriggles and writhes, trying to free itself. It pulls up, then drops again, slicking the blade with blackish blood, and shrieks again. On my back, Charlie whimpers.

Nathan stands back from his handiwork and watches as it goes through death throes, spindle legs kicking, claws thrashing, making that strange, shrieking cry. At last the claws close one final time. It is motionless, but I still don't trust it. It could be faking. It could be alive and waiting and lurking. That's when I start to shake.

24

Charlie does not let go. We are all frozen. Keene's arm is still drawn back with the bat, ready to strike again if the probably dead thing shows any sign of moving. The adrenaline is starting to wear off, and I'm becoming aware of the depth and number of my Charlie-related injuries. I am oozing blood.

Jenny comes scrambling up the stairs, calling, "Did you find them?"

The intrusion breaks the freeze and drops everything back into normal time.

"We split up to look for you," Keene says. He drops to his haunches, relaxing his swing stance. "We couldn't tell where the shouting was coming from, and we couldn't find Little."

"He's in there," I whisper, motioning behind me. Charlie lets out a howl and digs in harder, not yet ready to believe the danger has passed. Everything hurts. Everything.

Jenny walks around me slowly, cautious of Charlie, who lets

go with one claw long enough to swipe at her. She opens the door. Enters. Shuts it again and calls out for Little. The voice comes from high and low, here then there.

"Let me help," Nathan says and reaches for Charlie. He's nearly rewarded with a bite for the effort as Charlie gnashes his teeth and screams gutturally. Nathan snatches his hand away, shocked. Charlie isn't like this. He isn't mean. Pesty and testy, but not mean.

Keene tries instead, extending a hand very slowly with the same result. He says, "Nathan, can you cover up the bird? Maybe he'll chill if he can't see it."

"Yeah." Nathan ducks into Keene's room and comes out a moment later with a white plastic laundry basket and a curtain. He puts the basket over the corpse, then drapes the curtain over the basket. He leaves and comes back again, this time with a pair of hand weights, maybe eight or ten pounders. These he puts on top, then says sheepishly, "Just in case."

I really, really like him in that moment, even through the pain and fading terror and low-throated grumbling coming from the angry feline on my back.

With the bird thing out of sight, Keene tries again, extending his hand to the cat slowly, whispering and muttering, making cooing noises. He gets Charlie between the ears, rubs, gets closer. This time, Charlie retracts his claws and comes away into Keene's arms, pads bloody, eyes wild. He squirms, malcontent at being contained, and squirts away. Without so much as a backwards glance for me, his savior, Charlie streaks down the hall to the stairs. He disappears to parts unknown, presumably to lick my blood from his paws. I see how it is.

"Keene, check on the baby," I whisper. That's all I can manage, that single whisper. It wants to be a voice, unconcerned, untraumatized, but I am not capable of normal, fully human speech. Bile is rising in my throat, tears are pooling in my eyes. "Make sure he isn't bitten."

"I woke up and he was gone," Keene says. "I was cold and I woke up and he wasn't there."

"Check on the fucking baby!" I scream, and here comes my voice at last, bubbling out like lava, burning the hallway with all my bottled terror and pain and fully justified paranoia. "Check on the baby! Check on the fucking baby!" I cannot stop screaming it, over and over and over.

"Holy shit," Nathan says, even as Keene takes a step back from me. He rushes into Mom's room after Jenny, anything to make my screaming stop. Nathan takes me by the shoulders. My eyes feel too wide, like they might pop out with the pressure of my brain. My jaw hurts, my throat hurts. "Are you bit?"

I shake my head, can't stop shaking it.

Nathan pulls me close, pressed up against him, and whispers in my ear. "Shur, he's fine. He's fine. The thing is dead."

"Little's safe!" Jenny shouts, bursting into the hallway. She tugs me from Nathan, wraps her arms tight around me. "He's scared. He pissed himself. Jesus, I nearly pissed myself, but he's fine, Shur. Really. Not a mark anywhere on him. You got there in time." She pushes away, takes me by the cheeks, looks into my rolling eyes. I can't even focus on her. My teeth chatter. I'm freezing, as cold as if I'd barreled into a frozen lake in my bra and underwear.

"She's going into shock," Jenny says to Keene.

We lost track of Little again. How could we have lost him a second time? What is wrong with us? What is wrong with *me*?

"What do we do?" Keene asks. He's got Shawn in his arms. I smell piss. I don't know if it's Little or me.

"Get her downstairs, elevate her head and feet. Put them together, maybe on the couch, and we need blankets. Lots of blankets. And boil some water for hot chocolate. Sugar helps. Do you know how to light the gas burner? The long lighter is in the cabinet with the water glasses." Jenny is authoritative and both boys hop-to without further prompting.

We're guided past the basket. There is nothing to see but curtain and weights, but I still do not look because I will start screaming again. Down and down the stairs, slowly. My legs wobble and shake, not sure they want to work. Eventually we get to the couch. Little snuggles against me, stripped from the waist down, still slightly damp. He sobs, his whole body heaving. I cry too. They cover us with blankets, a whole pile.

"Maybe we should light a fire," Keene says.

Jenny shakes her head. "It'll be fine in a few minutes. Talk to them. Keep them alert."

I say, "My fault. Should have told someone to watch him. Should have told you where I was going." Little snuggles in closer, so close he's practically part of my skin, cool and damp, thumb corked in his mouth. Had I really believed I was the one to think for the group, to keep us safe? I'd no sooner thought it than I'd nearly gotten the baby eaten by a monster. What's wrong with me?

"No. We all lost track of him, Shur. Jesus, you can't be on top of everything all the time." He runs a hand through his black hair, which is getting a little greasy, I notice with strange clarity. I'm seeing things in pieces: hair, his eye, the mantel. Not the whole of anything. My eyes can't process it all right now; my brain is broken. He digs for my hand under the blankets. "He went looking for you, that's all. You thought we had him. That's on us, not you."

"I should have woken you guys up."

"No, you did the right thing. Everyone sort of shut down but you. We all need to be more alert."

Jenny returns with the bag I packed, already pulling out clean clothes. She drops it beside the couch and says, "Okay, big boy, time for underpants."

Keene says, "I'm already wearing underpants."

It doesn't get the laugh he hoped for, and Jenny ignores him. She coaxes Little's legs out from under the blanket. He grumbles and kicks, but Jenny's been helping get Little dressed his whole life, and she manages to get both feet into the right holes. A pair of sweatpants follows and, now that she has his attention, she says, "You want hot chocolate, kiddo?"

"Is the monster gone?" he whispers.

"Oh yeah. Keene hit it with a baseball bat and then Nathan stabbed it with a giant knife, and that thing is d-e-a-d dead!"

"Are you sure?"

"Yep. Keene, are we sure?"

"Deader than dead, buddy."

"He hit with a bat!" The giggles turn to howls of laughter, maybe a little more hysterical than I'd like, but he comes out from under the blanket. "He hit it like it was a baseball!" When the laughter starts to taper off, he leans forward and asks Jenny very seriously, "Can I have marshmallows in my hot chocolate?"

Little kids bounce back so fast. I wish I could feel his relief and optimism and love of marshmallows. All I feel is cold and stinging and terror. And anger at myself.

The giggles start again. He wriggles out from under the blanket and is off like a shot. Keene follows but returns with the first aid basket a few seconds later, handing it to Jenny. "You want help?"

"Is there any leftover hot water?"

"You want hot chocolate too?"

"No, dumb ass. To clean out her wounds?" Jenny says, rolling her eyes.

After Keene delivers a bowl of hot water, he leaves so I can strip off my shirt without traumatizing him with the sight of sister boobs. Jenny has to help—the drying blood is already bonding the cloth of the T-shirt to my skin in a sticky, crusty mess. As each puncture and cut is exposed to air, they sting and burn. Cool air hisses between my teeth, and Jenny mutters, "Just a few more. It's almost loose."

She dips a cloth into the water over and over, wiping away at the edges of the injuries before she goes back in with the antibacterial. The liquid, in a clear blue bottle, numbs as it cleans, the only way Little's scraped knees and elbows can be disinfected without waterworks and wailing. She slathers ointment into the worst of the cuts and punctures and covers a half dozen with Band-Aids of varying sizes. There are only two she seems really concerned about, matching, bloody shreds on either side of my neck where Charlie really dug in. These she bandages before declaring, "You are fit for service."

She hands me a clean T-shirt, which I pull over my head. "What a fucking day," I say.

"You're telling me. Is the sun even down?"

"No. It's like 3:00 p.m."

"I hate this dark. I hate everything about this situation." She reaches out her hand. "Hey. You did good, you know?"

"I almost got my brother killed."

"No, we all almost got your brother killed. In our defense, murderous mutant bird wasn't covered in the YMCA's babysitting course, right? So maybe cut yourself a little slack. He's alive because you're fast."

"Sure."

"Don't give me that tone," Jenny says, amused and exasperated. "I can see you prepping the self-flagellation, Shur. That's a dangerous road, and your mother would not approve."

"I guess." A thought occurs to me. "Did you see it? The butterfly in the box? I mean, did you *not* see it?"

"What do you mean?"

"In Mom's room. It's gone, like disintegrated. That's what I was looking at before the bird... Anyway, how could it have rotted so fast?"

She shakes her head. "I don't know. Bugs break down pretty fast in nature, although a lot of time that's scavengers picking away at the body. I saw a colony of ants dismember live crickets once. Nothing I ever need to see again." She shudders. "But I just don't know. It kind of explains how we've never found them before, though, not like in amber or whatever."

One more mystery to not solve, I guess. Maybe the turkey corpse upstairs will do us all a favor and disintegrate into nothingness so I don't have to worry about anything that might still be growing inside, trying to find a new host.

"Maybe…" I say, and I stop, swallowing hard.

"What?"

"Maybe it's time for us to get Bill. He said if we really needed him that we could put a candle out front and he'd come."

"Did he mean it?" She stops midgesture, hand still on the last bottle. "Like, could he get here?"

"He did last time. It's not like he just waltzed across the street. He took his truck."

"You think he'd come, though?"

I nod. "Yeah."

She considers for a minute, tapping her long fingers on the bottle's cap. She never paints her nails, but they're usually long and immaculately shaped. I see now that they're broken and jagged. Another sign of the times. She says, "We should talk about it with the boys."

"Between the thing upstairs and the people with the guns…"

"Not sure they're going to be an issue anymore," she says and gives my hand a quick squeeze.

25

Day drains from the house. On the second floor, it backs out through the sun-soaked towels and blankets over the windows. The first floor is a perpetual dusk of candles and flashlights. Beyond the boarded windows, the rustle of wings is a constant.

Charlie will not come upstairs, so I go to him, bowl of food in one hand, water in the other. I set the both down on one side of the tent's opening. He climbs gingerly out of the tent, where he's hidden himself away in one corner, and stares at me. Charlie is ready to bolt at the first sign of alien movement but, finding none, eventually comes out and eats. It's the good stuff, the wet with a little leftover chicken mixed in. A "congrats on surviving another encounter with monsters" dish. When he's had his fill, he disappears back into the tent with a tail flick and one final look over his shoulder at me, like, "I know what you did back there, so thanks."

The washing machine crapped out with the power, and a load

is rotting inside. I pull the stuff out. It stinks in that way only stagnant laundry does, so I throw it into an empty basket to hand wash later with Little's pants. The clothes in the dryer smell fine. I fold them mindlessly, something to do with my hands. Overhead, someone else is making dinner, taking a turn at being domestic. Helping. The thing in the hallway was a wake-up call. A wake-up call to a nightmare? Is that a thing? I don't know, but at least they're hustling around now, checking the windows, gathering up blankets, putting together a toolbox full of things that can be used as weapons in a pinch.

I say, "See you in a bit, Charlie," and head back up the stairs, carrying the clean laundry with me.

In the kitchen, Little is sitting in Jenny's lap, tears streaming down his face. "But I want to watch it!"

"But we can't, sweetie. There's no power."

"We can use the computer again!"

"The computer died," Jenny says, trying to be patient. "It uses power too. The battery is all out."

"But you can make it work!"

Jenny shakes her head, and he lets out a long, low, pained howl. It hurts in my soul to hear it. His comfort is gone, his retreat into the world of Elsa and Anna and goofy-ass Olaf. No Mulan. No Genie. No Moana and her brainless chicken. Just us and Charlie, the dark, and real terrors lurking everywhere.

"That candle stinks," I say, setting the laundry down. It's gingerbread, sticky sweet. In theory, it should be cheerful. Hopeful, like the holidays. In the enclosed space, it's more like drowning in sugar.

"Yeah, not one of her better ones," Keene says without looking up. He's got the emergency radio, a bright red plastic thing that takes batteries, but has a hand-crank too. We're not quite to hand-crank territory yet. He's fiddling with the dial.

"Anything?"

"The signal keeps coming in and out. I'll get it."

"Where's Nathan?"

"Checking the upstairs windows." Keene looks at Jenny. "You want me to take a turn?"

She shakes her head.

"I'm going to start cooking," I say.

"We have dinner going," he points out, waving in the general direction of the stove, where two pots and a pan are simmering away over flickering orange and blue flames. "I'm on it."

"Yeah, I mean everything else. The power isn't going to come back on soon."

"What about…" Jenny cocks her head backwards, awkwardly. Bill's house is, technically, behind her, but I get the gist.

"What about what?" Keene asks.

"We were talking about signaling Bill," I say.

He doesn't say anything but looks up at the ceiling, then to the side, then back at the radio. Classic Keene processing. Not a yes or a no, not an anything. He's thinking. "It'll be crowded over there."

"He's got guns and food."

"We've got food."

"So you don't think it's a good idea?"

"I didn't say that. What do you think, Jenny?"

Jenny sighs and smooths Little's hair. He continues to wail. "I think we're fine here unless people come. Or Not-people."

"Not-people," Keene repeats. He presses the off button on the radio, conserving the power.

"So, do you think we should signal him?" I ask.

"I think we shouldn't have used the spaghetti," he says and runs a hand through his hair. Still greasy. "Too late now." He rises and goes to the stove, stirs a pot, pokes sausages in the pan.

"Well, I think we should try to signal him at least," Jenny says. "Maybe he can bring us a gun, or we can give him the other walkie-talkie so if we really *do* end up needing help, we have a better way of communicating than jar candles."

After dinner, Little rubs his eyes and yawns, clearly exhausted. I say, "I can take a turn with him."

Keene says, "Nah, it's fine. Maybe we'll sleep in the basement tonight. In the tent. Charlie's already down there."

My brothers head downstairs but leave the door open. Keene has a book, something for school. He's still hopeful, then, that we'll be going back. Soon. This year. I'm not convinced his hope is anything more than denial. My homework is collecting dust at the bottom of my book bag.

I take stock of the fridge again. There's plenty I can cook on the stove. We can keep most of it in the fridge and freezer, start to deal with it tomorrow.

"You need to rest," Jenny says, then, "Close that door. The stuff will last longer. I'll help tomorrow."

"Me too," Nathan says.

"Sit," Jenny says to me. To Nathan she says, "Can you put the candle outside? Like we talked about?"

He salutes her smartly and takes a broom and a jar candle.

"What's the broom for?" I ask as he disappears toward the den.

"Light it inside, open the door a crack to push it out, use the broom to get it farther," she explains.

"That's clever," I say.

"His idea." She wiggles her eyebrows suggestively. "He's smart."

"Oh, quiet," I say.

"All set," Nathan says, coming back into the kitchen. "Rescue is on its way. In theory." He turns on the radio and messes with the antennae for a while, alternating between that and the dial. I cannot stand the stink of gingerbread any longer. I retrieve another from the box in the pantry. Clean Cotton, this one says, with a picture of linens flapping on a line under a butterfly-free blue sky. I set it down, light it, blow out the old one. Now there is a mixed stench of cotton and cookies, and I feel nauseous.

"—not coming," says a voice, staticky on the spectrum.

"Oh! I got one!" Nathan says, triumphant. He tweaks the knob back and forth. The static falls away, and the voice is crystal clear, or as clear as it can be on AM radio. AM always sounds like it's coming from across the world, even when it's from the college station across town.

"Hang in there," the second voice says. "I know, unpopular opinion, but hear me out. Take us, for example. We're only still on the air because we have redundant power sources, specifically for natural disasters. We never thought we'd have to use them. We've been holed up in the studio for, jeez, Stewart, how many days has it been?"

"Nine? Ten? Who knows?"

"It feels like three months. Three *years*. But we're doing as well as can be expected. We're following the guidelines. And I'll tell you something else. We're up pretty high, and the worst of the butterflies aren't up here. This morning, yesterday, it was like looking down at a velvet curtain. Nothing to see. City eaten by smog."

"Just gone," Stewart agrees.

"But today, it's only *almost* that bad. I know, that sounds like nothing."

"Nothing burger."

"Nothing sandwich. Right. But, and maybe it's my imagination, I think there are fewer of them. I think they're starting to die. You know that thing about big dogs versus small dogs?"

"What about?"

"That small dogs live a really long time. Twenty years, sometimes. But big dogs, take your Great Dane or Great Pyrenees, those live maybe ten years. Could be it's the same with these. Small butterflies, how long do they live?"

"I'd take a caller now to ask that, but clearly we cannot. So, I'll guess...a few months? A season? A year?"

"Depends on the species," Jenny mutters.

"Huh?" Nathan asks.

"Species specific," Jenny says, louder. "It's a huge range. Two weeks to a year, give or take."

"Why do you know everything?" Nathan asks.

"Highly speculative," Stewart says. "But, it might give us hope. Let's say they usually live a year. Are you saying these will live six months?"

"Oh, I fucking hope not," the other announcer says. "What I'm saying is that if what we saw isn't a fluke, or wishful thinking that their numbers have peaked, then we should know for sure tomorrow or the next day, then maybe their lifespan is a few days. A week."

"Suicidal mating," Jenny says. She's talking to herself.

"What?"

"Life span and suicidal mating," she says.

"What are you talking about?" Nathan says.

Jenny gives a deep sigh, the one she gives when she's the smartest person in a room (common) and no one else understands her (also common). She says, "The one upstairs died a few hours after it bit that bird."

"Right. Maybe it was injured."

"Or, maybe it did its job and died. There are a ton of species that die after having sex. Or giving birth. I did a whole report on that in Advanced Biology."

"These aren't mantis. Mantises?" Nathan says. "You get what I mean. They're big."

"Size is irrelevant. Take squid," Jenny says.

"Squid live forever. That's why they're giant."

"They don't, though. They die after sex. The males, I mean. If they all died after sex, there wouldn't be any more squid."

"Shut up!" Nathan says, but it's not a disrespectful shut up, more of a "this is news to me" proclamation.

"The females die after giving birth. They only live up to five years. So," Jenny says, "if this is like that, then these guys could be right about life span. If these things *don't* infect something, maybe they live awhile. If they do infect something, they die. Maybe that's their version of giving birth. Like...zombie wasps."

"Tell me that is not a real thing," I say.

"Oh, too late," Jenny says, her mouth twitching in an almost-smile. "They lay their eggs inside cockroaches and when the eggs hatch, they eat the cockroach."

"Eww! Why doesn't it just leave before that happens?"

"That's the zombie part," Jenny says. "The wasp stings it in the brain first, then lays its eggs in it. It sits there like a living buffet waiting to be consumed."

"I'm going to barf," Nathan announces.

"So, I'm thinking," Jenny continues, now on a roll, "that this thing bites its victim. Chews it up good, right? The eggs get laid from its mouth."

Nathan gags and covers his own mouth with a fist.

"Then when the whatever dies, the body decomposes and the eggs end up in the soil. But that's why they die—the adults I mean—they're done laying eggs."

"So they're all female?" I ask.

She shrugs. "That happens in nature."

"What does that mean for us?" I ask.

To this, Jenny shrugs. "I honestly don't know. If they're right, the monsters might be dying out on their own. That won't help us with the infected humans, though."

Full night, restless quiet. Keene sits at the kitchen table with Nathan, listening to the radio. The two guys, Stewart and his friend, have been replaced by a woman reading from an old newspaper in a halting, strained voice. She sounds constantly on the verge of tears, and I cannot stand to listen. I retreat to the den, where Jenny and I read by candlelight. We unearthed a fancy candelabra from the credenza in the dining room. It comes with long, white candles, a whole box of them. The setup feels Victorian, like I should be wearing a flowing nightdress and wandering about the house, candles raised, and haunted by ghosts.

"You're going to burn your retinas if you keep staring into the flames," Jenny says without looking up from her book. She has a stack of them beside her, liberated from Mom's bookshelf. She could have taken one at a time, but Jenny has set herself a challenge. I don't know what it is, exactly, because she didn't *say* she's challenging herself. I just know her. She's decided to read that whole pile, and the only real question is, does she have a deadline or is it about getting through them before this disaster ends? My own book is barely dented, some closed room murder at a high school. I might trade it for something more romantic, less death-y.

I open the book's cover to try again.

Thump.

"Did you hear that?" Jenny asks.

It came from the porch. Maybe Bill is here. But...does that make sense? At night, the butterflies seem to settle down, covering every surface as they rest, wings twitching. This is a less dangerous time, but even if Bill thought it was an emergency, he wouldn't have come without his truck, and we didn't hear an engine.

The noise, again. Unmistakably closer. *Thump. Thud.* Heavy treads on the porch. Moving side to side, window to window. Maybe trying to see in.

"I don't think that's Bill," Jenny whispers.

From the other room, Keene calls, "Is that you guys making that noise?"

Jenny rushes to the kitchen doorway, a finger pressed against her lips to silence him.

The next thump is from the window on the side of the house facing the driveway: the dining room. I follow the sound's progress as it moves to the next window. Then the next. It stops sometimes for several seconds. Once, I think I hear glass break.

Keene's face is white as cottage cheese under his lank hair, and he retreats to stand guard at the basement door, putting himself between Little and this new threat.

It reaches the back door. *Thump thump.* Knocks, as if politely asking to come in. Another tinkle. Broken glass. The wood shield holds. The storm door slams, and I jump, swallowing a metallic scream that tries to escape my throat. Jenny is clutching Nathan's sleeve so hard the fabric has bunched up tight against his arm, but he doesn't seem to notice.

It continues around the house. Finally, we hear it on the porch again, back where it started.

The front door doesn't have a knob. It's more of a lever-like thing, with a big, heavy deadbolt above it. It's metal. Solid.

Trembling, I press my eye up to the peephole.

It's dark. Not our usual suburbs dark, but deep-in-the-country dark, with only the stars and moon for light. That almost-full moon hangs high in the sky, throwing beams down through the dissipating clouds. Beyond the porch, mica chips in the pavement sparkle like diamonds. I curse that moon. Because I can see. I can see the monster at my door.

It bangs with both fists, face obscured by the motion. Sounds are shaken loose from its maw—guttural, raging. It backs up and looks at me. It can't know I'm here. It can't. But it's staring straight at me through the peephole, right into my eyes. It is worse than the turkey vulture, worse than Joe Arroz's arm chunk. The clothes are black, cargo pants, black jacket. No ski mask, that's long gone. And no hair. As it stares at me with those inset eyes, I wonder how much it can even see. Are they even eyes anymore? Will they fall into its skull? It leaps forward at the door with surprising speed, and I almost scream, but my confidence in the door's strength steels me. It hits the metal again and again, sending a fine, diamond spray of black blood or some other, more sinister, liquid arcing in the moonlight.

And then, with one final, furious glare over its shoulder, it retreats back down the steps. I follow its progress across the street to the ruined house with a pickup truck parked in the living room.

"The door will hold," I tell the others, but I'm looking at the candle Nathan put out. It's kicked over, smashed on the front path. Not just broken, but flattened, stomped.

The thing came because we showed it we were here with the candle.

26

A day and a night pass, and another day without more movement from across the street. Bill does not come. We do not dare put another candle out again so soon. Maybe these human monsters will die of their infections. Maybe the butterflies will go back to hibernating.

There is very little to do. I cook and cook and cook. Little colors and plays with Play-Doh. The basement has taken the place of the den, becoming a debris field of toys and games, Legos and picture books. We take turns with him. He naps too much.

The temperature drops in the house further, but it's still comfortable enough with sweatshirts. I have made enough bacon to feed us all for a week. I drop some in Charlie's dish, and it disappears. He comes out of the tent to shit and eat and stays hidden the rest of the time.

Jenny is on her fourth book. The pile is shrinking rapidly. Keene is teaching himself the next lesson in Algebra 2, doing homework that hasn't even been assigned yet. And Nathan paces. He checks the windows over and over, upstairs, downstairs. Upstairs again.

We are on edge, and there is nowhere to put that nervous, quaking energy.

On the radio, Stewart and his friend cover the same ground. Other channels come in distantly, but it's more of the same. Cities on fire, no easy way to get rid of the butterflies. The White House is giving daily briefings, but we hear it secondhand. Same with the CDC. Stay inside, quarantine if bitten.

"That doesn't mean help isn't coming," one announcer says. She sounds tired and sad. Her voice sags like speaking is too heavy a load. How long has she been on the air, trying to reassure people like us? "Widespread communication isn't possible. No one was prepared for a disaster like this, so sudden, right? So don't give up hope." She might be talking to herself.

Jenny sets her book down beside her on the couch and uncurls her legs. "I'm going to light a fire."

"Knock yourself out," Keene says. He's coaxed Little out of the basement and is trying to set up an elaborate Matchbox race track he found in Mom's closet. It was probably meant to be a Christmas present. The bright orange and yellow plastic strip stretches out across the carpet in a broad oval. So far he's had no luck with getting the pump that fires off the cars to work, and Little is losing interest.

I'm thinking about moving more cans to the basement and

cooking the things in the freezer that are mostly thawed. Another pound of bacon. A pack of Italian sausage. The camping cooler is filled with ice, and it'll keep stuff cold for ages, maybe even a whole week, as long as we don't open it too much. Once the ice melts…well, I don't want to worry about that too much right now.

"We could get a game going," Nathan says, brightening. "You guys have UNO or something?"

"That's a good idea!" Jenny says. "I'm so bored."

Keene waves at the cabinet beneath the TV. "You know where it is."

"Throw Throw Burrito!" Little exclaims. He claps and bounces. He really likes the throwing part.

"You pick a game," Jenny says to me and Nathan. "I'll get the fire going. Keene, stay there and continue to be grumpy."

"It's my thing," he mutters.

The fireplace has glass doors to keep the New England winter winds from blowing down the chimney. In a normal year, this wouldn't be a fireplace night: It would be a firepit night. We'd be around it in the backyard, Mom with a glass of wine in one hand, me and Keene staring at our phones in the dark because we never learned how to just sit and *be*. We're learning now. Mom would have the baby monitor with her, balanced on the arm of her blue Adirondack chair. If we make it out of this, I decide, I'll leave the phone inside when we're around the firepit. I wish I had done better.

There are a couple of logs by the fireplace year round, and at least one easy-light chemical log. Those burn for hours. For one fleeting moment I have a doubt: What if we're still here in winter? Will we need those logs? But three logs aren't going to be the difference between freezing and surviving. Let Jenny have her fun.

Jenny sits cross-legged in front of the fireplace. She opens the doors and plops the chemical log inside, wrapper and all.

"Don't forget to open the damper," Keene says without looking up from his failing project.

"I know how fireplaces work, dumb ass," she says.

"Of course you do. You could probably build one out of mud and rocks," Keene says.

"Actually," Jenny says, reaching in to jiggle the damper. Then she screams.

———

We hadn't heard it in the chimney, of course. It wasn't like a squirrel, or a bird or bat, thrashing around, making noise. The chimney's liner is stainless steel. It wouldn't have been able to get purchase to climb out, didn't have enough room to flap. It must have fallen in, dropped like a stone, sat on the damper waiting to die or for food to come along. And then Jenny did.

She's still screaming when she pulls her arm out of the fireplace. The butterfly is attached to her forearm, a monstrous thing a solid foot across. It flexes its wings, ecstatic. Chewing. Digging in deeper.

"Get it off!"

Keene is up and moving toward her, putting himself between Jenny and Little. Nathan takes Little in his arms, even as he asks, "What's wrong?" He's craning his neck toward the fireplace, toward the screams. They disappear into the kitchen.

"Don't rip it off!" I shout. "It'll take the flesh with it. We need to pry it loose."

"Please!" The pain in Jenny's voice is syrup-thick. "Please!"

"Lie down," I tell her. "On your belly and put your arm out as far away from you as you can, okay?" If it does let go, it might go straight for her neck or her face. Her soft belly.

Whimpering, Jenny goes to her knees, then lowers to the ground with my help, her arm and the butterfly held out. It doesn't seem to notice or care that she's moved.

"What are you going to do?" Keene asks, running a hand through his hair.

"Find something sharp. Bill's knife. Fast!"

He doesn't question. He's gone and back in a moment.

Jenny's hyperventilating, gray with shock. Her body is on the carpet, her arm on the brick hearth. Blood drips steadily from below the wings, *drop drop drop*. When her arm moves, it smears.

"Cut off its head," I say.

"What?"

"I'll hold her arm down, and you, like, grab it by the head and cut it off. Then we'll pry it loose."

"Holy fuck," Keene says.

"Hurry!" Jenny screams. "Please, Keene, do something! It's *eating me*!"

Whey-faced, Keene drops to one knee. His hand hesitates over the thing's head, where oversized antennae wave, probing and testing for threats.

"The mouth is underneath," I say. "It can't bite you." Beneath my hand, Jenny's arm is warm and wet. A black crab legs brushes my skin. I flinch but hold on.

"Right." He grabs both antennae in his fist. At first I think they might pull right off, but the thing is sturdy, built for combat. When Keene tugs up, Jenny moans. Then *whish* and the head comes away in Keene's hand, dangling. The body writhes and convulses, and Jenny lets out the most awful gagging and grunting. They both lie still.

"Is she dead?" Keene asks.

I let go of her arm and reach instead for her neck. There's a pulse, steady, not very strong. "Alive. Throw that head in the fireplace, we need to get the rest off of her and clean the wound."

"How?" Keene asks, motioning at the butterfly's morbidly still-clamped-on corpse. "Try the legs first?"

"Yeah." I reach under the wings and find the legs. On the other side, Keene mimics the motion. I gather them up in both hands. They are thick and spiny and feel unpleasant against my skin. "On three?"

We count together, then tug in opposite directions.

"Shit," Keene says as a leg tears off in his hand. The butterfly is no closer to coming off. Blood pools beneath Jenny's arm, smearing brown on the brick. "Now what?"

"We pull the jaws open?" I say.

"Not with your bare hands, not with those teeth," Keene says. He pushes upright, very pale. "I'll get gloves."

I stroke Jenny's blond hair and try not to throw up. We were going to play card games.

Nathan comes back in Keene's place. He has a pair of leather work gloves and a bunch of dish towels. "Keene told me what you want to do. I'll do it."

"Maybe I should. She's my best friend."

"I'm stronger," he says. "Let's do this. Hold her arm down. And still. I'm going to...figure out where to put my hands."

I pin her wrist on one side and clamp my other hand around her triceps. "We should really have Keene, in case she wakes up. She might thrash."

"He can't."

"He can. She needs him more than Shawn does right now." I call Keene's name. Then again. Finally, he appears in the doorway. "Come here," I say.

"But the baby?"

"Where is he?"

"In the basement with the cat."

"He'll be fine for a few minutes. Sit on her. On her back. I'm going to hold her arm down, you're going to hold the rest of her."

His expression is dubious, but he straddles Jenny's prone figure and presses both hands against her shoulders.

Nathan gives us both a nod. I'll bet he wants to do his face-slap thing for luck or whatever, but he reaches under the butterfly instead. His eyes are pointed up at the ceiling as he feels his way along. "I have the edge of the mouth on this side...wow. This thing is really dug in. Let me just..." He repeats his search on the other side, then looks up. "Ready."

He pulls in both directions, straining. We're close together. I can smell her blood and his sweat as he works the jaw. The muscles in his neck stand out, his face darkens with the rush of blood.

Jenny's head, by my knee, moves. She comes to, finds herself immobilized. Maybe she's remembering what happened, because she starts to freak, tries to roll, tries to move her arm.

"Jenny, no!" I cry out. "Nathan's getting it off. Hold still!"

She settles, but begins to sob, her forehead pressed into the carpet, gulping in air.

"Almost," says Nathan. Then, with a grunt, he bumps backwards into the fireplace, taking the thing with him. It cracks. We all hear it as it comes off, the jaw snapping at the hinge. He throws it into the fireplace alongside its disembodied head, on top of the chemical log. He fumbles for the matches on the hearth. It takes a few tries before he manages to light one. Nathan lights the entire pack and throws it in. The beast begins to roast in the dancing green and orange flames.

"Close the doors," I say. "Just in case there's something airborne."

He shivers and pushes them shut.

Jenny moans again, and I realize we still have her pinned to the floor. I snatch one of the dish towels and wrap the wound as Keene clambers off. She lets out a squeal. Her eyes roll back in her head and she's out again.

Keene is gone like a shot. Maybe it's because he wants to check on Little in the basement, or maybe he wants to be as far away from the burning monster as he can. Or maybe he wants to escape the fact that Jenny is now almost certainly infected.

27

leave Jenny with Nathan in the den and go to the kitchen to start boiling water. With the pot on the stove, I shout down to Keene. He comes back on the stairs, pale-faced.

"Keene, I need you. You can't hide," I say, my voice breaking.

"I know," he says.

"Seriously. Are you with me?"

"Yeah. It's just…it's a lot." Before I can point out that it's a lot for all of us (especially Jenny), he adds, "I'm with you. I promise."

He follows me into the den. Jenny is still unconscious, her face pressed against the floor. The dish towel on her arm is dark with blood.

"You guys bring her in into the kitchen. Just give me a minute to clean off the table," I say. Nathan nods grimly.

Back in the kitchen, I wipe down the table as if prepping for surgery (which I suppose I am). I gather as many dish and paper towels as I can find, preparing for oceans of blood. By the time the boys return with Jenny's limp body, dripping blood from the oversaturated towel, I am as close to ready as I can be.

I am not ready.

Nathan and Keene gently lay Jenny flat on the table. Her arm is a useless, dead fish by her side. The dish towel bandage is bordered with tiny dancing cats. Red creeps toward them through the white fabric. It'll have to be burned, I realize.

The dish towel and the arm.

"What do we do?" Nathan asks. He's back to tapping his hands on everything: jeans, shirt, shoulder, pockets. Always in motion.

"Is the water boiling?" I ask.

Keene glances at the pot. "Almost."

"We should...grab the medical supplies and see if there's rubbing alcohol or peroxide. Anti-bacterial ointment." I do not mention that I am thinking about cleansing the wound with fire. Are third-degree burns better or worse than parasitic infections and necrotized flesh? Better, I suppose.

Keene takes this as an order and disappears, leaving me and Nathan standing over Jenny. I take the meat scissors from the knife block.

"What are you doing?" Nathan asks, horrified.

I look at the scissors and realize he thinks I'm about to cut her. "Her shirt," I say.

"Oh." His relief is obvious. "What should I do?"

"Turn off the burner. We're going to flush out her wounds with the water."

I pick up Jenny's arm. It feels hot to the touch already, but that could be my imagination. I hope it is. The sharp scissors make quick work of the sweatshirt fabric. *It reminds me of you*, she says when she borrows it from me, always that same one, her favorite. I'll owe her a new one, I guess.

Sleeve, dish towel, and scissors all go into the stainless steel sink where the parasites can die a cold, metallic death with no host. I put a fresh towel under her arm.

Keene returns with the basket. "I found a box of latex gloves." He hands a pair to me. "Where do we start?"

"Scrub up. Flush the wound with the water, then the alcohol, then…"

"Then the ointment?"

"I…um," I start, then chicken out. Who do I think I am, a doctor? No. Can't think like that, must be brave. I shove myself forward. This is Jenny that needs saving. "We should cauterize the bites." There's silence and silence. No one says anything. "It's dumb, I'm sorry," I say in a rush. "I saw it in a movie."

"It's a good idea," Keene says.

"Seriously?" Nathan asks.

Keene shrugs and picks up a flat box with a cat on the front. "I was going to suggest we give her this."

"Charlie's heartworm meds?" I say.

"Look, if she's going to die if we don't do anything, we should at least try everything we can think of," Keene says. "I read the box. I don't think it's poison for humans, and we know it kills parasites. It's all we've got."

We're staring at each other, round robin, each looking to someone else for an answer about the right thing to do, but none of us knows.

Then Nathan says, "What if it doesn't work? What if she turns?"

"She's not a freaking vampire," I snap.

"I'm sorry, I'm sorry," he says in a rush. "I'm not saying...I mean, what if, though? If she's infected and gets like the bird."

Like his mom. Like the thing at the front door.

"I thought we'd starve," I say. "I made so much bacon."

Keene drops a hand on my shoulder. "Yeah, it's hard to predict how the apocalypse will play out."

"What happens if she's infected? What are we supposed to do? It's Jenny!" My voice sounds desperate even to me. Broken.

"It's okay, Shur. We can do this," Keene says. He straightens up, squares his shoulders, like he's playing the part of the strong older brother. "We'll talk about what happens later...later. For now, you guys wash out the wounds. I'm going to heat up a knife or a spoon or something."

"A knife?" Nathan asks, eyes widening.

"It's not 1643, I don't exactly have a hot iron available," Keene says. He makes himself busy with examining utensils for a surgical candidate.

The wounds are hideous, but almost symmetrical, one set on either side spanning her entire forearm, a series of deep, ugly gashes in a jagged pattern. Dozens of them. Each one oozes blood. The flow is not fast, she won't bleed to death, but it's bad. I wash the worst of the blood away, and the holes immediately fill again.

We put a deep pan, the one my mother roasts the turkey in at Thanksgiving, on the floor beside the table. I hold Jenny's arm out over it as Nathan carefully washes first one side and then the other. Pink water streams down and disappears into the pan's black bottom. One more piece of cookware never to be used again. We repeat the exercise with peroxide. It fizzes and bubbles in the wounds, like a witch's brew in a cauldron. In her unconscious state, Jenny's face twitches in pain. As we are finishing, wiping the arm clean and lying it beside her on the table on a clean towel, she wakes.

Jenny blinks several times, then she realizes where she is and what happened. She lurches, struggling to a sitting position, and already screaming in panic. "I have to go! I'll turn into the thing upstairs! Not safe!" She's pushing at Nathan and clocks me one in the jaw by accident. I see dots in my vision and know I'll have trouble chewing my next meal. But I don't care. I don't care because the only thing that matters now is keeping her inside, safe. Giving her a chance.

Keene says, "Dude, stop. We'll put you outside in a minute."

"What?" I scream.

He raises an eyebrow. "What did you think would happen? We'd keep her in the den and wait for her to eat Little? Jesus, Shur." He's smug. I hate him, he's my brother but I swear to God, I hate him. "Besides, I have a plan worked out."

"No! No, no, no!" Now Nathan has to hold me back instead of Jenny, who has calmed considerably.

Jenny reaches out and puts her good hand on my arm. "Stop," she says. "Listen to him."

I don't want to listen to him. I feel betrayed. Stabbed. Murdered. Keene says, "We're going to cauterize your wounds first. You need a fighting chance. Then, you can go to the barn. The same way you guys got to the car. It'll take a long time to walk there, but you can do it. I'll fill a backpack for you. Water, food, all the stuff. We have antibiotics for after, because your burns will probably get infected."

She nods. Her eyes are fever-bright, traumatized. She won't make it to the barn. We know it. She knows it.

"I'll drive her," I say.

"No," Jenny and Keene say together.

"No. I'll go alone. And you might need the car later," Jenny says, so quiet I can barely hear her.

I open my mouth again, but Keene holds up a hand. Dismissive. "Ever burn yourself ironing clothes?" he asks Jenny.

"Once."

"Then you know how it hurts." He opens his palm. Two pills lay on it, flat, alongside a longer, pinkish-brown rectangle. He says, "Mom's painkillers from her surgery. Take them now."

"Won't they make me drowsy?"

He shakes his head. "Prescription ibuprofen, nothing fancy."

"And this?"

"Heartworm meds."

She stares down at it and then says, "Smart, Keene."

"He's literally going to be the death of you, and you're praising him?" My voice is high pitched, almost as angry as Jenny's when she shouted at Nathan. Almost. Some part of me, some tiny, tiny, hated part, wonders if he's right.

"Bottoms up," Keene says, handing her a glass of water.

She throws the pills back, then chews the heartworm treat, flinching. "Jesus, that's bad," she says.

"I have to pack the bag," he says. "If you want to say your goodbyes, this is the time. And maybe lie down and rest a few more minutes. You've got a long trip ahead of you. And, to be honest, I think the cauterization is going to hurt worse than the bite."

"I hate you," I tell Keene, and I mean it. My heart stings with venom.

"I'm doing what needs doing," he says. Nathan looks between us, not sure what to do, and Jenny pushes him aside.

She grabs my hand, pulls me closer. "Talk to me," she says. "Please. I need you right now. Please, Shur."

It takes everything I have not to go after Keene, to punch him, scream, throw him down a flight of stairs. Everything. But Jenny's eyes are haunted and scared. In the end, I shove aside my rage and throw my arms around her. There will be a time for reckoning later.

———

Nathan fetches a pillow from the couch and puts it under Jenny's head. She lies down as Keene suggested, conserving strength for her cauterization and death march. I am crying already; I cannot stop. Tears leak from my eyes in a continuous flow as she blinks up at the dark ceiling.

"Make sure Keene packs her books," I tell Nathan, then regret it at once. Will they be too heavy? Does it even matter?

Nathan squeezes my shoulder from behind and disappears to gather the books, to pass them on to Keene.

"Shur," Jenny says.

"I never want to see the den again," I say. "Or my room. Or anything in this house. It's all ruined."

"It's not, though," she says. "You still have Little. You have Keene and Nathan. And Terrible Charlie."

"I want you. I want my mother and my father. I want my old house and my old life."

Jenny smiles. She says, "You want to hear something awful? Like really? Sometimes when I sleep over here, I hope I die in my sleep."

I suck in breath, completely involuntary. "What?"

"My life sucks. I mean, parts of it are great. You. School is good. But home. Fucking home. You know how it is. How bad. This is my safe space. Here, with you guys. Your mom is amazing. You, of course. Even the cat. When your mom bought me that trundle for Christmas, I thought I'd explode. It wasn't my own room, right? Just a bed? But still."

"Well, you're here a lot."

"My mom got me that sweater the same year, you remember? The red one with the panda on it?"

I want to laugh, can't quite get there. It was horrible, that sweater. Very not-Jenny. Her mom barely knows her.

"That bed said something. Welcomed me. If I'm going to die, this is where I want to do it, Shur. This is my home."

That does nothing to slow the tears, and I swipe them away.

"I'm dizzy," Jenny says. "Wouldn't it be funny if an allergic reaction took me out?"

"Oh my God," I say. "Are you reacting to the heartworm thing?"

She shakes her head. "I don't think so. I'm not feeling sick. Just...thick. Anyway. Don't be hard on him. Keene. He's thinking straight. You aren't."

"Shut up."

"Seriously, Shur. You know Keene. He wouldn't do something like this for no reason. That thing at the front door..."

"That thing at the front door isn't you. We could lock you up somewhere. A bathroom!" This feels inspired, brilliant. "We can, like, shut you in."

"What if I get out? What if I do something I can't take back?"

"You wouldn't."

"You don't know that." She puts a hand to her head. "What is this shit?"

"The ibuprofen? It's from Mom's knee surgery."

"How bad was it?"

"You remember the brace."

"I didn't know it was this bad. Seriously, Shur, I feel dizzy..." Jenny smacks a hand to her forehead. "That asshole."

"What?"

"Your brother drugged me!" She tries to get upright, grabbing onto the front of my shirt, pulling. She doesn't have a lot of strength and her dead arm is useless. "Keene!" Jenny screams. "You asshole, get in here!"

Nathan is there again, materialized from the shadows. "Hey," he tells Jenny. "Hey. Calm down. Lay back. Relax. You're having a bad reaction. It happens, right? It'll pass."

"I hate him," she grumbles, but Jenny lies back onto the pillow. She balls her good hand into a fist. Scowls. Her eyes slip closed, then open, then closed. It goes like that on and off, until finally they close and stay closed.

Nathan calls, "She's out."

Keene comes in from the other room. No backpack. Nothing. I say, "What the hell?"

He says, "That wasn't Advil. I gave her Mom's sleeping pills."

"How did you know to drug her?"

Keene shrugs. "I didn't. I brought down all the pills. When

she started in, I thought we might have a fight on our hands, so I drugged her. Still hate me?"

Hate him? A hot flare of shame shoots from my gut to my face. "No."

"Good," Keene says. "Let's burn the ever-living crap out of that wound and decide what's next."

28

Cauterization: The stink is the worst part. Jenny is out cold thanks to Keene's quick thinking, but I cannot bring myself to help, no matter how much I want to. It smells like roasting pork, or the bacon I've been cooking. Nathan and Keene do it, and I cannot even watch. I sit on the first step of the basement stairs and face away. They flush the burns with water and pack them with slushy ice from the freezer. Jenny lets out a high whistling noise in her sleep but stays unconscious.

They are thorough, and I am unreasonably hopeful.

"Done," Keene pronounces and strips off his gloves. The contents of Mom's first aid basket are strewn everywhere, across the counter, the table, the floor. Keene tosses the gloves in the garbage and starts to collect everything, rearranging them in a haphazard pile.

I have an idea. "We can close her in Mom's bathroom," I say. "Nail the door shut."

Keene nods slowly. "That's good. There's a toilet. Light from the skylight."

"What if she...you know," Nathan says.

I don't have words, but Keene says, "Then she'll be locked in. Where is she going to go? Out the window? We can nail that shut too."

"No escape," Nathan says softly.

"It's not forever," Keene says.

"Unless it is," I say. We avoid each other's eyes. I add, "I'll start getting stuff." I don't wait for anyone else to offer to help.

I try to reframe the prep in my own head. It's a camp out. It's a small studio apartment where she's living on her own for the first time. A fun adventure. Anything but what it really is: a quarantine for a body under siege in a house under siege.

Nathan wants to help, but I shoo him away. He and Keene both look withered and diminished. I rescue the stinky ginger-bread candle from where I banished it to the bathroom. Maybe it's strong enough to drown out the smell of cooked Jenny.

I have a list. Of course I have a list. I collect things into Jenny's school backpack and an oversized reusable shopping bag. Her laptop is dead, so no need for that. The remaining pile of books. So optimistic. Her journal and a pencil. A spare pencil too, in case the first one runs out of lead. Granola bars. A huge bag of flavored popcorn, soup cans with pop-tabs. A jar of peanut butter, a box of cereal. Pears, apples, shriveling grapes in a plastic sandwich baggie. Packets of Goldfish crackers and fruit gummies. Enough food for a good, long time. No bacon.

In the basement, I'm foraging in the spare blanket bins when a small voice asks, "Did the monster get Jenny?"

Little sits at the opening of the tent, safely on his side of the barrier between his fortress and the rest of the world.

"One bit her," I say.

"Is she dead?"

"No, honey, but she could get sick. She's going to camp out in Mommy's bathroom for a while until she's better."

"Is the monster dead?"

"Keene killed it," I assure him. "Cut its head right off and threw it in the fire."

"Good," Little says. "Shur, are more going to get in?"

"I hope not." I don't want to lie, but I also don't want to scare him more than I need to. "You're safe down here."

"Can I stay down here and play Legos with Charlie? I don't want to see the monster."

"Sure," I say, ruffling his hair. He's taking it a lot better than I am. For now.

In the kitchen, Keene hands me a small, rectangular box and a pill bottle. "This is what I could find. The rest of Charlie's heart-worm meds and the antibiotics from my ear infection. I thought there might be more in Mom's medicine cabinet, but there's not." He pauses. "I emptied the bathroom of anything sharp. And I filled the tub with water. In case something happens to the supply."

"Thanks," I say. I squeeze his arm. "Sorry I thought the worst."

"I wanted you to think the worst. She had to believe it." He kisses my cheek. "But, thanks. I don't like my little sister thinking I'm a monster."

"Twelve minutes younger," I remind him.

"And a foot shorter. You're an Oompa-Loompa."

<hr />

The hamper remains over the reeking bird corpse, the sheet over the hamper, everything pinned by weights. I skirt around it, listening for movement that does not come, and then go to my mother's abandoned bedroom.

Keene has lit candles, one on the dresser, another on the nightstand. I bristle. I will never get used to the idea of unattended candles and the potential for burning down the house. The room flickers with uneven, restless light. I take the pillows from the bed, even the decorative ones, and carry them into my mother's bathroom, her private oasis. The left wall is dominated by a jacuzzi tub, and the tub is partially filled with water. A long window normally overlooks the carport and, beyond it, the barn. Right now it overlooks nothing because Keene has covered it with the blanket from his own bed, nailing it in place. If something comes crashing into the window, maybe the blanket will stop it. Maybe not.

I unload all the stuff from the bag and backpack into the vanity and set about making a bed in front of the jacuzzi. In Mom's closet, I find a bunch of yoga mats and colorful blanket-like wraps, the ones she wears around the firepit. Along with the basement blankets and pillows, I set up the most comfortable nest I can, under the circumstances. It seems inadequate.

Overhead is the ominous black night. Rain patters on the skylight. The glass is double thick, insulated. Jenny will have some sunlight, at least. More than we have downstairs. I put a half dozen spare candles under the sink, a flashlight, batteries.

Finally, the walkie-talkie. In case she needs us or in case we get even more separated. I try not to think about that, about if something gets in the house and we have to flee to the basement or, worse, leave. Our world is shrinking and receding and becoming smaller and smaller with each hour. With each new intruder.

29

I guess it's time," I say.

Jenny is still out on the kitchen table, drooling in her uncon-
sciousness. Keene prods her in the ribs a few times with his index
finger to no response. He sighs deeply, the sound of a very put-out
man doing a job he does not want. "Get her feet," he says to Nathan.

Together, they maneuver Jenny out of the kitchen and
through the den, pausing at the base of the stairs. They prop her
against the front door, legs splayed out like a little kid fallen asleep
playing. Her head lolls forward, chin not quite touching her chest.

"She doesn't look this heavy," Keene complains.

"Dead weight," says Nathan.

"Can we not use that word?" I snap.

"Fine. Unconscious weight."

They pick her up again. I take the stairs by twos and wait at
the top, chewing my nails as they start the long trek. Jenny's arms
flop to the sides, bouncing.

The mess under the hamper is starting to ooze a strange, rotten-meat smell into the narrow confines of the hallway. I pluck the weights off and set them aside before the boys make it to the top. It has to be moved; there isn't enough room for them to get by.

I lean hard against the plastic, pressing down, and slide it toward the wall. A strange noise erupts from inside and I squeal, leaping backwards, nearly tipping the basket. The smell is worse. *Gas.* I realize. I shove the basket against the wall and drop the weights back on top. *It's only gas. Decomposition.*

A depressed carpet line marks where the basket was, and the center is stained black. The stink rising from this spot is gag-inducing. It's slick, evil.

"Hold your breath when you get to the top," I call down to the boys, and gag again.

They maneuver into the hallway, and Keene says, "Holy shit, what *is* that?"

"Rotting corpse," says Nathan. "Move faster."

I guide them around the stain. The last thing we need is for one of them to slip, dropping Jenny right into that mess. They follow my flashlight beam down the hall, through Mom's room, and into the bathroom. Overhead, the skylight is a dark, watchful eye.

When Jenny's settled in the mass of blankets and pillows, we watch her for several minutes.

"Do you think she'll be all right?" Nathan asks.

Neither Keene nor I answer.

I leave Elmo turned off for now, to not waste batteries. She'll wake up and turn it on. Or she won't. But I don't want to think about that.

"We should go," Keene says, taking my hand in his.

They nail the door shut from outside. It's loud enough to wake anyone not dosed out on sleeping pills, but no answering noise, no pleas or objections, come from the bathroom. When they're done, we stand in front of the dark doorway like we're waiting for something. Permission to leave, maybe. But nothing comes.

———

Our flashlight beams play over the hallway floor and walls, settling in a trifecta on the sinister, stinky stain where the vulture had been before our passage. Silence from the basket.

"We should get rid of it," I say.

"We could leave it," Nathan says.

"No, she's right," Keene says. "It could still be dangerous even dead. There could be a million larvae in it. It could be sending spores out into the air."

"How are we going to move it?" Nathan asks. "I don't want to touch it."

"No one should," Keene agrees.

"How about if we slide it onto a blanket or a sheet, then bundle that up like a sack, then we throw the whole thing in the fireplace?" I suggest.

Nathan shrugs. "I think that'll work."

"Worth a shot," Keene says.

We're running seriously low on blankets, but I manage to scrounge a sheet from the abandoned load in the basement. It stinks of mold and is stiff to the touch. New sheets: add that to the list of stuff we'll need to replace for Mom. Keene and I shake it out, placing it over the stain, careful to avoid contact with that black spot. I'm already thinking of pouring bleach or emptying an entire can of Lysol onto it when we're done. It looks vile, malignant. Cancer of the carpet.

Nathan nominates himself to do the actual moving of the basket. He sets the weights aside, presses down like I did before, but this time in reverse, tugging the bird along.

"It weighs more than I thought," he comments.

"It's probably bloated with gas," I say, but maybe it's also loaded up with parasites. I gag.

"Guys, step on the sheet so it doesn't roll," Nathan says. Sweat drops down from his temple to his cheek. He's moving slowly, carefully.

We both help, stepping on either side of the sheet's edge to pin it in place. Nathan lifts the edge of the basket enough to get it over, then nudges it. There's tugging on the sheet as the vulture fetches up. I imagine one of those clawed black arms hanging on for dear life, trying not to be caught. It only lasts a second, and then he has the entire basket on the sheet. He stands, breathing hard, more from fear and holding his breath against the stench than from exertion.

"Who's going to carry it?" Keene asks.

"I'll do it," I volunteer, not really wanting to, but not wanting anyone else to have to either. "If one of you guys can open the fireplace and light the fire?"

Keene nods. "I'll light it."

"Do we have lighter fluid or barbecue stuff?"

"Vegetable oil," he says. "It'll burn."

"Good," I say. "Help me get the corners. Nathan, get ready to lift up the basket on three. Keene, we'll come together fast, give me your corners, and we'll spin it shut."

They both nod.

We count to three. It feels like everything is an exercise in prepping for the worst lately: cutting off heads, pushing candles to the porch, cauterizing wounds, now bagging corpses.

"I hate this," I say as Nathan lifts the basket. As he does, Keene and I rush at each other, each holding two corners of the sheet. We come together. Keene hands me his corners and I pull the cloth tight in my fist so the sheet becomes an impromptu bag with the turkey vulture inside. Before I close the bag's mouth, I catch a glimpse of the disaster in the bottom.

It's a half-second glance, the kind that burns into your brain as a photographic plate, unshakeable, seared in forever.

No one else sees. "We need to hurry." My voice betrays my horror, as much I try to stay calm

"What?" Keene asks. "What was it?"

"Go," I say. "Get the doors. Get the oil."

The makeshift bag is heavy, heavier than I thought, like Nathan said. The corpse can't weigh more than a few pounds, even bloated, rotting.

Infested.

That's what I saw. Writhing, wriggling. White. Brown skin bursting open like a dropped melon. I want to vomit, but I force myself to keep it together. I haul the bundle down the stairs, held out in front of me, not wanting it to so much as brush the front of my sweatpants. Nathan opens the glass fireplace doors fast, and I shove the mess inside on top of the ashy remains of Jenny's attacker. There's not much left besides some shards of its exoskeleton and a strange smell, like roasted fish.

Keene is there with the oil. He shakes it in, saturating the sheet so the brown bulk of the thing is visible against the fabric. He steps back and digs a book of matches out of his pocket. "Bombs away," he says and lights a match, tosses it in. The flames roar upwards more violently than they did with the chemical log. Nathan slams the doors shut. Instantly, the room is filled with the stench of rot and flesh and cooking things.

"I might be a vegetarian when this ends," Nathan says and rushes from the room. I think he's going to puke.

Keene and I stand there watching the vulture burn. The fire pops, the sheet blackens. "What did you see?" he asks.

"I don't know. It was just a moment, but it looked like maggots."

He says almost brightly, "Maybe that's all it was."

"Maybe."

Keene folds me into a hug. "Those things aren't inside Jenny."

"We don't know that."

"But we don't know that they are. We did everything we could. Cleaned her up, gave her pills, cauterized the wound. She's safe in that room, can't hurt us, can't hurt herself."

My eyes are leaking. I can't tell if I'm crying or if they're watering from the stench. I don't want to talk about Jenny right now or think about whether those things were maggots or parasites or the squirming children of the killer butterfly. I need to get bleach from the basement. I won't feel right until I've disinfected the hell out of that carpet.

"Give me your clothes," I say. "I think we'd better all change."

It feels wrong to sleep in the tent, but I don't want to be upstairs near the fireplace. The corpse and it passengers have been reduced to dust. Nothing moves in that gray pile of ash, and we closed the damper after a few hours to ensure no more visitors come in that way.

There is no sound from the walkie-talkie. It's maybe 10:30 p.m., but it feels middle-of-the-night late. Charlie and Little sleep squashed together. As I climbed into the tent, Charlie hissed at me, maybe scolding me for being upstairs for too long, but now he's snuggled close to his boy.

I want to cry, can feel the heat creeping up my throat toward my cheeks, tugging down at the corners of my mouth, but I fight. I don't want Little to wake up and see me like that. And if I start now, I'm not sure I'll be able to stop.

I want my mother.

We agreed to keep a jar candle burning in case one of us wakes up in the night and needs the toilet, and for Little, who might panic in the dark. It casts a weak glow. Keene lies on Little's other side, arms behind his head, staring up at the tent's orange ceiling. Beyond the opening, Nathan is in the same position, contemplating the rafters.

"I keep waiting for things to get better," Keene says quietly. "It hardly seems real. It has to end sometime."

"I know."

"But it's not getting better. It's getting worse. I thought we were safe inside, I really did. When Jenny and Nathan went to the barn, I thought we were all being melodramatic. Even after what we saw happened to that bakery lady. I'm a fucking moron."

"No," I say. "An optimist maybe, but not a moron."

"You and Jenny were the smart ones. Cover the windows. Do the research, make the food. What was I doing?"

"Taking care of Little."

"Yeah." He spits it, angry. "Treating it all like a damn babysitting job until Mom comes home to take care of everything."

"Keene, we're kind of learning this as we go."

"We're all Little has," he says.

"That doesn't make us adults," I say. "Besides, who's prepared for shit like this?"

"Bill," he says and manages a sharp laugh. "Seriously, Shur. What if we killed Jenny?"

"You said it yourself. We did what we could. Everything we could. Mom couldn't have done anything different."

He's silent for so long, I think maybe we're done talking for the night, but finally he asks, "Why are you like this?"

I bristle. "A hot mess?" I don't want to be in the judgment zone now, not here, not with Jenny upstairs maybe dead and two corpses turning to ash in the fireplace.

Keene says, "Well, you are, but you're not too. I mean, how are you just going and going and going?"

"I've had breakdowns, same as everyone."

"Not the same," he says.

"Yeah," Nathan says from out of the dark. "Not like the rest of us. You're handling it like you were made for it."

I want to laugh and cry and scream. Instead, I say, "All this time since Dad died, I've been waiting to lose someone else. And now it's real. I don't want to lose you guys. That's all. I'm trying so hard not to lose anyone else." The tears do come then. They flood my cheeks, and I can't stop the pulling of my trembling chin, tugging the corners of my mouth down and down. In the dark, I see my father's face and my mother's eyes and Jenny's grin. I am losing and losing and losing.

Keene pushes himself upright and reaches over the sleeping baby and now-watchful cat, who is unhappy to be disturbed. He leaps out from between us and saunters out of the tent. A moment later, he thuds onto Nathan's bed.

"Hey," Keene says. "I didn't mean to make you cry."

"*You* didn't make me cry. It's everything. I'm being as strong as I can, Keene, but what if it isn't enough?"

He doesn't have an answer but holds my hand in his. I want him to tell me I don't have to be the strong one, but Keene doesn't say that either. It would be nice for someone, anyone, to tell me we're in this together, that they're going to do what they can to protect me, but all that comes through the dark basement is Charlie's purring. No reassurances.

30

I f I expected sobbing or hysteria from the other side of the nailed-shut bathroom door, I'd have been disappointed. No wailing. Maybe that's the sound of Jenny's pencil scratching away in her journal, or maybe my memory is quietly supplying that detail. Jenny, normal and whole, doing normal and whole things on the other side. Anyway, above that sound, real or imagined, comes a different kind of scratching. Spiny crab feet on every surface. Scraping. Digging.

We've reached another noon. Jenny is alive and awake but will not talk to me in more than grunts and the occasional two or three words.

We check on her in turns, me and Keene and Nathan, knocking and asking if she's okay, trying to make conversation. Sometimes she'll answer, most of the time she doesn't. Keene goes back and forth between mournful and exasperated when she doesn't reply. Nathan's taken to reading to her from a romance novel he found in my mom's nightstand. And me, I just talk.

I fill her in on what happened after we drugged her, on why we did it, the vulture's final resting place. I do not mention the maggots. The room is lit by filtered sun through nailed-up towels, made brighter than other rooms by my mother's insatiable love for white. White dresser, walls, white sheets, cream carpet. White bathroom.

In the bathroom, Jenny says, "Are you still out there?"

"Yeah."

"You should go take care of Little."

"The boys have him."

"You can't stay up here with me forever," Jenny says.

I ignore this. "Will you please tell me what's happening, Jen? Do you feel different?"

She falls silent again. The bathroom is big enough to pace. I imagine that's what she might be doing. "The same," she says after a while. "My arm hurts where...the burns, I mean. I might take a nap now. You should go."

"Please don't shut me out," I say. "We're trying to help, Jenny."

"I know," she says.

"You're mad."

"I'm not mad," she says. "I'm a little pissy that you locked me in here instead of putting me outside like I asked, but I'm not mad. I know you guys love me."

"Then talk to me! Did you eat? There's soup."

"I had a granola bar and some water. Listen, Shur. You need to promise me—"

I know where it's going and cut it off clean. "No. We're not going to think like that."

She doesn't speak again, no matter how many times I say her name. Eventually, I say, "You have the walkie-talkie. Please call me if anything changes. It's just for a few days, I promise." She doesn't answer. Before I leave, I add, "I love you." She doesn't answer that either.

***

There is nothing pressing to do, which is bad, bad. My brain is reaching the edge of its tether and really needs to be busy. Usually, when I get like this, I'll go for a run. Not an option, so I get Little out of the basement.

"Come on," I say. "We're going upstairs. You stink and we need to wash your butt."

"Don't wanna," he declares, crossing his arms in a miniature imitation of Keene.

"Yeah, I know," I say, "But we have to share a tent with you, child, and you *STINK*. No one wants to smell your butt. Not even Charlie."

This earns a giggle. Charlie's ears twitch at the sound. "But then can I watch *Frozen*?"

"You know the answer, *but* I was thinking you can sing me *Frozen* songs and we can make cookies."

"What kind of cookies?"

"Sugar cookies, probably?"

Little's nose crinkles as he considers this offer. "How come we can make cookies with no lectricity?"

"We can light the oven the old-fashioned way?"

"What's that?"

"Black magic."

"What's that?"

"I was kidding. Matches. We'll use matches. Which you are never, ever allowed to touch, right?"

He still doesn't move. "I don't want to go near the fireplace. Because of the monster." He hangs his head. "I'm not brave like Moana."

"You don't have to be brave. We burned that monster up. And also, you don't have to go in there. Want to know a secret?"

"What?"

"No one wants to go into the den because of the monster. If you come upstairs, we're going to stick to the kitchen and the bathroom. It's safe in there. Will you try that?"

Little nods slowly, his head bobbing up and down. Tufts of fluff stick out over each ear. He needs a haircut.

Charlie follows us to the base of the steps and no farther, nose raised. Tail twitching. Sniffing for predators? Apparently he does not like what he smells because he sits, unwilling to climb the stairs. I choose not to take this as an ominous sign.

The bathroom off the kitchen only has a toilet and sink, not a whole shower, but I guess it doesn't matter without hot water. I set a pot on the stove to boil. It might be a bit much to wash Little's hair, but I can at least give him a solid wipe down. Aside from the weak light, it's almost a normal moment.

He gasps and dances around the little throw rug. "It's cold!"

"The water?"

"No! The air! I'm cold! I want to be done now!"

"Then let me clean the stinky parts, dude," I say. "The sooner you smell nice, the sooner you get warm clothes."

"I do not like no lectricity!"

"Electricity."

"Lecricty?"

"E. Lec. Tris. It. E."

"E. Lec. Trict. E."

"Yeah, it's pretty sucky." I get him clean, then toss the cloth into the sink. "Drying time, short thing."

When he's suitably dressed for a long day of going absolutely nowhere farther than the kitchen, I herd him back to the table and sit him down, make him lunch while he jabbers away on various topics ranging from Things He's Seen at Day Care to Things He's Seen on Television.

"Where are Keene and Nathan?" he asks from around a mouthful of jelly sandwich. I had given the peanut butter to Jenny. Little doesn't seem to mind.

"Making sure the windows are covered good."

"So no more monsters get in."

"Right."

I stand in front of the oven, prepping to light it and stop. We have no eggs, no milk, no cookie mix. The vegetable oil was used to burn the vulture corpse. Even if I can light it, the control for the temperature is electric. I drop into a chair and begin to laugh at the futility of it all, shaking my head, unable to stop. Tears fall. My abs hurt. I can barely breathe.

"Shur?" Nathan and Keene are back. "Are you alright?"

I can't answer. My body continues to heave with laughter that isn't really laughter. My brain is all about the screamer.

Keene drops to one knee in front of me, takes my hands in his. "Talk to me."

I manage, "We can't make cookies!" and double over again. My face hurts.

Little asks, "What's happening?"

"Shur's overtired," Keene says. "You know how you get all crabby when you don't get enough sleep?"

"Yeah and sometimes I get real mad!"

"It's like that."

"I could make hot chocolate," Nathan says, and that sets me off into another gale because we can still make hot beverages like civilized people, even if we can't bake cookies and my best friend is sealed in a bathroom.

I bolt to the bathroom just in time to reach the toilet. There's not much. Just bile and some mushy cereal remains.

That takes the wind out of the fit. I reach out with a trembling hand and flush the mess away. Everything hurts. My head, my stomach, all the muscles in my neck.

Back in the kitchen, Little seems to have taken my fit in stride and is working his way through a second sandwich. My stomach lurches again, but then settles.

"Nerves," Nathan says, handing me a cup of water and pulling out a chair for me to sit in. "You want a blanket or something?"

I shake my head.

"Did you take your pills?" Keene asks.

"Yeah. Last night, so at least I didn't just puke them up."

We stand around the table. No one seems to know what to say to me. Finally, Little says, "Don't worry, Shur. We can make cookies from Play-Doh. Play-Doh tastes good and you don't have to cook it!"

"That's a great idea," Nathan says, laughing "Let's do it."

31

By dinner, I almost feel normal. New normal, not old normal. More myself. I light the burner to heat up a can of ravioli for Little's dinner. The walkie squawks and Jenny's voice comes through tentatively.

"Shur? Are you there?"

In my haste to snatch it, my fingers brush the red plastic, sending Elmo's face into a spin on the countertop. The boys all look up from their coloring. They have spent the time since lunch babysitting me and Little, playing card games, coloring, keeping Little from eating Play-Doh. He's tired from being busy. He's almost happy. Even Charlie has come part way up the stairs, although not all the way to the kitchen.

"I'm here!"

Keene is already on his feet, ready for the worst.

"Can you talk privately? Fast?"

"Sure." My stomach flip-flops, convinced she's about to deliver *the* news. She's worse.

"I'm in the bathroom. What's happening?" I close the door behind me.

"There's someone coming toward the house. It looks like they're all in black. The people from the crash, I think."

"What? How do you know?"

"I took the cover off the window. They're coming from that direction. I think they're headed to the back door. You need to do something. Get in the basement."

"Maybe it's help," I say.

"It's not help," she says. "Hide!"

I rush out of the bathroom and say, as brightly as I can, "Jenny had an idea! You and Little can try cooking this on the camp stove downstairs. Like real camping!"

"What?"

I'm already turning off the burner, grabbing up the pot handle, and thrusting it into Keene's hand. "Now."

He catches my expression and says, without breaking eye contact, "That will be so fun! Come on, Little! You get to make your own dinner like a big boy."

Little asks, "Can I bring my picture?"

"Yep." He doesn't ask but gives me his "What the hell?" expression.

"Someone is coming," I mouth.

Keene rushes Little down the stairs. I hear them clattering and Little's upbeat question about if cats can eat ravioli. I push the door shut and wish I had something to secure it with.

"What's up?" Nathan asks. He's abandoned the table, has a hand on one of Bill's big knives.

"Jenny said we're about to have visitors."

"The thing from the porch?"

"I don't know."

"Back door?"

Before I can answer, Jenny's voice drifts from the walkie, still on the counter. "Shur, they're close. I can't see them, they went underneath the carport."

In the silence of the kitchen, every outside noise is amplified. Scraping and scratching. Vague movements of my brothers in the basement. Then, a sneaky, stealthy sound, the screen door being pulled open. It could be missed if you weren't listening for it, hadn't heard it a thousand times before. A whisper of metal and air.

The door knob rattles. Doesn't budge. It rattles again, stops. Outside, no voices, no discussion. Insect noises. Thirty seconds pass. I can hear my heart, or maybe it's Nathan's. Blood in my ears. Our ragged breathing. A minute. Nothing.

Nathan whispers, "I think they gave up."

A vicious thud, a hideous whack! Someone kicking the door hard, then again, and again. The wood is thick, but the lock is old. Not dead bolted like the front. I see everything in perfect clarity again, like before, pieces of distinct detail disconnected from every other detail. The door seeming to bulge, bowing inward against the pressure. The wood around the lock splintering as it gives. The door explodes inwards, followed by a leg clad in the tattered remains of black cargo pants.

The black night outside framing a nightmare.

A man loses his balance and falls inside, landing with both hands square on the kitchen tile. His head snaps up and he growls. It's not a human sound.

His face is not a face anymore.

There isn't a lot of time to consider more than that fact, that he clearly was human, but what remains is pure infection, boiling up to the surface of his rotten, putrid skin. Oozing, ready to split. As he pushes upright, his hands leave a slick of slime on the floor. He's fast, moving straight at Nathan.

Nathan is ready with the knife. He swings it, but halfheartedly (or at least it seems that way to me). The thing blocks his arm. Before I can move to help, a second one is coming up the steps. Another person or thing like him. Longish hair on half of her head. No hair on the rest. Shorter than he is. She's trying to get inside, but I hurl myself at the door, slam it in her face.

A scream of rage and frustration comes from under the carport. The door is hit, hit, over and over again. She's getting a running start. Backing up. Bolting up the steps, hitting the wood full force. I time it. Four seconds. Once. Twice. Three times, like clockwork. On the fourth run I snatch the door open just before she hits. She spills into the kitchen, momentum carrying her, tripping her up.

Like the monster fighting Nathan, this thing is no longer entirely human. Her eyes are still there, but red, filled with blood, even the irises. The nose is mostly gone, and a garishly purple-black tongue squirms at me, too large for her mouth. The only normal things are her straight, white teeth. They gnash as she struggles to get up.

I don't hesitate like Nathan. I kick her while she's down, right in the ribs. Hard. The air oofs out of her and she drops all the way to her stomach, arms splayed. She rolls onto her back to face me.

This is her last mistake.

Again, that sense of time-lapse, of specific details, too bright. Individual pieces of a whole puzzle. I drive my knife down into her throat. Not her. It, the calmer voice says. Its mouth snaps, blood eyes roll. The knife connects with something hard, crunching. Spine, maybe. She/it bucks then lies still, swollen eyelids drifting closed.

No time to think. I leave the knife in her, turn to find Nathan.

His hesitation has cost him. He's pinned to the floor, holding the rabid thing up and off of him with every ounce of strength he has. His fingers are dug into the flesh of the monster's exposed upper arms, literally into, and brown goo oozes out. My first thought is for the door, for the butterflies that might get in, but there's no time to deal with both. I grab one of my mother's cooking knives out of the block, a giant, pointy one, and bury it into its back, right between the shoulder blades.

I think I scream, but that could be all in my head. The thing does not fall, but gropes at its back, gurgling, then rises and stumbles. Brown, like the fluid coming from its arms, drips to the floor through the torn black T-shirt.

It shuffles at me, arms out, shrieking. I grab the first thing on the counter my hands find—the toaster. I swing it by the cord and get in a lucky hit, right to its face. It grabs the toaster and yanks.

Then Nathan has it from behind and hauls it toward the den. I take the rest of the kitchen in two steps, yank the knife from the dead girl's throat, and run at it. This time, the knife hits something vital. The creature—I can't think of it as anything else—slips from Nathan's grip, no longer struggling, dead before it hits the floor.

Nathan limps to a chair and collapses, panting hard, face covered in sweat, hands slick with that weird brown goop. His shirt too. We stare at each other, breathing hard.

"I think my ankle is broken," he says. "I'm going to pass out." His eyes roll back.

"Nathan!" I cry. "Stay with me!"

His eyelids flutter a few times.

"Deep breaths. Come on. Deep breaths."

"I'm awake. Shit, man, this really hurts." He's pale.

I dart across the kitchen and close the door as best I can. The frame is damaged, a mess of raw wood and splinters. It won't hold against another attack.

I go to the top of the stairs, open the door. "Keene! I need you!"

Keene sprints up the steps. He has a hatchet in hand, ready for action. "Holy shit," he says, taking in the scene.

"Nathan's hurt."

"Bitten?"

"No, he messed up his ankle. We need to get these things out and secure the door."

"Oh shit. Okay." A pool of brown spreads from the corpses. "Oh shit. I'll take them." He scowls at their matching black clothes.

"No, you stay with Nathan. I can do it, but you need to make sure nothing comes in with me."

"Shur, they're deadweight. How are you going to manage?"

"I just am." I'm strong. Stronger than he thinks. Motivated.

Filled with adrenaline. Right now I could climb Everest. While we discuss, a stench is unfurling from the bodies. It smells like the dead vulture but amplified. Grotesque. No candle will cover it.

I run to the front closet and grab everything I can find of use. A pair of my mother's snow pants and her thickest winter jacket, the one she bought for snowblowing the driveway (which Bill always did anyway). A ski mask. I'm already pouring sweat from exertion. Now I'm broiling and lightheaded, ready to pass out, puke, or both. Ski gloves so thick, my fingers feel planets apart from each other.

I yank up the hood and return to the kitchen.

"You going snowboarding?"

"I don't want to get bitten," I say. "This is the best I can do."

"And what am I doing?"

His questions are irritating me, but instead of screaming, I say, "I'm going to drag these things out. You stand here and close the door behind me, beat anything to death that comes in. And get the bleach out, boil water. We need to sanitize."

"If one comes in, what do I hit it with?"

Jesus Christ. "Knock it down with a broom, end it with your hatchet. The broom is in the pantry."

"A broom and a hatchet," Keene repeats.

"Let's get it done." I tug open the broken wooden door. The screen door has bounced shut, keeping out any additional winged guests. Outside, it's a pleasant, warm fall night. Wings whisper everywhere, but the underside of the carport is mostly empty of insects, except two by the far end. They've latched onto the crossbeam, wings together in quiet repose.

The knives come loose from the male corpse with a wet

squelch, like a spoon from pudding. I tug the body by the legs until it's closer to the door and lay it beside its female counterpart. They rest side by side, his feet near her head.

At our father's funeral, he'd looked asleep. It was horrible. For weeks, Keene and I both had nightmares that he'd sit up in his coffin. In mine, his eyes and mouth were stitched shut, and he screamed and screamed, trying to pry them open. In Keene's dreams, Dad's head rolled off, and then the rest of him came out, trying to get us.

This is worse. The bloated forms seem to be putrefying before our eyes. The skin literally crawls. Something inside is alive and trying get out.

I hoist the man by the armpits, sure I'll feel writhing through his clothing. The gloves are thick, so all I feel is my own sweat dripping from my fingers. "Get ready. Close the door as soon as I'm out." The stink of the man's head so close to my face envelops my whole world. My eyes water.

I hitch the man up, tightening my grip, and nudge the screen with my back. It swings lazily toward the siding. He is a sack of weights, and I will be hurting tomorrow. But it has to be done. I drag him backwards, careful on the steps. Two of us with broken ankles would be disastrous. One is bad enough.

With one eye on the two butterflies, awash in my own sweat, I drag him a dozen steps down the driveway and drop him. The head bounces on the blacktop and I flinch.

When I turn back, I'm greeted by a dozen butterflies on the siding. They are beautiful, vibrant, startlingly huge. Disinterested in me. Maybe they can't smell me, maybe they're just tired. Maybe these are reaching the end of their lifespans, monster butterfly old age. Down the driveway and over the lawn, along the street, they swarm in a river. Gaps in the flow, here and there. Maybe it's my imagination, but they do seem less numerous than the day of the truck crash.

The second body is up. The wound in her neck has collected a pool of dirty brown slime. Her pocket bulges. I flick the snap up, find a wallet. It's girlie. Powder blue with an embroidered flower.

"Why do you want that?"

"They were people."

"People who tried to kill us."

"Someone might want to know what happened to her," I say and set the wallet on the table.

Outside, I deposit the second corpse near the first and check his pockets. No wallet. A pocket knife, a good one, the kind you can't take on planes. I slip it into my coat pocket. Should I say a prayer? They were people. Even if they did open fire on the neighborhood out of some misguided need to protect America. They were still people who, until recently, had jobs and families and hopes for the future. Hobbies. Likes and dislikes. And now they're victims, dead things rotting under a carport, filled with wriggling monsters.

I shudder and go back inside.

32

We have new problems to discuss while Keene bleaches the floor on his hands and knees.

Nathan's ankle is clearly messed up, more than just twisted. It's not taking his weight and most movement causes him to turn pale and nearly vomit. It's likely badly fractured, even if it's not a clean break.

The door is splintered and unsecured, leaving us with a massive security problem.

And, finally, there were at least five, maybe even six people in that truck when it crashed. We saw one eaten. Two are outside. That leaves two, maybe three, unaccounted for.

"Door next," Keene says.

"Do we have any supplies left?"

"Not that works for this." He reaches to scratch his face, realizes where his gloved hands are, thinks better of it. The bleach water is tinged brown.

"Maybe we could put the table against it?"

"That won't work," he says. "We need to lodge the door shut. Like with a doorstop. Anything else can be pushed aside with enough force."

I swear at the lock. "Why did Mom put a heavy-duty deadbolt on the front and leave this flimsy thing?"

"It's not like we have a lot of break-ins around here," he says.

"And yet here we are." I pick up the walkie-talkie. We're overdue to give Jenny an update. "Jen, are you there?"

Nothing.

"Talk to us. Are you asleep? Wake up. We got rid of the things that came in. How are you doing?"

More nothing. Not even the fuzz of static.

Immediately, Keene says, "Don't."

"Don't what?"

"Think the worst. The batteries probably died or else she dropped the stupid thing in the bathtub. It doesn't mean anything."

"I saw a thing in the basement," Nathan says. "It could be a doorstop."

"What?" I ask, distracted.

"It was on a shelf with the toolbox. This metal thing, like, this big." He holds out his hands a few inches apart. "Thick. Shaped like an L."

"Oh my God, did she keep that?" Keene asks. He wipes sweat from his head with his forearm.

"What is it?"

"I tried to make her a box in shop in eighth grade. The welding didn't take, but she insisted it was the most beautiful thing she'd ever seen."

Once the cleanup is done (and the knives are soaking a bucket of bleach), Keene retrieves his abortive box project from the basement.

"How is this a box?" I ask, taking it from him. I turn it over in my hands. A flat, quarter-inch thick metal piece, maybe four inches long and two inches wide has been welded to a shorter piece at a 90-degree angle so that it resembles a fat 3D letter L.

"It's the bottom and one of the short sides, see? I never even got the lid on because the whole thing fell apart. I got a pity C– for effort."

"Well, on the upside, it's getting a second life now," I say, handing it back. It'll be perfect if we slide the long part under the door and secure it to the floor. If someone tries to shove the door open, it'll get caught by the short side of the L. There are no holes in the metal, but we have Mom's drill and plenty of screws.

While Keene works, I spray down my coat and gloves with Lysol. There's nothing on them but some faint brown streaks, but they feel tainted. We're quiet, all in our own zones, Keene and me working, Nathan swimming in a world of pain. Little humming away in his tent with Charlie, coloring by flashlight. Jenny having gone radio silent.

"I think," I say to Nathan, stirring him from his half-doze, "it would be safer for you in the basement. You might be able to slide down on your butt."

"I don't think that's going to work," he says. "It hurts kind of a lot."

"Keene could help you down. Like a human crutch."

Nathan shakes his head. "I'll never be able to get back up if there's an emergency."

He seems determined to spend the night up here, and I'm disinclined to argue right now. "We can set you up the couch."

"Basement is safer, dude," Keene says.

"I can stay up here with him," I say.

Keene raises an eyebrow.

"You can, if you want," I offer.

"No. It's fine. I'll hang out with Little and Charlie."

———

Nathan tries to rest on the couch, leg propped up, blood full of over-the-counter pain killers. We've got a couple of chemical cold packs, and I wrap these around his swollen ankle before doing a check of the house.

I check each window one by one. I rattle the back doorknob, really tug at it, but the door is solid. Nailed in place, metal door-stop to keep it from budging. Even if I wanted to go upstairs and look out the window at the house across the way, I would not be able to see anything in the dark. Instead, I force myself to sit at the table. Empty candle jars fill a recycling container by the door, but Mom's supply seems endless. Keene found another whole box of them in the basement. One of these new ones throws a ring of light across the table, enough to examine the dead girl's wallet by.

I unsnap the cover. It's not a very big wallet. Her license on top. Marie St. Clair. Under the license is a college ID, expired by a couple of years. Maybe she still uses it to get student discounts. She's pretty, in a basic way. Perfect hair. I think of it now, half of it gone along with her deteriorated scalp. That hair was long and brown, layered around her shoulders. Straight teeth in a smile, wide set eyes. I can't tell their color. I wonder who's missing her, who's wondering where she is and if she's locked down safely. The wallet has a few one-dollar bills folded over, a random key, a heart sticker with the color rubbed nearly clean off. I close it all back up and put the wallet in the cabinet near my pills. Someday, maybe I'll be able to turn it over to someone and give them closure.

I take my pills out, pop today's. I haven't forgotten them since the vulture.

I try the walkie-talkie again. "Jenny?" No answer. Maybe I should go upstairs, knock on the door, at least try to talk to her. Get her to tell me what's going on in her head, in her arm, in her body. I shake a few Advil out of the bottle on the counter, careful to make sure there's enough for Nathan. I hurt all over already.

33

Little's nose wrinkles at the smell in the kitchen, which has mellowed to a rank mixture reminiscent of old fish and salty ocean breezes. It's past his bedtime. He sits at the table in front of a pudding cup, a spoon clutched in one hand, eyes on the door. The job Keene has done is effective, but hardly elegant. Screws and nails jut out everywhere, punctuated by the makeshift doorstop.

"The monsters got in again, huh?" Little asks.

"Eat your dessert. There are no monsters here."

"Then what was all that noise? And how come I had to stay in the basement? And how come Nathan got hurt? And why is it smelly in here?"

"Nathan fell over," I say. "He's resting his leg."

"Did he get bit? Is he going to have a campout with Jenny?"

"Eat your pudding," Keene tries again. "No bites. Just a hurt leg."

"How come the door looks like that?"

"Monster protection," Keene says.

"Oh. How is Mommy going to get in?"

"She has a key to the front door," Keene says. He's starting to sound exasperated.

I grin at him and pick up Nathan's water glass, along with another dose of Advil and a fresh cold pack from our dwindling supply.

Nathan is stuck on the couch, leg propped. He is bored and uncomfortable, with an unopened book beside him and fingers tapping on the mattress.

"How's the leg?"

"Sucks. How's Little?"

"Unimpressed with Keene's carpentry skills. Past that, you know...he didn't hear much."

"Thank God for that."

"Yeah."

"I was thinking, if you want to send him in before he goes to bed, I could read him a bedtime story? So he can see I'm not bitten or anything?"

I force a smile, but it's a bit sad. A bad-news smile. "He doesn't want to come in here," I say. "Because of the fireplace."

"Oh. Yeah, that makes sense. Listen, Shur, if you want to sleep downstairs tonight with Little and Keene, I'll be fine on my own. Just leave me one of the knives."

"Trying to martyr yourself?"

He sort of laughs, looks down at his lap. "Nah, I still expect you to come to my rescue if anything goes wrong. But if it was me, I'd kind of want to be with my family after a day like this."

"I do," I say. "I want to be with them, but you're our family too. Right?"

"Not the same."

There's no good way to say this might be all any of us have left, so I don't. Instead, I say, "We're going to take turns staying with you. We want you to move to the basement, but"—I hold up a hand as he starts to object—"no one is going to rush you. We don't want to make your leg worse. I'll be back in a few minutes."

In the kitchen, Keene doesn't seem ready to let go for the night. He says, "Are you sure you want to stay up here? I can do it."

"Tomorrow."

"If his leg is better tomorrow, we'll bring him down too." He pauses. "You think there are more of them." It's not a question. "Yeah, me too." He rises from the chair and stretches.

"Shur said we could have ice cream when we got home," Little says, pushing away the empty pudding cup.

"That was ages ago."

"Is there ice cream?" Little asks.

"No, but there are cookies," I say.

"Ooo, what kind of cookies?"

"The chocolate chip kind."

"Mommy's special cookies?" Little asks, eyes wide.

"Yeah, and you've been such a good boy, I bet she'd want you to have two!"

"Three."

"Two and you have to brush your teeth."

"Oh, fine," Little says, sounding so put out that we both laugh.

After they're squared away, ready to leave us for the night, Keene kisses the top of my head.

"What was that for?"

"For being my badass, neurotic sister," he says.

"You said ass," says Little.

"Yeah, yeah, whatever. Say goodnight to Shur."

"Goodnight to Shur!" Little shouts and throws himself at me, climbing my legs with some help. Every muscle aches, but I squeeze anyway. He wraps his arms around my neck and whispers, "Tomorrow, all the bugs are going to be gone, and Mommy is going to come home!"

"Oh really?"

"Yep!"

"How do you know that?"

"I just know," Little says, his face solemn. "You'll see."

"Well then," I say, "we'll have to have pancakes in the morning to celebrate."

"Yay, pancakes!"

"Yes, yay for pancakes," Keene agrees. "See you in the morning, sister."

"See you guys. Sleep sound."

They close the door behind them, and I wish I could do more to lock them in safely. For now, being watchful will have to do.

———

"You need to use the bathroom?" I ask Nathan, taking his empty glass from the end table.

"Yes. And it's going to suck."

"That's the spirit," I say.

He slides to the edge of the pull-out and swings his good leg out, followed gingerly by the bad. I sit beside him so he can put an arm around my shoulder, and we struggle upright together.

He groans.

"I'm sorry," I say.

"It's not far, I'll survive." It takes forever to get across the kitchen to the bathroom, and both of us are bathed in sweat by the time we arrive. I leave him at the door.

The kitchen is stagnant. I wish we could open a window, a door. Anything.

It takes Nathan an age to finish, but he does not call for help (thank God). I hear water running, then he's hopping into the kitchen, wincing with every movement. I put myself under his arm again, and we begin our three-legged race back to the couch bed.

"Maybe tomorrow," he says, "we could move the gym mats up? I can sleep on the floor. Closer to the bathroom."

"It'll be harder to get off the floor," I say.

"Oh. Right."

Once he's back on the couch, leg propped, I look at the ankle again. It's bad. Huge. And he smells terrible. So do I. Tomorrow I will boil water. Being clean will make everyone feel better. More civil. Normal, even.

As I cover his good leg and body with the blanket, careful to leave the bad foot untouched, he says, "This reminds me of the dentist."

"This blanket?"

"Heh. No. Marking time. The dentist, or like doing burpee sets."

"You've totally lost me," I say. "Did you get hit in the head?"

"No, I just have too much spare time lately."

I climb into bed next to him.

"Not sure Keene would approve of this arrangement," Nathan says.

"I can sleep on the trundle if it bothers you."

"Nah, it's fine. You want to…" He puts out his arm and invites me closer. I accept the invitation, move in closer to him. It's intimate. Nice to be held.

"Tell me about the dentist. He makes you do burpees?"

"Yeah, you don't brush your teeth, you do burpees. No flossing? That's laps."

"You're funny tonight."

"Someone has to bring the humor, right? But what I mean is that you start a thing, and it feels like it's forever. The start of a dentist appointment. Start of a workout."

"Spanish class."

"Algebra 2 for me. But it's a routine. You know how it's going to go, how it's going to end. When the pain will set in, when you'll want to quit, when you'll realize it's almost done. When it's over."

"Except this doesn't have an end."

"Right. Right. That's what makes it suck. It not only has no end, but it also broke our routines. You get up, get dressed, talk to your parents, go to school. In the summer, you go to work or whatever, hang with your friends. Same rhythms. Now, we can't even tell when day or night is without checking the clock. It's all fucked up."

"Everything familiar is gone."

"Yes. Well, not everything, but enough stuff so that what's left doesn't even feel familiar anymore. It feels like…"

"Like the memory of another life."

We're quiet in the dark. His arm is warm around me. I feel almost safe. Almost happy.

"I was going to ask you to homecoming," he says into the gray darkness.

"Really?"

"Maybe next year, right?"

"I think I would have said yes," I say. "You never really let on that you were going to ask me..."

"I'm bad at flirting," Nathan says.

"If we get out of this, maybe can we go on a date? A real one?"

"Yes. That would be amazing. Just you and me. No Keene. No Jenny."

I bite my lip hard, and it takes him a second to realize that I've stiffened. "Oh, God, sorry. Sorry. I didn't even think."

"It's okay," I lie.

———

After Nathan's breathing deepens to steady snores, I roll off his shoulder and settle into my own space, staring up into the void above. The room's jar candle eventually consumes itself, hissing out in a final puff of white smoke. The house is still.

I'm almost out when I hear knocking. It might be a figment of my pre-sleep brain. I snap awake, listening, but nothing comes again. Then there: *knock knock knock* at the window in the dining room. I rise with my bare feet and pick up the flashlight with one hand, my newly acquired pocket knife in the other. I keep the flashlight low, beam sweeping the baseboards. This is unnecessary; no one can see me through the wood, but it feels safer.

When the knocking comes again, it's right on the plywood. It breaks off, starts on the other side of the dining room at the next window. I follow it. It's testing. Trying to lure us out? Looking for its friends?

The noise happens at every single window. It progresses toward the back door. To the kitchen.

Bam! Bam! Bam!

I scream and jump. Someone or something hurls itself at the door over and over, trying to get in. Something inhuman. A hand falls on my shoulder and I nearly scream again, but I whip around to find Keene beside me, hatchet in his hand. Ready.

From the den, Nathan shouts, "What's happening?"

"Stay there," I yell back, and from outside, animal noises, grunts, screams of rage fill the air. Sawdust shakes from the screws and nails. The makeshift stop does not budge, but the would-be invader keeps trying. It goes on for minutes that feel like hours. Relentless.

But the door holds.

After a final prolonged rattle of the knob, of the whole door, the screen door bounces hard off the siding. The onslaught is over. For now.

34

Nathan eats cold Pop-Tarts alone in the den. Keene doesn't want to talk. He keeps his eyes on the table, not ready to discuss what happened last night. Little eats pear slices and babbles about how the basement smells like cat poop, a sure indication that the litter box needs changing.

But Keene turns to the stairs as soon as he's done eating.

"Hey," I say. "We need to make a plan."

"No we don't," he says.

Little watches us, attuned to our moods. He says, "Can I go downstairs now too?"

"No," I say. "You need to change your clothes and wash your face."

"Can I take a bath in the tub? I want to play with my ducks."

"Sorry, kid, not yet."

Little pouts. Keene pouts. Everyone gets to pout but me, and I am not in the mood to deal with this nonsense.

"You know," I say, "this isn't just about keeping them out. There's stuff to do. Clothes, Nathan's leg, food supplies. Coming up with a plan for if we have to leave. I can't do it alone."

I could, if I really had to, I know. Fragile, broken Shur.

Keene grunts, hand on the rail.

"We got caught out, Keene. If Jenny hadn't been looking out the window...and after last night, we know they're coming back."

"Come on," he says to Little, who gives me a grin and squirts away downstairs. Traitor.

I put water on to boil, a huge lobster pot's worth of it. Maybe they all want to smell bad, wear rancid clothes, but I don't. I will wash towels. I will wash underwear and T-shirts and pillowcases and my own armpits. They can all stink while they wallow.

The water will take a long time, so I sit at the table with the emergency radio. Our friends at the high rise haven't been around much lately, or maybe their power source finally blinked out. I tour the dial, up then down, listening for signs of sound beneath the static.

And then, here they are. Or one of them, at least.

"...and if you've been listening, you know I'm by myself now. The butterflies are definitely thinning. I want to make that clear. Jesus, I know I'm talking to myself, but maybe someone is out there."

"Come on," I say. "Tell me something I can use. Give me some good news."

"Alone is worst," he says. "Alone is worst of all. Anyway, I want to take some callers. I'm desperate to take some callers. Do you guys know that was always my least favorite part of the job? I hated talking to callers. Messed up, right? A talk show host who hates callers? That was Stewart's thing."

The other guy, then. Not-Stewart. Have I ever heard his name? I can't remember. I picture him sweating in the studio under the emergency lights, breathing stale air, talking without even knowing if anyone can hear.

"Some callers were a blast. They would tell us the craziest stories. Keep in mind, this was before all this butterfly shit, so it seemed a lot...funnier. One caller from New Mexico wanted to know how to get a tarantula infestation out of her car. At the time, I thought her story was farfetched. Something out of sci-fi show or a sitcom. She comes back from a weekend away, goes to run an errand, and boom—her car is crawling with tiny, newly hatched creepy crawlies. We sent her to the guys on Car Talk, nothing we could do but laugh and sympathize. Another guy called us blaming the Democrats for hunting restrictions. Why? He got chased three blocks by a flock of pissy Canadian geese." He laughs, sort of. "Those stories don't seem so funny now.

"Anyway, most people who called in were angry. At the government, at us, at the Democrats like that guy. They'd spew hate at anyone who would listen. Just crazy, crazy shit."

Where is Stewart? I don't know if I want to know.

"If I get out of this, I never want to see another booth like this again. Studios are dead to me. I don't know what I'll do. Photography, maybe. Happy things. Kid portraits. Dog portraits. Engagements. Or maybe I'll become a nurse. Hokey, right? But I feel so helpless. I want to help people. I want to take action, but I can't. I can't do anything but sit here and talk to you, because going outside means...well, you know. For now. The butterflies are leaving, you guys, but the infected..."

I lean forward. What are they; how long do they stay sick? Can they be cured? Is the government coming?

"Not going to talk about that," he says. "But here's your hourly reminder. AM bands 1640 through 1670 and your low 500s. I haven't gotten much from them, but those are your emergency broadcast stations. Try. Keep trying. Don't give up. And if you make it out and you heard this, come find me. I want to shake your hand." He begins to cry, loud, hoarse, braying sobs into the microphone.

35

spend the day stewing over Keene's pouting. I scrub clothes until
my hands are red and wrinkled. When I run out of laundry, I
turn to twirling the radio dial and worrying. Now and then I'll
grab a few snatches of words around the 500s. A handful of dispa-
rate phrases, not enough to piece together into a coherent thought.

I peek in on Nathan a few times, but he's passed out cold on
the couch. I don't want to revive him to a world of pain just to
keep me company, so I leave him to his nap.

Upstairs, Jenny refuses to answer me. "Come on," I say, almost
whining. "Jen, this is ridiculous. If you're sick, we'll deal with it.
Can you just...please..." But no amount of cajoling on my part gets
so much as a grunt from the other side of the door.

Eventually I get tired of being by myself. I'm angry. I clomp
down to the basement, making as much noise as possible on the
steps to announce my arrival.

"I have an idea," I say, stopping with my feet on the bottom step. The stairs, painted a nondescript gray, are dirty. And why wouldn't they be? Before this week, we never thought of the basement as anything more than storage space. Not living space. Now I am acutely aware of dust and sand in the corners, cobwebs overhead, dead bugs, bits of rubbed-off paint.

Keene does not come out of the tent where he and Shawn lie together.

"It is the middle of the day," I say, sounding ridiculously like our mother. "You two cannot sleep forever."

"Why not?" Keene asks. "Do I have somewhere to go?"

"You could come help."

"You've got it under control."

"I think we should try the candle again," I say. "They already know we're in here, so there's no risk."

"Yeah, Shur, that's good. Real good. You don't need me."

"Fine. I'm going to check on Jenny. Feel like doing that?"

"I haven't heard the toilet flush."

"What?" I'm confused.

He sits up and leans into the tent's opening. "When the toilets flush, they make noise in the pipes. I know the kitchen one because I hear it twice, once through the floor and then in the pipes. I haven't heard any other flushing. So, she's not using the toilet. Unless she's shitting in the sink, I don't think you need to bother checking on her."

That bit of bad news delivered, he disappears back into his lair.

I grapple with this for a second. Could she be dead? No. Not Jenny. Jenny would not go out of this world so quietly. Maybe she *is* shitting in the sink. There's an explanation, but not death, I'm not prepared to accept that.

"Dude, you need to stop feeling sorry for yourself," I say. "I can't do it alone!"

"You don't get it, do you? There's nothing to do. Light the candle if it makes you feel better. Check on Jenny. Hell, cook some more bacon. You don't need me for any of that."

I sit down next to Nathan. There's a new awareness between us, something electrical, the slightest spark. I say, "I'm going to try the candle again tonight."

"Is that smart?" he asks. "Last time…"

"I get it. But they obviously know we're here already."

"Yeah. Maybe it's our best option. I don't really see another way out. Especially not with my leg like this. I'm about as useful as Little."

"I'm not sure I did the right thing for us, telling Bill we'd stay here."

"Hindsight and all that, right? You don't even know that he's alive over there."

I choose to believe Bill can survive anything. "Anyway, I'm going to pack up a few bags to get ready. And I'm going to tell Jenny."

Nathan looks away, suddenly interested in imaginary fluff on the blanket under his leg.

"Look," I say. "I have to try to talk to her."

"Do you?"

"What's that mean?"

"We haven't heard anything in days. If you open the door—"

"Who said anything about opening the door—"

"It's a natural assumption. She's not answering, you want to know, turns out she's infected—"

"Are you serious? Do you really think I'd put us all at risk like that?"

"I think you care about her a lot," Nathan says. Now he does raise his head, locks eyes with me. My face burns with rage and humiliation. After all this time and all I've done to protect us, he thinks I'd just open the door?

"She only has enough food for a few days. I need to know if she's coming or staying." I spin on my heel and head up the stairs. Behind me, I can hear him shouting my name, calling me back, telling me not to do anything stupid.

With the vulture corpse gone, the hallway is a little less stinky, but only slightly. I give the stain a wide berth, even though the carpet has been bleached a funny shade of yellow that nothing could have survived. Mom's bedroom is dusty and brighter than downstairs, like last time. I knock on the bathroom door.

"Jenny?"

Nothing comes back, not even a whisper-scratch of pencil.

"Jen. Listen, we're thinking about trying for Bill's again. We can't leave you without knowing..." There's no good way to end that sentence. *Without knowing* sums it up but doesn't say enough. "I need you to answer. I know you're trying to take one for the team, but please. You know how I feel. Stop with the silent treatment. Just tell me how it is. Are you dying? I promise not to open the door if you're infected. I swear on my dad."

But she still doesn't reply. I hear feet on the stairs, Keene coming to scold me for being an idiot, now on a mission to grind in his feelings on the futility of my plan making.

I drop to my knees, then lay flat against the carpet. The pile is too high, blocks any view under the door. It's snug against the wood.

"That's not going to work."

I look up, already scowling, ready for a fight, but Keene waves a drill at me. "If you want to see, we can drill a hole."

I choke back a noise that is both laugh and sob.

"Was that a yes?" Keene asks. I run to him, flinging my arms around his neck. He hugs me back with his free arm. "I can't have you knocking the whole door down."

"I wasn't going to!"

"I know that." He ruffles my hair, looks embarrassed. "I'm sorry."

"I know that."

He grins and points to a spot on the door. "There? That short enough for you, Oompa? Stand back. I hope this bit is long enough." The drill meets some resistance. He pushes harder, leaning into the operation. The smell of warm wood fills my nostrils as sawdust floats down on the carpet. Finally, Keene stands back, stoops, squints. "That's it."

I peer through the hole. The main window is uncovered. Light spills in from everywhere, interrupted by moving black shadows. I angle myself this way and that, trying to get a better view through the tiny hole. "I can't see her."

"Maybe she's up against the door or in the shower?"

"Maybe." I shift. The pile of pillows is just there, nested against the jacuzzi tub and..."Oh shit," I say.

"What's wrong? You see her? Is she..."

"No," I say. "She's not in there at all. She left a note. She's gone."

36

Are you sure?" Keene asks.

"Look for yourself."

He hunches to see, both hands flat against the wood. Given his height, it takes him a minute to spot what I did. The note, nestled in the blankets, facing the door. "That's a note with your freaking name on it. Shit. She went out the window, didn't she? That's why we didn't hear the toilet. She was gone."

I think back to that afternoon lifetimes ago, days ago, when the scribble of her pencil filled the world.

"Why?" he asks, pushing his lank hair away from his face.

"I guess the answer's pretty obvious," I say. "She was turning."

"But she was contained! Why leave?"

"I'm not sure she...when they're like that..."

"She wasn't thinking rationally?"

I shrug.

He balls both fists, smacks the door with the heels of his

hands. Once, twice in an expression of intense irritation. "Why is she always such a pain in the ass?"

"She probably did it to protect us," I say.

"That doesn't make me less mad. She's irritating as fuck sometimes, but she's still family." He sighs and throws himself against the door, back first, tilts his head. His Adam's apple bobs. "I guess we can open it up. Get the note. It'll free up a tub."

I pretend to quote him: "On the downside, your best friend is dead, but on the bright side, you can wash your ass?"

"That's not what I meant."

"I know, I was trying to be funny."

"Well, don't, because you're fucking not."

I want to punch him but grab for his hand instead. "Keene. I love you. She loved you too, in her own way. Sure, she found you super annoying, but you know she'd trip a bitch down a flight of stairs for you."

He smacks his fist backwards against the door again. "This wasn't supposed to happen."

"Yeah. That's going to be this year's slogan. Let's open the door, big brother. I want to see that note."

***

It takes almost as much time for Keene to undo the screws and pry open the door as it did to close it up in the first place. My job is to listen for stealthy creeping within. Just in case. Keene works the drill, unscrews, pushes the pry bar. Sweats and curses. Finally, the last nail is out and he reaches for the knob.

"Ready?"

I nod. He hands me the pry bar.

Just in case.

Neither of us are ready to bash her head in, but neither of us is ready to die either.

He turns the knob slowly, then kicks the door open, staying safely back. Part of me expected it to thump against Jenny's dead body, proving why we couldn't see her in the most gruesome way imaginable, but the door swings in, bounces off the wall, and comes lazily back. Keene stops it with one hand.

The bathroom is empty. There are signs of Jenny everywhere. Her nest, the blankets disheveled. Her books. Fruit rinds, empty cans. A discarded bandage. She's collected the refuse thoughtfully in the bathroom's tiny garbage can.

"I wonder if she left while they were still in the house," Keene says.

"Or right after." I pluck the note from its resting place on the blankets. I know Jenny's writing as well as my own, and this isn't quite right. She wrote with her left hand. Of course. The right would have been a mess. The letters of my name are awkward, juvenile. Slanted wrong. The page is torn from her diary, the edge jagged, ripped from near the seam. Beneath the note, the mute Elmo walkie-talkie stares up at me.

The note doesn't have much to say, but Jenny wouldn't have wanted to leave without some goodbye.

Shur,

You asked if I was changing. The answer is, I don't really know. Maybe I'm imagining wiggling in my arm. I can't see anything, even with my phone light right in the wound. It doesn't look infected, but I have a fever and I swear it's there, that wiggling and wriggling. So, I'm going to go. I don't want you to have to deal with a monster in the house if I turn. I heard those things come in, then the banging. I think you guys closed it all up. I want to know how everyone is, but I'm afraid of the answer. I want to know. I don't want to know. So, I'm going to go. Oh, God, Shur, I thought we'd end up in the city, sharing a shitty apartment. I'm going to the barn, so if you head in there after...be careful. I might be there. Don't come after me. I'll either take care of myself or I'll die, and either way, there's nothing for you to do. You were my best friend. You guys were my real family.

Love,
Jenny

There is something very not-Jenny in that note, like her brain was occupied by bad thoughts or fever. Or physically occupied, I think, and shake it off.

Keene kneels beside the cabinet under the sink. "Her backpack is gone. She took everything we left her."

I hand him the note. He scans it. "Sounds like the fever talking. If I had a high fever, I'd probably be feeling worms under my skin too." He kicks the cabinet. "Dumbass. She should have stayed."

I fight the urge to drop onto her pile of blankets and refuse to move for the rest of the ordeal. If I stop moving now, it's for good.

Someone else will have to take charge. There is something nice in that thought. Someone else could take a turn being the adult. I'd like to be a kid again, with run-of-the-mill, real-world anxiety that meds mostly manage, stress dreams that, in retrospect, seem tame, and a therapist who scribbles down my thoughts and tells me they are perfectly normal.

I wonder if my therapist survived.

"We should probably throw those blankets outside," I say. "They might have parasites."

"I don't think that's how parasites work."

"Well, I don't know how they work, Keene," I say, "But that's how smallpox spread."

"That's a virus."

"Can we just..."

"Fine. If it makes you feel better."

We close the bathroom behind us, and the bedroom door after that, although there is nothing left in either room to protect or be protected from.

37

Watching night fall from inside my mother's bathroom, next to the drained tub, feels like a new experience. I stare out into the yard through the uncovered window, desperate for a view outside my own walls.

I picture Jenny in the barn with a blanket. With her backpack. Comfortable on the couch, sleeping off a fever.

Another picture tries to slip in, Jenny with her skin falling off, bloodred eyes, hair missing. Gnashing teeth.

The sun dips below the horizon, and the butterflies dip and float along with it. They rest on the carport's roof, peaceful from this vantage. Not a care in the world. They don't seem to be hunting. There are fewer, much fewer. That's relative, though, to the worst of their numbers, when I couldn't see the street through the peephole. They're no longer the blanket they were but are still worse than they were forty-eight hours in.

Thinning though.

I take a cold shower. The water stings my skin and wakes me up, uncomfortably so. The pain of it drives my anxiety backwards as my brain focuses entirely on being unhappily frigid. I wash my hair, which has become greasy and unruly, but I do not have stamina to condition. Outside the shower, the air is warm and pleasant. I wipe the cold shower water away with a towel stiff from hang-drying. It scratches.

My brain struggles, humming, talking over itself in half-formed sentences. It abandons them, picks up new threads. Worrying itself, rubbing like a stone or a coin, compulsive. This happened a lot after Dad died, before the meds and therapy started to help me cope. To get control of my brain. Back then, I hadn't been able to think at more than a cursory level. I couldn't read, I couldn't watch TV. I did jigsaw puzzles by the dozens. Lego sets, pulled from the depths of Keene's closet. Anything with teeny, tiny steps helped. Like taking a shower.

One foot in the underwear hole, the other foot. Pull up. Nothing to process, no one asking questions. I can hear myself now, a little. Sweatpants on the legs. T-shirt over the head, towel-dry my hair. The noise is receding.

Keene starts dinner while I'm showering, various cooked meats from the shrinking collection of what's remained cold in our cooler, and ramen noodles.

"Are these still good?" I ask as he hands me a cold Italian sausage wrapped in a paper towel.

"Yeah, but the last of the ice is almost melted. We're going to have to toss the rest in the morning."

"Mom would freak if she saw us eating sausages like this," I say. "She'd call us feral."

He nods. "I miss her yelling about manners."

When we're done with our sausages, he takes a pair of bowls to the basement, and I take a pair to the den. Feeding our children.

Nathan has seen the note. It's set aside on the end table next to the useless lamp. He doesn't say anything when I hand him the bowl of ramen. Maybe he wants me to bring it up. I don't. We eat in silence.

When we finish, I take our bowls back to the kitchen, come back with the broom and a fresh jar candle. "I'm going to put this out, then it's my turn tonight with Little. Do you need anything? Keene will be up in a few."

"You don't want to talk about it?" Nathan asks.

"Not really."

He sighs. "That note sounded kind of dire."

"I really don't want to talk about it," I repeat softly. I know the candle is seafoam green, but in the dim light, it's one more shade of dark gray. I light it, open the door a crack. Out onto the porch it goes, set down over the threshold, then I give it a gentle push with the broom. It bumps over the boards but goes easily enough. If Bill is there, it's right in his line of sight. Dark shapes flutter, and I retract the broom fast, close the door, throw the bolt.

I am beyond tired. It's deep in my bones, like I want to hibernate. In fairy tales we read as kids, there were always monsters in eternal slumber, and I remember thinking, "How boring! Who would want to sleep forever?" But now, in the shit light, with another shit night ahead of us, and more shit days and nights after that, I finally get it.

38

n the basement, I poke Little awake. He's only dozing anyway, as disinterested in the world as I am.

"Come on, up and at 'em, lazy."

"Don't wanna."

"Me neither, but we're gonna."

"Why?"

I have no real answer. Hopelessness spreads down my back like cold water from an errant ice cube, but there's no way to explain existential despair to a four-year-old. Instead, I say, "I think we should try to make s'mores."

"I. Don't. Want. To!" He rolls over and hides his face.

"Dude. Me neither. I don't want to make s'mores. I don't want to sleep in the basement. I don't want to stay inside or smell bad or not be able to watch *Frozen*. It all sucks. I'm bored and you're bored and even Charlie is bored."

"Charlie isn't bored," Little says. "He's a cat. Cats don't get bored."

"Sure they do," I say. "Why do you think they knock things off shelves?"

"Mom says that's because Charlie's a dick."

"That is not a nice word," I say, stifling a smile.

"That's what Mom said. She said I shouldn't say it, but I'm telling you what she said."

"It's fine just this time," I say "But you shouldn't say it, even if you're talking about Mommy saying it. It's not a nice word."

"What does it mean?" he asks and sits up, suddenly interested.

"It's a kind of bad word for...man parts."

"You mean it's a penis?" he says and begins to giggle. "Dick! Dick! Dick!"

"Hey! I said not to say it, not to say it a whole lot!"

"Dick! Dick! Dickity dick!" Little claps his hands in rhythm, making a song of it, and I pray my mother will forgive me when he inevitably does this in front of her. Clearly not all of me has given up hope that Mom will come home.

"Shur, teach me more bad words!"

I note a crust of ketchup on the front of his T-shirt from some earlier meal and say, "Let's change your shirt, then I'll teach you a new bad word."

"For real?"

"Yeah, if you get into clean clothes and come out of the tent to play with me, I'll teach you two bad words."

"What if Mom finds out? Is she going to spank us?"

"Only if you use them in front of her."

This lures him from the tent and onto the throw rug.

He giggles maniacally and tries to push my hands away as I change his clothes, but I am victorious. "Teach me a new bad word," he says.

"Hmm," I say.

"You promised!"

"I'm thinking! I know a lot of really, really, really bad words, but I can't teach you those, or Mom is going to do more than spank you."

"There's more than spanking?"

"I'm being hyperbolic."

"Is that a bad word?"

I nod. "Yes. Yes it is. It's a very, very bad word that Jenny taught me, that means exaggerating."

"What's 'exaggerating'? Is that a bad word too?"

I shake my head. "No, exaggerating is a very nice word that means you're making something out to be way bigger or sillier than it is. Like Terrible Charlie is the fattest cat in the whole world."

"He's not!"

"I know! That's exaggerating!"

"Hyper...bolic," he says. Then again proudly, "Hyperbolic! Hyperbolic! Charlie is hyperbolic! Tell me another one."

"First, I think we should make s'mores. Unless you still don't want to."

"I guess I do," he said, shifting from foot to foot. "My feet are cold."

"Clean socks," I say, and help him with those too. With that done, I grab him and pull him close without warning, smothering him in a hug.

"You're squishing me!" he grouses but doesn't try to pull away. "You're clean. You smell nice."

I say, "Thanks, tomorrow you can smell nice too." I feel lighter. That hug and those moments pulling Little just a bit out of his funk and back into the semi-real world has softened the blow of Jenny's departure the tiniest bit. Reminds me of what I still have. The tired is still there, but his simple joy in curse words has charmed some of the black away from my edges.

We make a mess of the camp stove and of ourselves. Charlie, who cannot have chocolate, settles for graham cracker bits. He rolls on his back, fat with satisfaction.

Little points to Charlie's penis. "Hyperbolic dick," he says, and I nearly choke on my dessert.

———

I wake almost refreshed in a tangle of cat and boy-child, relieved we had one night without unwanted visitors—at least as far as I heard. Little's head is stuffed up against my neck, his leg thrown over my torso. The cat has taken over my legs, and I swear he smiles at me when my eyes open. It brings me back to that first night, when we thought things might straighten themselves out. When we believed the authorities were coming. That Mom would be home soon.

I slide out from underneath both boy and cat and head upstairs. Keene greets me with bad news. "I don't think Bill is coming."

In my mind's eye, I see the worst; Bill's house burned to the ground, Bill's shambling, infected form sprawled on the lawn, Bill's zombified wife eating one of his limbs on the roof of their house.

"Something attacked the candle," he says. "It was banging on the door for hours."

So much for no unwanted guests. How did I sleep through that? "Do you think it was attracted by the light?"

"I don't know. Hey, buddy, how was your night?" he asks Little.

"Dick!" says Little.

Keene gives a drawn out, tortured sigh. "I left you alone for one night."

Little giggles and runs into the bathroom.

I get his cereal out, shake it into a bowl. There's no more milk, but he's never been picky about that.

"What if it's Jenny?" Keene says.

"What?" I almost drop the box.

"The thing outside…it could be her."

I sit down hard in the nearest chair. "Oh," I try. My brain is stuck on that one syllable, somewhere between, "No!" and "Oh my God that makes so much sense."

"It might not be," he hurries to add. "It could still be someone from the crash. We thought there were a bunch, right?"

"Five or six," I mutter, hardly hearing myself, turning this new potential nightmare over in my mind.

"And we only know for sure what happened to two, so…"

Three. But Jenny and I never told the boys about the third.

"But it could be," I say. My voice is soft, a whisper, even though I've meant it to be a statement, an agreement, a logical acknowledgment of a thing that could be true, like it might rain tomorrow or the Red Sox might go all the way this year.

Of all the things that could be true, this is the most surreal.

Mom could be dead. Bill could have tried to make a seafood casserole out of the crab parts of the butterflies, and Helsinki could have burned to the ground, and the Mayan empire could have been wiped out by this same plague. But this is making my brain hurt. Jenny could be a monster, trying to break into the house. Or not. Schrödinger's Jenny, at once monster and not.

———

Nathan winces as we round the corner of the kitchen table. His hand tightens painfully on my shoulder. Little has half his games out, perusing his options as if diamond shopping. He glances at us once in a while, waiting for a victim to sit.

"Do you want to stop?"

"Not yet," he says.

We've been walking him every few hours. We take a lap around the downstairs, through the kitchen, into the dining room, back to the den. Reverse. His ankle looks awful. He should probably be in a hospital. How many people are out there right now like him? Broken arms, legs, worse?

"You've had enough," I say. "Really. Time to rest." He doesn't object as I pull out a chair. His forehead shines with sweat. Carefully, I prop his leg up on another chair. I get him a glass of water, more Advil. We're running low. He throws the pills back and gulps down the water.

His butt has barely touched the chair when Little pounces. "Nathan, will you play Go Fish with me?"

Nathan, still ashen with pain, says, "Sure thing."

"You don't have to say yes," I tell him.

"Where else do I have to be?"

"Hey!" Keene comes galloping up the stairs holding the emergency radio in his left hand. He plunks it down on the table, looking pleased.

It fuzzes static.

"That's the radio, congrats," I say.

"Shut up. Someone is on one of the emergency channels... hold on." He leans in, messes with the dial, tweaking this way and that. A faint sound almost resolves to a voice, slips away again.

"—Barrymore," a voice says clear as day, then static again.

"Oh my God!" I say, "Try again!"

The words come, separated by long stretches of static. "Imperative you continue to stay...and...coming.... help is...mobilized." Gone again. Static and static.

"It'll be back," Nathan says encouragingly after a few minutes, seeing Keene's obvious disappointment. "Why don't you try upstairs? I'll hang with my man, here." He and Little grin at each other.

Keene snatches the radio eagerly. I trail him up to my mother's room, then into the bathroom. He sets the radio down on top of the toilet tank and bends, fiddling.

"—from President Barrymore." A woman's voice, deep, serious, full of authority. Clear, but AM distant. She could be anywhere in the world from a deep-earth bunker to our den. "This is a pre-recorded message of the Emergency Broadcast System, updated every twelve hours. This is an automated message on behalf of President Barrymore. Standby to receive. President Barrymore has issued a continuing order for the protection of the people of the United States. It is imperative you continue to stay secure in your location, away from doors, windows, and other points of entry. The Army, Air Force, and National Guard have been mobilized. Help is coming. Repeat, the Army, Air Force, and National Guard have been mobilized. Help is coming. Containment operations are underway. It is imperative that you stay in your homes or other secure locations. Stay away from the infected. If you are bitten, thoroughly clean all injuries with peroxide or alcohol and quarantine the infected in a locked, secured location. Repeat, the infected must be quarantined in a locked, secured location. This is a pre-recorded message of the Emergency Broadcast system, updated every twelve hours."

It starts its loop over. We listen again, then again, unable to tell how far into the twelve hours it might be. When will we get another update?

I punch his shoulder. "Dude!"

"News at least. It's something."

"It is." I know he wishes it would say something new, something more immediately optimistic.

"Guys!" The scream from Nathan is more than a demand for an update. There is real fear and, with it, Little's cries. Something falls over downstairs, a chair maybe. Without further thought, I grab the radio and follow Keene, already in motion, out the door.

We burst into the kitchen. It's empty, the deck of cards neatly stowed in their pack beside a boxed Memory game. Judging by the mess of marbles, they were interrupted playing mancala.

"We're down here!" Nathan calls from the basement.

Keene grabs a knife and I run down the steps.

Nathan's face is a rictus of howling pain, but his panic is worse. "Something was on the porch, Shur. We could hear it out there." He latches onto my arm. "It's trying to get into the dining room through the window. We heard a weird creak, like wood being bent. Like when you pry it."

Prying. Like something clever with a crowbar trying a new way to get in.

Little's face is pale and frightened again, peering out from the tent's opening, one thumb in his mouth, the other slung around Charlie's neck.

"Stay here."

"Where else am I going to go?"

"Right." More needs to be said, some sort of reassurance, but there's no time. "There's a book in the tent. Fairy tales." Nathan looks confused, so I add, "Read to Little. Distract him. And you."

I bolt up the stairs and close the door behind me. "Did you hear Nathan?"

"Yeah." Keene hands me Bill's other uber-blade, the first tight in his right fist. He has a hammer in his other hand.

And here it is, that noise, the creepy, stealthy sound from the window, just as Nathan said. It creaks. Stops. Creaks. There is no voice, no snarling or rage, only patience. It's working slow. I can picture it (her) there on the other side, face pressed against the siding, maybe standing on a box to get height. Bloated. Butterflies lighting on a gnarled arm, curious, probing, smelling infection, taking off again. And it (she) works on, singularly focused on getting in.

"Hey!" Keene shouts and bangs on the wood hard once. Twice. "Fuck off!"

It stops.

It starts again. First the scrape of something being jammed under the wood. Then the patient, patient pressure.

Keene bangs again, but this time it doesn't bother to stop. The sound just keeps on.

"For the love of..." Keene murmurs. He examines the nails and screws. At the very bottom, two nails have pushed away from the wall the tiniest bit. He hits them with the hammer, bangs them back in tight.

If the thing is dissuaded, it does not show. It carries on with its project. Patience, that motion says. I can do this all day and allllll night. I can do this forever. Can you? Little pigs, little pigs, let me come in.

———

It finally stops around 6:00 a.m. It's my watch. Keene is asleep in the chair in the den, or trying to sleep, anyway. Instead of shaking him awake, I listen to the absence of sound. Where will our visitor go now? Into the barn? Under the car? Into the neighborhood to hunt?

She might have a nest of blankets and a few remaining shreds of our food.

Jenny? Jenny, is that you? Did you take the candle to keep us from talking to Bill? You knew all about that, Jenny.

As I contemplate the plywood, my brain is bright and dark at the same time. Dark from lack of sleep, a night spent in the twin rings of yellow light thrown from a pair of candles. Dark with fear, with worry.

But bright with the spark of an idea. We have been defensive so far, small animals in tight holes. We might be able to wait it out like that, like the message said. The Army and Air Force could be here soon with pesticides or flamethrowers or simple guns.

But.

The thing outside is not expecting us to go on offense. We might have the element of surprise. If we have the guts.

If I have the guts.

It might not be her. It might be anyone. It might be a neighbor, or a friend of Marie St. Clair's from the truck. It could be Bill. A stranger. The mailman.

It's not.

I wanted to fight. To leave the cave behind and defend my home. I wasn't expecting to do it against my best friend. This is what I've dreaded all these years, have lost sleep over. Losing. Losing my loved ones the way I lost Dad.

There's something new in my chest, unexpected. It's a hard, red coal of anger. It's at Jenny for leaving, at Dad for dying, at Mom for not being here. It chokes up in my throat. I am angry at the thing outside for trying to take whatever is left, angrier still that it's Jenny outside trying to take everything.

I don't want to kill her, but I can't have her back. So what choice is left if I want everyone else to live?

39

Early in the morning, Keene and I prep for my scouting trip. Sun lights the white bathroom. The plan is that I'll climb out onto the overhang, cross to the carport, and see what there is to see. If there's someone—something—out there that needs handling, only then will one of us risk going out the front door to confront it. This way, I'm still at risk from the butterflies but don't have to add in the potential of being attacked by anything infected.

A butterfly, asleep on the overhang, is startled. It flaps its wings a few times and launches into a blue morning sky. The monsters are almost back to the level they were that first day. Few and far between. Still, I'm not especially excited about climbing out onto the overhang or onto the carport. It only takes one bite. I'm suited up again in my winter clothes, knife in my pocket. Ready for battle. I'd feel better in chain mail.

"I'm sweating my balls off," I tell Keene. Moist breath bounces back into my face, icky and ripe.

"If you had balls."

"I did before I put this on, and now they're gone, and that's the story I'm telling my grandchildren."

"Grandchildren. So optimistic." He peers out the window. "Nothing to see but butterflies and blue skies."

"So the Army isn't coming down the street?"

"Nope."

"I guess I'd better do it, then," I say. "Hugs for luck."

He holds out his arms, so I can wrap mine around his lanky torso. I can barely feel him through the layers. He can't hug back; he has a broom in one hand and the hatchet in the other. "Be careful."

"I'll be right there," I say, pointing to the spot I mean.

"Yeah? So be careful anyway."

It's a challenge to maneuver out, even though the window is large. The padding makes everything harder. I overexaggerate every movement in my desire to neither fall to my death nor be bitten. Ski goggles color my world pink. I don't need them for the sun or snow glare, but they provide a useful barrier over my eyes. Another few inches of skin covered. A pair of butterflies approach. I hold perfectly still. They hover for a moment, checking me out, then flutter off.

If they're dying off, the yard should be littered with corpses, piles of wings and legs and teeth. But there's nothing, exactly like in the bin, where even the leftover legs have disappeared. There may be a fine, foreign dust on the fall grass, but I can't tell for sure through the pink tint.

I squat on the asphalt shingles and contemplate the move to the carport.

"Can you handle this?" Keene asks. "I can do it instead."

"Just remembering I don't love heights."

"Can you see anything from there?"

The goggles are fogging with my breath in the cool morning. "I might have to take these off."

"Keep them on."

"I'm going across. The view from here is shit." I can see up the driveway to the mailbox and across to the neighbors on that side of the house, but that's about all. There's a gap of maybe three feet, not a huge space, but it's still vertigo-inducing to see pavement and the house step below. Overhead, a cluster of butterflies move along on their lazy way, at least a dozen in all. They pay me no mind.

Before I can overthink, I take a giant step across, placing a boot on the carport's edge. The metal clangs and the whole structure shakes. I stand straddling the gap, surprised by the sound and the motion, not sure if it'll hold or tip.

"It's fine," Keene coaches. "Keep going. Bend forward slowly and get your knee and upper body down, then pull your other leg over. You've got this."

I drop my hands to the metal surface. It's like doing a stretch for soccer, maybe a lunge. My back leg stays on the roof. I look back in time to see a butterfly settle on my snow pants. It ticks its wings. I hear Keene's soft intake of air.

Slowly, careful to stay steady (and not daring to breathe), I bring my stiff, straight leg and its hitchhiker across the gap. The stolen folding knife is in my pocket, and I free it gently with one hand. It drops from my fat, gloved fingers to the carport's roof, clanging like a bell, like an alarm.

The butterfly, disturbed by the noise, pushes off and disappears over the roof.

I let out my breath and pick the knife up.

"Jesus," Keene says.

I have a thick tongue, dry throat, and no words. A pair of binoculars hangs around my neck. They aren't great ones, a basic pair Mom sometimes took with us to concerts if we had bad seats. I hold them to my eyes. The adjustment dial is awkward under the glove's thickness, and it takes me several tries to focus. I'm hoping the binoculars will help me pick out anything that's hiding, especially in the thick bushes and trees at the edge of the property or in neighboring yards.

I turn in a circle looking for our attacker.

Looking for Jenny.

If not for current circumstances, this would be a perfectly normal day, almost exactly like the day all this started. There's the barn, same as always, door shut. The neighbor's house peeking over the top of the arborvitae line separating our properties. The street, devoid of traffic. Bill's house, shut up, quiet and dark. His neighbor's house, another line of pines, a fire hydrant.

Movement at the back of the yard catches my eyes on the next turn, near the not-yet-fall-touched tree. There's a tall, wooden fence there, containment for our back neighbor's Scottish terriers. I fix the binoculars, adjust with my fat fingers. Animal? Butterfly?

Jenny?

I see nothing. My heart beats hard and fast in my ears under the thick hat.

"Do you see her?"

"I don't—" My heart seems to stop for a beat. There, right up against the fence, crouching behind a bush. Movement. Too large to be an animal. It's squatting, shuffling.

I see red. Not clothing. Blood. There is no clothing I can make out, not even with the binoculars. The thing is brown all over, still alive. It has a raccoon clutched in its hands, rips at it with its mouth. I force myself to watch, to not vomit the nothing in my stomach up onto the carport roof.

It's the right size to be Jenny. Smallish, but also sex-less. It could be a short woman, a boy. It could be anyone.

Jenny. She didn't want to go far, didn't want to leave us. Here she is, a monster.

"I see someone," I say, and my voice is calm. It takes me by surprise, hearing myself like that. I turn away from her, do another full check of the area. Looking for others. Any indication this might be the people from the truck, and not my wayward friend, all on her own.

Not alone, she has a raccoon, I think, and that time I almost lose the battle with my stomach.

I see no one else, no matter how many times I check.

"Coming back," I tell Keene. He steps back as I make the half leap then helps me in through the window. He slides it shut and latches it before turning to help me with the layers of my safe-suit.

The air is blessedly cool against my skin. Keene takes each layer and hangs it along the edge of the tub to air dry, so saturated is it with all my sweat. My lips feel chapped and burned. He hands me a bottle of room-temperature water and I gulp it down.

"I think I saw her," I say. "No clothes or anything. Hair was gone."

"What was she doing?"

"Eating," I say, and he doesn't ask what.

"She was alone?"

"Just her."

We look at each other, understanding what this means next. One of us has to take care of her. Put her down. That will be the last gift we can give to Jenny—an end to her suffering and the beginning of a new chapter of ours.

40

B ut are you sure it's her?" Nathan asks. He's antsy and wants to pace but is stuck on the trundle bed. It's pushed against the wall outside the tent so he can sit up or get up easily by pushing off. Not that he's able to go far. He can hand-over-hand around the basement, leaning on supports or the stairs or walls to get to the toilet, but that's about it. He's frustrated with his own limitations and inability to help.

"No," I say.

"I just..." he starts. "I don't know what to do with this."

"Yeah," I agree.

"But you guys think you should..." He cuts himself off, doesn't want to say. We're whispering side by side while Keene reads to Little behind the makeshift curtain, with Little perched on the camp potty, pants around his ankles.

"We don't know," I say. "You heard that noise. The prying."

"It scared me," he says. "It wasn't like the pounding."

"Right." He gets it at least, and my chest eases with relief. I thought he'd fight us, scream at us, but instead Nathan is thoughtful. "Tell me again about the butterflies?"

I've told him three times, recounted our adventures in turns with Keene as we keep Little contained to the basement and unaware of what's going on. Nathan might not have panicked, but Little will for sure. "Way fewer. One landed on me and took off again like it was nothing."

"But you think it didn't smell you? Didn't register you as food because of all the layers?"

"I mean, best guess? Didn't register me as food or already ate."

"But there are fewer." His head bobs up and down. "Fewer. That's good. Oh God, I feel so freaking useless."

"You're not, though. You're kind of critical. We literally can't do this without you."

"Oh come on," he says.

"No, seriously. We're trusting you to keep Little safe. He's... you know..."

"The most valuable thing you have?"

I wouldn't have thought to phrase it that way, but it's accurate. "Yeah."

Nathan puts an arm around my shoulder. His fingers are cold. "I get it. You want to keep him safe."

"And you. And all of us."

"Yeah. Jesus, how am I supposed to keep it together?"

This, I have recent and very painful experience in. "I know how you feel, Nathan. When you guys went to the barn..."

"Yeah. And me, babbling on about macaroni and cheese."

"It was good macaroni and cheese."

"It was awesome. When this is over, I want that again."

"Me too."

He takes my hand and squeezes it. "I get why it has to be done. Like, logically? But I still don't want you guys to do it."

"Me too."

"It's Jenny." His eyes roll toward the ceiling, and I wonder if he's crying, or trying not to. "And going out there...it's a little too real."

"But that's the thing, Nathan. It's all real."

"I know."

We've already talked about all the ways it could go wrong. Noises he might hear. What might be waiting in the yard. How hard it will be to manage the baby and the cat with a broken ankle if something happens to me and Keene. But if something gets in and downstairs, it's better to have a plan, to talk about all the bad things that might be and prepare, than to pretend we've totally got this.

Because we don't. Jenny might not be alone out there. Or she might have a plan of her own. Or one of us might get bitten.

So many things could go wrong.

"The door locks from this side, which isn't helpful. Keene rigged up some rope to the deadbolt on the hatch. You'll loop it around the knob, once you're inside, okay? Keene will show you how. If someone tries to open the door, they won't be able to."

Nathan nods, looking miserable.

"I'm putting the car keys in the hatchway, and we'll leave the inside door open. Keene will put Charlie in his carrier in there too. And a flashlight, plus a blanket to cover you all if you have to go out. If things go wrong..."

"Up and out, into the car, drive away."

Assuming no one has sabotaged the car.

"One more thing," I say, wanting to end the conversation, but also never wanting it to end. "The secret knock. So you know it's us."

Nathan laughs, the misery momentarily passing from his face. "You could just say 'it's us.'"

"Humor me." I knock twice, pause, three more times. "That's me."

He reaches over and pulls me into a tight hug, his breath tickling my ear. "It's going to be okay, right?"

"Sure," I say with a lump in my throat. "Of course."

Keene has stalled Little as long as he can. Little skips over, trailed by Charlie, who streaks into the tent. He knows something is up.

"Hey, Little," I say. "Me and Keene have some stuff to do upstairs. You're going to hang out down here with Nathan for a while. You need to do everything he says. Be a very good boy."

"What are you going to do?" Little asks.

"Clean up some stuff," Keene says vaguely.

"Oh." He considers. "Then can we make s'mores again? That was messy."

"Sure," I say.

"Can I jump on the bed?" Little asks Nathan.

"No, it might break. How about we read a book?" He lifts up "Verdes Huevos y Jambon," one of my mother's perpetual attempts to better Little—a second language while his brain was still blank, infant-swimming classes, preschool karate classes, and a dozen other things to enrich his babyhood.

And here we are, trying to keep him not-dead, our best form of enrichment yet.

"Can I bounce?"

"Yes, on your butt," Nathan says. "But only away from the edges. You don't want to crack your head open."

"I'm not an egg!"

Keene's hand finds mine. We want to hug Little and say good-bye, but we also don't want to scare him. This will have to do. Keene makes an excuse about containing the cat while we're gone and gets a scratch for his efforts. I put the survival gear into the hatchway while Little is distracted. Together, we trudge up the stairs to the kitchen and close the door behind us on what's left of our family.

This is the plan: Keene will go out the front door, around the side of the house, take care of the thing in the back yard, and book it back. I will stand guard and open the door when he returns, whether it's at a dead sprint or his own leisurely pace. We'll each have an Elmo walkie-talkie. Nathan and Little will stay near the hatchway in case they need to make a sudden exit.

I'm having second thoughts.

"We have to," Keene reassures me. There are so many reasons to do it. But we're not hunters. And between the two of us, I'm one who's actually killed...something. I don't want to think of Marie St. Clair or her nameless friend as someone. The infection killed the someone part. Still, will Keene be able to do it when he's not under attack? Will it attack? Will he freeze up?

"I should go."

"It's my turn," Keene says. "You did the roof thing."

"That doesn't count."

"Sure it does. Help me with this stupid coat. It's too small."

The thick snowboarding jacket slides up over his shoulders, and I tug the hoodie of his sweatshirt loose. It pools against his back.

"You probably should have said goodbye to Little," I say.

"No need. I'll be right back. Jesus," he says, tugging at the crotch of his snow pants. "Should have lost the jeans first. Anyway, it's going to work out fine."

I hate when he dismisses my worry, but it's probably bravado. He doesn't want to go, but he doesn't want me to go. And he doesn't want me to see his fear.

"My therapist says I'm angry at Dad for not getting to say goodbye," I blurt. We don't talk about my therapist. That is, I don't talk about my therapist. Sometimes, he or Jenny or Mom try, but I shut it down. It's bad enough I have to be in therapy, forget chatting about it.

"We did say goodbye to Dad," he says.

"Maybe it was enough for you," I say.

"This isn't goodbye, Shur." He pulls the goggles down over his eyes. "Look. We can talk about it when I get back. Let's focus on the job."

"I love you."

"I love you too. That's why I'm doing it. For you and Little and Nathan."

"And Mom."

He doesn't respond to this but turns toward the door with the knife in hand, unsheathed. "Ready?"

I wind his scarf around his neck, the final piece of protection. "I guess."

"Listen. If I'm wrong and I die out there, I give you permission to be really, really angry at me for as long as it takes to get over it. And you're right, this getup is hot as balls."

I peer through the peephole out onto the porch. No one to see. Almost no butterflies. Hand on the deadbolt, a click as it opens.

"Don't take any risks, don't hesitate. She's not human anymore." I drop a shaking, sweating hand to the doorknob. "Keene, you're my best person. I can't lose you."

"Ditto, sis. That's why I'm going and you're staying. Back in five." He digs in his pocket, liberates Elmo with his free, not-knife-wielding hand.

He's out the door and onto the porch with a clomp of his boots. I softly close the door behind him and throw the lock.

We've agreed that I'll keep watch from the window in Mom's bathroom. I push open the door, trying to slow the rampant charge of my heart. I feel sick and frightened, but there's nothing to be done about that. I blink in the sudden light and brace myself, maybe half expecting to see a ghoulish face pressed up against the glass, fumbling for a way in. There's nothing more menacing there than a lingering butterfly sunning itself on the carport roof.

I wish we had more than the two walkie-talkies so I could tell Nathan what's going on, but maybe it's better this way, because, if I did tell him, Little would hear. Still, spread out like this, I feel like we're so exposed. Outside is supposed to stay outside; inside is supposed to stay in.

"Are you there?" I whisper into Elmo's plastic face.

It takes a second before he comes back. "Yeah. These gloves are a nightmare to press buttons with. I'm at the corner of the house. I just passed under the carport. Not a lot of butterflies."

"Do you see anyone?"

"Not yet."

Elmo falls silent. I can't see him from this angle. If the butterfly wasn't parked right there, I might risk opening the window to lean out. I pace, impatient, bare feet on the cool tile.

"I see her," he says.

"Are you sure it's her?"

Silence. "I can't tell. It's like you said—her size. It's all hunched over." He pauses. "I just can't tell. I'm going to get closer."

"Please be careful."

"I am," he says. "I'll tell you as soon as it's done."

I press against the glass again and this time catch a red flash, Keene's coat. He's creeping low at the edge of my line of sight. Maybe red wasn't the best color for stealth. Maybe we should have thought that through. Maybe the thing can't see him, has its back to him. Maybe he has half a chance at striking before he's seen. That would prevent a struggle and any real agony. To either of them.

Movement from the barn. My eye is drawn that way, not sure what I've seen but then, there it is. A second person, a new threat emerges from behind the barn, but I lose it fast because of the crap angle. It's a person, definitely a person, or a thing, oh God maybe it's a thing and not a person at all.

"Keene!" I shout into the walkie. "Look out!"

From downstairs comes a sound that I've heard in my dreams,

in my dark nightmares, driving me awake in my own sweat choking back screams. A sound we were waiting to hear when we took turns guarding the window in the dining room.

A huge crash. Wood hitting the floor.

Something has made it inside.

41

As I creep down the front hall, fast and quiet, I whisper rapid-fire into the walkie-talkie. "Keene!" I say. "Someone's inside!" Then, hoping he heard it, hoping he's not grappling with the second person, hoping, hoping I'm not talking to myself and already alone in the world, I snap the radio off. If he is there, I can't have his reply give away my position. I push all these thoughts aside. There is no room for anything but defending the house.

Pressed against the wall, I take the stairs carefully, trying to make no noise. The air sounds wrong, sounds open. Boarded rooms are muffled and stagnant. Noise goes nowhere. Now, outside floods in. Wind. Rustling leaves. A breeze pushes up the stairs, kisses my cheek. There's flapping in the dining room. The drapes.

I'm not alone. I can't explain the feeling, the sureness of it, but it's true. No one should be here, but someone is here. Someone is close. Aware of me. And I, aware of them.

He steps out of the dining room as if greeting me, squaring against the base of the steps and blocking my way forward. He—it—is a decaying bear of a man, still wearing the scraps of a black sweater, black cargo pants, the black combat boots I knew he and his friends would have on, but never actually saw. His fists are huge, how can human hands be that big? My giant knife seems inadequate, a toothpick compared with the mass of him. Skin, brown and black and white, mottled together, ripe, rippling. Red eyes. Bleeding gums when his lips part into a malicious grin. He takes a step toward me.

I have to lead him away from the others, away from the kitchen and the stairs, distract him long enough to end him. Maybe the others will be safe if I do this. How can I warn Nathan? My mind whispers their names, Keene, Little, Nathan in a litany. The soft breeze carries a breath of fall and the stench of organic things left in the damp dark for too long. Carefully, I move my left foot back up one stair, feeling along the wall for support. I do not lose contact with those sunken, determined eyes.

He bolts at me without warning, fast despite his size and condition, but I'm ready—was born ready. I am sheer adrenaline alight on terror's wings. I stampede up the stairs, down the hallway, straight to my mother's room. There is only one place to go. I must lure him outside, through the bathroom window without getting caught. Without getting bitten by him or the butterflies.

I catch a lucky break. His momentum sends him stumbling on the last step, ricocheting into the wall. His slick hands leave a trail of slime as he pushes off, head up, eyes locked onto me. I slam the door and throw the lock. It won't hold long.

The bathroom. I charge across the room, fumble with the

window lock, throw up the sash. His shoulder hits the outer door. Bam! Bam! Bam! I fumble with the screen. It comes loose in my hands, and I push it out, letting it fall into the gap between the roof and the carport. It hardly makes a noise when it hits, light as it is, or maybe I just can't hear anything past the blood rush in my ears.

The last *bam!* is answered with splintering. The bedroom door ricochets against the wall with a noisy thump. I think of my mother yelling at us not to slam doors, a rogue thought, then I'm out the window and squatting on the roof with nothing but my inadequate knife for defense, rough asphalt scraping my feet.

"Come on," I mutter. "Come on." Keene is nowhere to be seen. There is a body splayed out on the grass, not wearing a red jacket, mercifully. Not him. No sign of the second attacker. Heavy footsteps echo through my mother's room. I can taste blood, taste bile. "Come on out," I mutter. In the open, I'll be able to outrun him. The few butterflies hanging around are complacent, still. Dying, I hope.

The beast is coming. He's in the bathroom doorway, taking up the whole frame, squinting at the bright light. I make sure he sees me. He comes to the window, confident. I am a cornered thing. As he reaches, I rise and make the big jump across the gap to the carport, hands shaking. I land badly, knee down. The entire structure rings, hammer on thin steel. I almost lose the knife, but manage to keep it, bruising my knuckles as that hand collides.

We consider each other for a moment.

"Come on!" I shout.

He brings one massive hand up to shield his eyes, considering me. Horribly, that smile again, blood and slime oozing from cracked lips. He reaches out and pushes the window closed, flicks the latch.

I am locked outside.

Terrified, raging at myself for being so easily tricked, I drop the knife off the carport on purpose, with the express intent of following it down. It clatters to the driveway below. The edge of the port is raw metal, too sharp to grab, so I cross back to the little overhang. It groans as it takes my weight yet again, probably not built to withstand people jumping onto it repeatedly.

I drop to my butt and scoot to the edge, one eye still on the few passive butterflies, and flip over only my belly. My sweatshirt rides up and asphalt rakes at the bare skin as I slide over the edge. I dangle by two sore, miserable arms, completely exposed if the butterflies choose this moment to attack. It's a drop to the steps below, but not much of one. I let go, land, stagger, and go to one knee. My bare feet sting with the impact.

On the crossbar, a butterfly sits, wings closed. I can't tell if it's awake, asleep, dying, or waiting. A few scant feet away, the decaying corpses of our two visitors bloat in the early fall warmth. The stench is horrific. Gas has inflated them; they are almost unrecognizable as human. The skin squirms with parasites, larva, maggots. A buffet. I back up, tearing my eyes away, and collect my knife from where it's fallen.

The butterfly on the crossbar launches itself straight at me.

It's fast. One moment it's at rest, the next it's pushing off, legs unfurling at the same time. It's like a hawk in final approach to a rabbit running in a field. The maw is already open, yawning to latch on. Some part of me, a feral part, the born hunter, lets out a scream of rage. Adrenaline and instinct meet at the knife's hilt, swinging. I catch the nightmare with a long slash of the knife, nearly removing a wing as I dodge to the side. It spirals to the ground, clicking and clicking, jaw and pincers snapping and angry. But not as angry as me. I slice its head off and cast it aside. It goes on twitching in its death throes, but I have no time for this.

I race to the front of the house and the bashed-in window. All around, the neighborhood is eerily silent, no cars, no movement. The truck is still parked in the living room of the house across the way, flags limp, one wheel off the ground. No neighborhood kids, no whine of mowers. The damp, shaggy lawn under my bare soles needs mowing.

Of Keene or the second attacker, there is no sign. I try the front door hopefully. Maybe I didn't lock it during prep? I know I did. I checked it three times. The door is, infuriatingly, locked.

I contemplate how to boost myself up through the gaping, jagged hole that is the dining room window without cutting myself to shreds. Before I can figure anything out, there is a click at the door. I jump back, knife up. The door swings open.

Keene stands just inside. He snaps a finger up to his lips. Quiet. He motions farther into the house. I nod, follow. He's shed his goggles, hat, gloves, and mask. They lay in a pile just inside. A huge, dark splash of blood (or something like it) covers the front of his jacket, emanating stink. There's no time think of what that stain means right now. Keene leads the way to the kitchen.

The monster stands there with the basement door wide open,

staring down, head cocked. Listening. Or smelling. Scenting prey. Easier prey than me or Keene.

Keene yells, "Hey! Ugly!"

His head snaps toward us. I know what Keene is doing: It's at once a warning to Nathan and a hope to distract this thing long enough for Nathan to take that warning and run (limp) with it. But the thing's entire body seems to flex. He moves without preamble, starts right for us, picking up speed. We don't wait either. I run into the den; Keene bolts toward the dining room. It follows him.

I slide back into the kitchen and close the basement door, pressing it shut until the latch clicks. I press my back against it. The house is quiet as the new game of cat and mouse progresses. I wish I could silently nail the basement door closed, but there is no time, no tools, no way to keep attention from myself long enough.

Why didn't we do that earlier? Why didn't we do a better job of securing them rather than a length of rope rigged to a door-knob? Because we never really believed something would get into the house, despite things constantly getting into the house. We thought the offense negated the need for defense. Again, I am angry at myself but, again, there is no time to contemplate anything but the situation unfolding. I force my mind calm. The trip outside was supposed to be the security, no point in second-guessing that now. Nathan must have heard, has had enough time to get Little inside the hatchway and secure the door with the rope. They are huddled in the dark space with only a flashlight for comfort. Maybe an angry Charlie is yowling, or maybe they are all silent. I tighten my grip on the knife and will my mind to stop, stop thinking, stop and focus. Focus on the sounds on this floor.

Quiet. A thump. Stealthy footsteps. More. Frantic, I try to see anything, movement, a glint of light, shadow. The footsteps are coming from the dining room...no, the den...no...

Keene backs into the kitchen from the den, knife held out in front of him. His hand is shaking badly. He crosses the threshold, tensed.

The thing is visible only for a moment before it leaps, almost before my mind registers that it's here; it's here with us right now, huge, the smell of it, the rage of it filling the kitchen. He, it, grabs Keene's arm, yanks it hard sideways and the knife skitters away even as Keene screams in pain and fear. That scream, that scream is my nightmare. One giant hand closes on Keene's throat, squeezing, pulling him forward even as Keene tries to dig in with his heels. I shriek and bound forward, but I'm rewarded with a fist to the face I never see coming. My mouth fills with blood, my vision is a field of stars on a black night. I find myself on the floor, on hands and knees, about to witness the death of my other half. We came into this world together. We will go out the same way. I scramble up and prepare to charge again, even though I see two, three, four of the monster.

And then the thing stops cold with a grunt, hand still squeezing Keene's throat. Maybe the pressure has lessened too, because Keene's own struggles become more vigorous, like he can breathe again. The monster touches its own chest with its free hand. Three long metal objects have appeared. They are needlelike growths, slicked brown and damp. As I watch, they recede a little, then erupt even more fully. The thing's grunting ramps into a high-pitched whistle, a punctured balloon, a kettle nearing full boil. It drops to one knee, pulling Keene down with it.

Keene grapples with the giant hand and rips free, staggering backwards until he bumps into the kitchen table. His throat is gray and bruised above the red coat. Tomorrow, he will have a necklace of a hand print. If we survive.

The thing balances on one knee, wondering at the growth in its chest. It touches one prong gently. In response, the thing retracts again, and emerges again. The red eyes roll up, and he keels over sideways, crashing to the floor.

There, standing in the entry to the den, just behind it, is Jenny. The handle of the pitchfork has been yanked from her hands as the thing fell over. She looks dreadful, sick and tired, dark circles under her eyes, in the same clothes she's been wearing for days. She has a makeshift sling around her neck, no longer holding her injured arm in place. The bandage is the only clean thing on her.

She says, "Are you guys okay?"

I give the only appropriate response. I burst into tears.

It's a long time before I can bring myself to let go of Jenny. I cling to her, sobbing, both of us needing showers and to burn our clothes. She holds on as tight as she can with one arm. The other is still a wreck, but her skin feels cool. No fever.

"Yeah, sure, you guys stand there and cry while I take care of the window," Keene grumbles, but pauses to kiss Jenny's forehead on the way by. "Glad you're alive, doofus."

"You're welcome for the life save," she says.

Just like normal.

"Come on," I say to Jenny, leading the way down the basement stairs.

"It's me," I call from outside the hatchway door, and then give the secret knock, *knock knock*, pause, *knock knock knock*. Just in case Nathan heard the fight upstairs and assumed the worst. I hope they're still in there. There's a chance they've gone outside.

Again. I say, "It's us."

There's some shuffling inside, and Nathan's pale face appears in the crack as he opens the door.

"Holy shit, Shur, I thought—" He stops abruptly as he sees Jenny and throws the door the rest of the way open, hopping forward. "We thought you guys were all dead. Jenny!"

She looks at his leg. "What happened to you?"

"Battle injury."

"He tripped over a monster," I say.

Little screams, "Jenny! Jenny! Jenny!" and shoves past Nathan. Nathan winces as his leg is jostled, but even the pain can't keep the smile off his face for long. He's radiant, like a whole mountain slid off his shoulders. Sure he is. He thought we were all dead; instead, he got a friend back.

"We were in the dark, and there was just a flashlight and a monster got in the house and Charlie was in the box and he was mad! Are you still sick?" Little is talking so fast, he might explode with excitement.

I shuffle past Nathan up to the hatch doors and slide the bolt back in place. No more surprise entries. I open Charlie's box, and he growls at me before streaking across the basement, straight to the litter box.

"The butterflies are almost gone," I tell Nathan.

"That's something," he says and holds out his arm. I slide under it, allowing him to half embrace me. He leans down and kisses the top of my head. "Man, this is the weirdest day. But good weird, right?"

"Right," says Jenny. "I need a shower, and I'm super hungry."

"Oh, of course you are," Nathan says. "But someone needs to fill me in on what happened."

———

Nathan's fill-in waits. First, there is an impaled corpse in the kitchen to be dealt with. Keene and I do that. I am so tired. We drag it outside together as Jenny stands guard with the broom. It doesn't take long, but I swear this body weighs as much as the other two combined. It drips slime, oozes blood. A dark pool stains the kitchen floor, and we leave a trail as we drag his heft to the door.

"I went to the barn," Jenny explains as we work. "The fever was bad, and I was sure I was turning into whatever this thing is."

"You should have stayed," Keene mutters. His voice is clogged. He's trying to breathe through his mouth to keep the stench from getting up in there.

"Maybe," she says. "I kept taking the antibiotics. I was really sick for a full day. I was laid out on your mother's couch in the loft, praying no butterflies got in, drinking water, eating soup right from the can. I think I slept for twenty-four straight hours. I did my business in a bucket."

"Tell Little, he'll love that," I say.

We pause at the door, both in her story and physically. "Ready?" Keene asks.

"Hey, I'm the one who's done this twice," I say.

The bloated, rotting bodies are still right where I left them, along with the now-still corpse of the one-winged butterfly that tried to mess with me earlier. Keene raises an eyebrow at me over the top of the dead monster's head. I rescue the dead giant's wallet before we leave him to decay beside his friends, but it will be a long, long time before I can bring myself to look at it or to think of him as human.

With the door firmly shut, Keene screws the doorstop back into place. Secure. Hopefully.

"There were so many butterflies still," Jenny resumes. "I figured I'd wait until I ran out of food. I've been watching for more of those things, or for a sign of the Army, or Bill, or anyone, but all I saw was that huge guy and another girl."

"The raccoon girl," I say, thinking of the dark blood all over the front of Keene's ski jacket. "We thought...well, we thought she was you."

There's a long beat of silence while Jenny absorbs that Keene was out there to kill her.

"Okay then," she says, pushing past this new knowledge. "What now?"

"We clean up the blood, bleach the floor. Get rid of these clothes, take showers. Figure out how to stand guard," I say, ticking it all off on my fingers.

"I'd like a shower," Jenny says softly. "And to use a real toilet."

"The butterflies are almost gone," Keene says again. I think he's saying it to himself. Not to us, but aloud, to make it more real. "Maybe it's almost over?"

"Now we wait," I say. "For the National Guard or Army, or Bill knocking on the door."

"For Mom," he says, so low I almost don't catch it.

"For Mom," I agree, forcing myself to sound upbeat. "For the power, for whatever. But if the butterflies are almost gone..."

"Then it might just be a matter of time," Jenny says.

"Can I come upstairs yet?" Little shrieks from the basement. "I want to see Jenny again!"

"A matter of time," Keene says, ignoring Little. His eye catches mine. Neither of us wants to come right out and say what we're feeling, but it's hope.

EPILOGUE

Normally I hate winter. I hate the cold. The snow is pretty, can be fun, even, but most of the time the world is grimy and barren, pocked with dirt, gutters lined with sand, black ice lurking in the driveway.

I will never hate winter again.

Winter came and the bugs died. I don't mean the butterflies—they were long gone—but the normal, seasonal bugs. I don't think I was ever so aware of just how many bugs there are in the world until I stepped outside into the sunlight after the crisis was over, right into a swarm of gnats. The mosquitoes and flies and bees carried on like nothing had happened. For them, nothing had, I guess, except there were fewer birds and other predators to pick them off. Even the harmless noise of crickets in the night sent me into a cold sweat. I prayed for winter, and now it's here.

"Close the damn door, Shur. You're letting out all the warm air." Mom is in the kitchen, cooking.

"Damn, damn, damn!" Little says from the couch.

"I heard that, young man," Mom calls. "That's not a word for you."

It was a week before Mom made it back to us after the butterflies died out. I thought it would be right away, and Keene's conviction that she was dead wanted to take root in my head so bad, but I wouldn't let it. My brain wanted to fill in every terrible scenario: She got bitten; she starved to death; that guy who was bitten in her office went nuts and murdered everyone. They treated his wound with stuff from the kitchen. Turns out that cold sunflower oil is as effective as peroxide at killing bacteria. Who knew?

There were lots of people like Jenny and that kid TJ from Jos's Insta post, who got bit and recovered. Then there were other people who weren't so lucky. The scientists said their bodies were sort of made for the pathogen. It moved like fire through their systems, wreaking havoc and torching everything it touched. Then there were people who were naturally immune. Got bit, and nothing happened except a gruesome scar. The government is super interested in those folks, in case they need to make an antibiotic or vaccine or whatever. For if the butterflies come back. But I try not to dwell on that, or I'd never go outside again.

After the butterflies were gone, there were power lines down everywhere and trees across roads, almost like a storm had happened. The "storm" was car crashes and fires, all sorts of man-made disasters. Also, the Army didn't want anyone coming out of their shelter-in-place until they had a chance to check out the living and dead alike. There were way more civilians than military, so that took a while.

Mom doesn't talk about what happened to her. I think it was

worse than she lets on because she's up a lot of nights, pacing. She's not so good with the dark these days.

I step out onto the front porch and close the door behind me. We're two days into a polar vortex, and it's so cold I can feel it in my teeth.

The neighborhood is mostly quiet. Bill's chickens survived the ordeal in his basement, and I can hear them clucking clear across the street. Bill brings us fresh eggs regularly. I think he feels sort of bad about inadvertently triggering the series of events that nearly got us killed, but he was defending the neighborhood. It's not his fault the Butterfly Militia hit a pole. And a house.

The house across the street is still empty, with a huge hole where the front windows used to be. I hate seeing it. A team came and pried the destroyed truck loose from the living room. There was a gunshot that day, when the Army went inside. We don't talk about that either.

The hum of an engine is coming our way. There's been a gasoline shortage for months, so hearing cars is uncommon. Even if there wasn't, there's hardly any place to go. So many people are dead or grieving, the world has sort of found itself in a strange wasteland in between the disaster and the before. Sun glints off the windshield of Nathan's dad's SUV as it turns the corner onto our street and here they are, the rest of our little family.

Behind me, Jenny throws the door open. "See? He made it even without your relentless stalking," she says, bounding down the stairs to help Mr. Iverson with the supplies he promised to bring with him today.

I move around to the passenger side of the car, where Nathan's sister, Trista, is already climbing out of the back seat.

Trista hugs me tight. We've spent a lot of time together, our family and Nathan's, in the past five months. Mrs. Iverson made it home (that's where she called Nathan from) and died in her own bedroom. Deliberate overdose. She left a note. None of them like to be in the house, so they're often over here, Nathan camped out in Keene's new room. Keene and I swapped rooms. I can't stand to be in my old room, even for a few minutes at a time, but he doesn't seem to mind the room's history. Trista bunks up with me and Jenny, and Ben stays on the couch in the den.

My mom has taken on the role of mother figure for both Trista and Jenny. Jenny lost her mom, but no one views her step-father as a loss. She cries herself to sleep at night sometimes and doesn't think I hear. Her scars are hideous, but she's proud of them. Proud of surviving.

"You want help with him?" Trista asks.

"I'm not an invalid," Nathan says, pushing the car door open.

"You sort of are," Trista corrects. She's not wrong. His ankle had to be rebroken and set with pins, and it's taking a very long time to heal.

"I've got this," I say. Trista grabs a box from the back seat and hurries after her father, who is already on the porch with a bag in one arm and an overexcited, underdressed Little in the other. Little adores Mr. Iverson. I can picture a world where he grows up not remembering a time when the Iversons were ever not part of our family. We're not supposed to know, but Mom and Mr. Iverson have been talking about all of us moving in together. This found family feels so important to me, and not just because I'm totally and completely in love with Nathan.

"Hey, beautiful," he says, handing me his crutch.

"Hey yourself," I say. "How's your pain level today?"

"Tolerable."

"Would you lie to me?"

He says, "I'll tell you whatever needs saying to keep that smile on your face."

I smile, because that's what I do when Nathan is around.

I reach for his hand before he can stand up, and he pulls me in close. Air puffs out from the interior, enveloping us in a warm pocket.

"I missed you," I say.

"I was only gone for a day."

"So you didn't miss me?"

"Of course I missed you," Nathan says.

"Well, you were only gone for a day."

He kisses me lightly on the lips, and an electric thrill goes through my body, exactly like it always does when he's this close.

"What did the doctor say?" I ask.

"Another month with the boot, then physical therapy," he says. "Keene keeps daring me to take the top bunk."

"Clearly he's trying to kill you."

"I don't think he likes that I'm dating his sister."

I giggle involuntarily.

"What's funny?"

"Dating," I say. "Like we've ever gone anywhere besides the barn."

"We went to the library that one time," Nathan says.

"I don't think it's a date if Little is with us."

"Someday I will take you on a real date."

"Oh, tell me about this date," I say.

"We'll pack a picnic lunch. You'll make that macaroni and cheese with chicken, and we'll take it on a hike to a beautiful spot," he says. "And we'll eat."

"I think you're more in love with the mac and cheese than you are with me."

"You could be right," he says, and I whack him lightly.

"Hey!" Keene yells from the porch. "Hands off my sister. Mom says to get in here so we can have dinner."

"I can't tell if he's happy we're together or is planning to kill me in my sleep," Nathan says.

"Could go either way." I don't tell him that Keene's good at masking his anxiety, but I can see right through it and he's a hot mess. That's between me and Keene, for now. Mom sees it, sort of, but not like a twin sees it. Feels it. I hate that he finally gets what I've been feeling all these years, but at least he's not alone.

"Alright, Mr. Iverson," I order. "On your feet. Let's get you inside." I help Nathan upright and hand him his crutch. He hobbles toward the house, but I can see improvement. If there's soccer in the fall, he might actually get to play. We'll see.

Once he's made it over the threshold, I stop to take another look at the barren street. Truth be told, we're afraid for fall. We're afraid for spring. The scientific community is confident in their theory that the butterflies hatch in a cicada-like fashion. They can't promise that it won't happen again, even though they're using special insectides designed to wipe out the eggs. And what if something even worse comes out of the ground next time?

Behind me, Jenny laughs and Keene grumbles. There's a fire in the fireplace and dinner on the table. For now, I can set my anxiety aside and live in this moment. The people I love are safe and together. I protected them as best I could, and they protected me. If it happens again, we have each other. We know just how strong we really are.

We survived.

ACKNOWLEDGMENTS

Writing a book is hard. Getting it published practically takes an act of God. To that end, I'd like to thank the many people who helped *Swarm* go from weird concept to actual book.

First, my sister Denise. She tirelessly reads all my drafts, from the really, really bad ones to the almost-there ones, and always has the best feedback. She is my biggest cheerleader and I'm not sure I could have done this without her.

My three besties, Anne Goulet, Easha Canada, and J Carbonneau have held my hand through different parts of my writing journey (and real life). Without a support system, writing (and real life) is an impossible endeavor. Although life has often kept us geographically separated, you've all always been a phone call or text away and your friendships have meant the world to me.

The best agent in the universe, Amy Giuffrida rescued me from querying hell and became my most vociferous advocate and strongest ally in the publishing world. Thank you, Amy, for istening to all my hairbrained ideas, helping me pick the strongest ones, and then selling the hell out of them to anyone who will listen. I know how lucky I am to have you.

Thank you to the amazing team at Sourcebooks. Wendy McClure, I live for your insightful and often hilarious commentary in my edit notes, and want to thank you so much for taking a chance on my debut work (and on me). Huge shout out Liz Dresner, Erin Fitzimmons, Thea Voutiritsas, April Wills, Natalie C. Sousa, Laura Boren, Lynne Hartzer, Neha Patel, Karen Masnica, Rebecca Atkinson, and Julie Larson. Thanks for being such an integral part of this journey.

Swarm was started during my MFA program. Thank God for the Interwebs because the high-residency MFAs of the olden days seem tailor-made for the young, independently wealthy, and childless. I want to thank the folks at Western New England for making their (actually) low-residency MFA accessible to working human adults, and especially for their diehard support of genre writers. Stephanie Wardrop is the writing goddess who cheered me on and brought me chips when I showed up to our residency recovering from a terrible cold. Anya Yurchyshyn and Pearl Abraham, my MFA mentors while I was working on this book, called out the garbage parts and let me know when I was on the right track. My learning was in the best hands!

The brilliant author Jennie Adams—you taught me the value of having writer friends and pulled me into a community where I felt I'd finally found my writing tribe. I love you to death.

And finally, my son Josh, my favorite monster—I love you more than anything.

ABOUT THE AUTHOR

Photo credit Adam Wright

Jennifer D. Lyle lives in Western Massachusetts with her family, including a son, three dogs, and an absurd number of parrots. She graduated from Western New England University's MFA program, where she learned editing is far easier than drafting. When not writing, she can be found reading, building LEGO sets, and watching horror movies with her eyes covered.

FIREreads

§ #getbooklit

Your hub for the hottest young adult books!

Visit us online and sign up for our
newsletter at FIREreads.com

 @sourcebooksfire

 sourcebooksfire

 firereads.tumblr.com